4/05

D0064842

GIVE ME TOMORROW

GIVE ME TOMORROW

Linda Sole

This first world edition published in Great Britain 2004 by
SEVERN HOUSE PUBLISHERS LTD of
9–15 High Street, Sutton, Surrey SM1 1DF.
This first world edition published in the USA 2005 by
SEVERN HOUSE PUBLISHERS INC of
595 Madison Avenue, New York, N.Y. 10022.

British Library Cataloguing in Publication Data

Sole, Linda
    Give me tomorrow. - (Country house saga)
    1.   Nannies - Fiction
    2.   Devon (England) - Social life and customs - Fiction
    I.   Title
    823.9'14 [F]

    ISBN 0-7278-6152-2

Typeset by Palimpsest Book Production Ltd.,
Polmont, Stirlingshire, Scotland.
Printed and bound in Great Britain by
MPG Books Ltd., Bodmin, Cornwall.

One

Hearing the wind howling outside and the patter of rain against the small windowpanes, Jessie shivered, trying not to think about what was coming. She'd been warned and now she was just going to have to take what was coming to her. She lifted her head proudly and looked straight at the woman sitting behind the imposing desk, determined to give no sign of the distress she was feeling.

'I'm extremely sorry, Nurse Hale,' Matron said, peering over the small gold-rimmed glasses she wore perched on the end of her nose. She was a small woman, thin and wiry, but carried all the weight of her authority. 'However, I have been instructed to tell you that your services are no longer required by the board of St Joseph's. You will be given a month's severance pay and leave immediately.'

'But that's so unfair!' Jessie said, a hint of anger in her normally soft brown eyes. The large, unflattering cap she wore over her reddish-brown hair made her features less attractive than they truly were, especially when her mouth was set in a stubborn line as now. 'If anyone has to leave it ought to be *him*. I've done nothing wrong, Matron.'

'I quite agree with you,' Matron replied and made a steeple of her hands as she considered her reply. It *was* unfair that Jessie should be asked to leave, but Doctor Acrington had refused to continue working at St Joseph's if the nurse was not dismissed. If it came to a choice between a senior doctor and an impertinent young woman, who had dared to complain about what the doctor had insisted was merely a silly mis- understanding, then the board was on the side of the man they both needed and admired.

Matron paused before speaking again. This dismissal of one

1

of her best nurses was against her own instincts but she must obey her instructions from the board. She did not look at Jessie as she continued. 'Had you agreed to apologize to Doctor Acrington I might have been able to simply move you to another part of the hospital and let the whole thing blow over, but since you refused . . .'

'Why should I apologize?' Jessie demanded, now indignant. 'I saw him with his hand on Nurse Rose's breast and I heard her ask him to let her pass, to stop bothering her. I heard his reply, and it was disgusting language. Besides, it isn't the first time this has happened. All the young nurses hate it when he's on night duty. They know he can't be trusted to keep his hands to himself.'

Matron was unable to meet Jessie's clear gaze because she knew that every word the girl had said was true. Acrington was a pest, but he had good family connections and donations had come the charity's way because of his association with the hospital. Besides, Acrington was a respectable man and had been decorated for bravery on the Somme, so it was unlikely that the board would take the word of a girl from London's East End against his. 'Unfortunately, Nurse Rose has refused to corroborate your story,' Matron said. 'She says that it was just an accident; the doctor bumped against her and she was just surprised, not upset.'

'That's because she's frightened of losing her job.'

Matron drew a sharp breath. The girl's defiance was beginning to annoy her. It was time to make an end of this nonsense. 'You came to us from the VADs after the end of the war, and I know you had been at the Front. You are a good nurse, but mistaken in your attitude towards this silly affair. As I said previously, I regret this incident, but I can do nothing more for you here. However, I have written an excellent reference for you. I believe you should be able to find another post quite easily.'

The angry protest died unspoken on Jessie's lips. So that was that then, she thought, leaving Matron's office with the reference in her pocket and Matron's good wishes echoing hollowly in her ears. She had always known this could happen when she made her complaint. It was the way of things, as her aunt had warned her.

2

'You can't win against them,' she'd told Jessie over their supper of cocoa and home-made seed cake only a few days earlier. 'Believe me, the establishment have it all sewn up between them. Keep your mouth shut and make sure you're not the one he catches off guard, that's my advice to you.'

'Oh, he doesn't bother with me,' Jessie had said and laughed. 'He likes them young. Besides, I'm too plain for Doctor Acrington – thank goodness!'

'I've never thought you plain,' Aunt Elizabeth said, considering her seriously. 'You used to look attractive when you bothered, Jess. You've lovely hair if you didn't scrape it back like that.'

'I'm twenty-six, plain, and any interest I had in looking nice ended a long time ago,' Jessie replied. 'I'm a good nurse and as long as I look clean and tidy that's all that matters.'

'I know you loved Robert,' her aunt said with sadness in her eyes as she looked across the scrubbed pine table at Jessie. She had witnessed her niece's grief, listened to her sobbing in the night long after it was over. 'But a lot of girls lost the men they loved out there, Jess. It doesn't mean you have to stop living too, love. Robbie wouldn't have wanted that for you; you know he wouldn't.'

Jessie knew her aunt meant well, but she didn't understand how it had been between her and Robert Greening. It wasn't just a case of her fancying the good-looking young soldier; it had been the real thing. Aunt Elizabeth wouldn't know about that kind of love. She'd married to escape the slums she'd been born in, settling for an older man with a nice little business. Harold Pottersby had died after six years of marriage, which for him had been happy enough – his wife was a good cook and a kind woman – leaving Elizabeth with a worthwhile sum in the bank as well as the house and bakery.

'Don't you ever miss Harold?' Jessie asked suddenly as she sipped her hot drink. 'You've never thought of marrying again, have you, Auntie?'

'Onc man was good enough for me,' Elizabeth replied and then laughed as she realized she'd fallen into the trap. 'But you're still young, Jessie love. I was much older than you are when I married. You shouldn't shut out the world. You could marry Archie Thistle tomorrow if you wanted – and then you wouldn't have to work at all.'

'Oh, Auntie!' Jessie cried and pulled a face. 'Archie is a dear, but he's fifty if he's a day. You know I would never think of marrying him. Besides, I don't want to marry anyone. I'm quite happy being a nurse.'

'That bookshop of his must be worth a tidy sum,' Elizabeth Pottersby had said shrewdly, unwilling to leave the subject of a man she considered highly suitable to be her niece's husband. 'It's a prime site on that corner and if they ever develop this area he could sell that property for a fortune.'

Collecting her possessions from her locker in the nurses' rest area, Jessie brought her thoughts back to the present and frowned as she wondered what she was going to do next. Nursing had seemed the obvious thing after Robert was killed in Belgium. It was only her dedication to the patients that had kept her going after she'd received the telegram telling her that her darling Robbie was dead. He'd been just one of thousands killed out there, falling into the mud of the trenches and brought back to a field hospital, just like the one where Jessie had been nursing that day. He had probably been crying for her as the soldiers she'd helped to tend every day cried for their loved ones when the pain and fear became too much for them to bear.

It was the fact that she hadn't been with him when he needed her that hurt so much. She hadn't been able to comfort him or kiss him or tell him that she loved him. Because of a mix-up she hadn't even known he was wounded until it was too late. And it was that knowledge that still woke her with tears on her cheeks night after night, even though he'd been dead for three years and the war over two. She wasn't sure that the hurt would ever stop. If only she could have been there, just to hold his hand, to tell him she loved him.

'Jessie, could I talk to you for a moment, please? I wanted to apologize.'

The girl's hesitant voice broke into Jessie's thoughts. She frowned as she saw Mary Rose, the girl she had saved from an unpleasant mauling by the arrogant Doctor Acrington.

4

'What for?' Jessie asked, her tone harsher than she'd intended because her thoughts were elsewhere, too painful to be shared. 'If you'd spoken out they would have given you the push, too.'

'Yes, I know.' Nurse Rose bit her pretty bottom lip to stop it from trembling. She was fragile in appearance but tougher underneath than she looked, Jessie suspected. 'I shall have to leave anyway as soon as I can find something, because Acrington will make me pay for this if I stop here. He won't like what happened, even though they took his side and not yours.'

'No, he won't,' Jessie agreed. 'I thought St Joseph's being a charity hospital and run by the Church they would listen to my story and support me, but I couldn't win against someone like him; he has too much influence. My aunt told me what would happen and she was right. Sorry I've made it awkward for you, Mary. I should have kept my mouth shut.'

'You did the right thing, but I was too scared to support you. I was told I would never work again as a nurse if I did – and nursing means a lot to me.'

'It meant a lot to me, too.' Jessie couldn't quite keep the resentment out of her voice, though she tried.

'I know. I really am sorry.' Nurse Rose took a scrap of paper from her uniform pocket and offered it to Jessie. 'I'm not sure if this is of any use to you. I was told about this job and I went to see her – Mrs Kendle – but it's not here in London; it's in Devon. I had an interview and she seems nice enough, but I couldn't go all that way. Ma's an invalid. She can't get about much, and she depends on me to shop and clean for her when I can manage it.'

Jessie glanced at the scrap of paper. It was an advertisement from the *Lady's Monthly Magazine* and was offering a post to a young woman with some nursing training to look after an invalid woman and help care for two children.

'But this isn't proper nursing,' she said, puzzled. 'You wouldn't think of taking a job like this?'

'I might. At least, I might if it had been in London,' Nurse Rose said. 'I've had enough of being told off by Sister and fumbled by bleedin' doctors that ought to know better. Excuse

5

my language!' Her cheeks were flushed and defiant. 'What I really want to do is nurse sick children. I'm hoping to find a job with one of the big hospitals where I can specialize – and I shan't do that if I get thrown out of here.'

'No . . .' Jessie wondered uneasily if she might find it difficult to get the sort of job she wanted after being sacked from St Joseph's. 'Well, thanks for this. I have to get home. Good luck for the future.'

'Good luck, Jessie – and I'm sorry I got you the push.'

'Not your fault. I dare say I shall get by.'

Emerging into the cool night air, Jessie pulled her short nursing cape up around her throat. Autumn had started early this year and the nip in the air warned of winter just around the corner. She shivered, but it wasn't just the chill wind that was making her feel cold. She hadn't thought that being asked to leave St Joseph's would seriously affect her chances of finding another job. After all, she had done nothing wrong, merely reported a doctor for making sexual advances towards a young nurse who hadn't welcomed them. Everyone, including Matron, was aware that she had been telling the truth, but somehow it was Jessie who was out of a job. Yet she had a good reference from Matron in her pocket. Surely that should count for something.

Jessie noticed the match-seller as she approached the queue for the tram that would take her most of the way to her aunt's home. He was an old soldier, she was sure, and pity stirred deep inside her. He had given everything for King and Country, including his health if that dreadful cough was anything to go by, but what had his country given him in return? Nothing, not even a decent job, or he wouldn't be standing here on a cold evening. So why should she have expected any better?

Jessie approached him, dropping half a crown into his tray and taking one tiny matchbox in return.

'Gawd bless you, luv,' he said and grinned at her. 'Not sure I've got enough change fer yer. Trade ain't that brisk ternight.'

'I don't want any change,' Jessie said. 'I reckon we owe you that, Tommy, and a lot more.'

'Pity there ain't a few more like you, luv,' he called after her as she walked away. 'Bleedin' government's forgot we're alive.'

Jessie had to run to catch her tram. She shoved the matches deep into her skirt pocket as she took out the money for her fare. She wouldn't be able to do things like that very often if she couldn't find herself a job pretty sharpish.

At least she wasn't desperate for the moment. Aunt Elizabeth had taken her in after her much-loved mother had died of diphtheria. There had been a lot of that kind of infectious disease about in the dirty little back streets around Bermondsey where Jessie grew up, and that year it had been particularly bad. Jessie's neighbour had taken it first and Ma had nursed her. Then it was her turn to go down with the dreaded infection and the doctor said it was hopeless from the start. Ma had taken it bad and she wasn't strong. She'd had too much work and worry after being left a widow with a small child to rear.

'Your mother was always the soft one,' her aunt said when she'd fetched the twelve-year-old Jessie to her house off Kensington High Street. It was a good address to have, Jessie had found when she'd applied to join the VADs, even if it was in one of the less posh areas of the borough. 'If Nell had looked after herself instead of others you wouldn't be here with me. Not that I mind, Jessie. I've no children of my own and I can do with a bit of company now my Harold has gone.'

Aunt Elizabeth wasn't one to fuss over things, and she didn't tell jokes or sing the way Ma had when she was happy, but her house was clean, comfortable and warm and there was always enough to eat. They hadn't gone short during the war, because Elizabeth Pottersby had her head screwed on the right way and had managed to scrounge extra food on the black market. Jessie had known she was lucky to be given a good home, because she might have gone to the orphanage if her aunt hadn't been so quick to claim her. She missed Ma, would have given anything to be back in the slum house with damp coming through the walls and often only an empty, aching belly to take to bed, if only her lovely, gentle Ma had been there to laugh and kiss her goodnight. Yet she had accepted

7

that her aunt was right: life had to move on; tears got you nothing.

Gazing out of the tram window, Jessie looked at the lights in the expensive shops they passed. At least things were beginning to get back to normal now that the war was over. There were more goods to buy for those who had the money and not so many queues for everything, but remembering the match-seller, she felt sad. How many more were there like him, and how long would it be before the government got round to solving the problem? Unions were making ominous grumbling noises, but it was going to take more than that to make the kind of changes that were needed in the poorest parts of the city.

What must it be like to live like the other half did? Jessie wondered as she saw people arriving at a theatre dressed in smart clothes and looking as if they'd never known what it was like to go without their supper. But maybe she was just feeling this way because she hadn't liked being given the push over that rotten business with Doctor Acrington. She was feeling sorry for herself, and there was no sense in that.

'You pick yourself up and start over when you've had a knock,' Aunt Elizabeth had always maintained, and that was what Jessie intended to do now. She'd lost her job because she'd spoken out honestly, but she was a trained nurse and it ought to be easy enough to get another position. At least she had a home to go to and a few pounds in her pocket. She was better off than a good many people.

Jessie took the pins from her hair, letting it tumble on to her shoulders with a sigh of relief that the day was finally over. She looked at herself in the mirror on the dressing table. The glass was a bit dull and the frame ugly, dark mahogany, but she could see that her hair shone with health. Robbie used to say she had beautiful hair, but then he'd thought she was lovely altogether.

'I loved you from the first moment I saw you waiting for the tram,' he had told her when they started courting. 'I wanted to speak to you then, but I thought you would give me a look for having the cheek!'

Jessie had laughed. She'd noticed the good-looking young man at her stop all right – and more than once – but it wasn't until the war started and he'd been wearing uniform that they'd had the courage to speak to each other.

'It might have been the uniform,' Jessie told him afterwards. 'You looked proud and handsome, but a bit scared, too, and I smiled because I wanted you to say something.'

Robbie had been working as a clerk at an insurance office before signing up and Jessie had worked at a teashop just round the corner from his office. Once they started to talk they couldn't stop and Robbie had asked her to go to a show at the music hall with him that night.

'I'd love to,' she'd told him. 'But how much longer are you going to be in London?'

'I'm stationed not far away. I'll be able to visit most weekends – until they send me over there.'

They'd had six months. Six wonderful, glorious months of happiness before Robbie went on his first period of active duty, and then ten days when he'd been given home leave. He'd seemed quieter and more reserved on his leave that time, but just as loving. Then on their last night she had sensed how much he wanted her.

'I wouldn't mind,' she'd whispered shyly, burying her face in his shoulder, 'if we did it – you know, went all the way. I love you and I know you love me.'

'It's best we don't,' he'd said and smiled at her so that her heart turned over. 'But when I come home next time we'll get a licence and get married – if you want to?'

'Of course I want to!' Jessie had said, hugging him.

'That's what we'll do then.' He grinned at her. 'I would've asked this time but I thought I might be rushing you.'

'Daft 'aporth!' Jessie teased. 'I would have married you two days after we first went out if you'd asked.'

Oh, what a lovely time they'd had that last night of his leave, whispering in the dark at the music hall, holding hands and making plans as they walked home. It was all going to be wonderful on his next leave, but before that had come round Jessie had joined the VADs and had been transferred to a field hospital in Belgium and Robbie was dead.

9

Tears were stinging Jessie's eyes as she laid her hairbrush down. She blinked them away, refusing to weep. She wasn't the only woman to have lost her man. Some women had been left with illegitimate children to bring up alone. At least that hadn't happened to her, and that was only because Robbie had been strong enough to resist for her sake.

Jessie summoned a smile. There was no point in letting things get you down; you couldn't change them so you just had to make the most of what you had. She had known real love once, and that was why she didn't intend to settle for second best. She would rather stay as she was than marry someone she didn't love, even if there were times when she felt desperately lonely, as if she'd missed out on something special. But she had managed to cope with her grief and disappointment, putting all her effort into making life better for her patients. She hadn't let Robbie's death destroy her. And she wouldn't let the board of St Joseph's put her down, either. She would find a job somehow, no matter how long it took!

'I'm sorry to inform you that the post you applied for has already been filled,' Jessie read aloud over the breakfast table that morning. Three weeks had passed since her dismissal from the hospital and so far there was no sign of her getting another job. 'They haven't even asked for my references or given me the chance of an interview. That's four nursing jobs I've applied for and they've all said the same. What's wrong with me? Surely there can't be so many trained nurses looking for jobs?'

'Work is short all round,' her aunt said and frowned. She knew how frustrated Jessie was at just sitting around. 'But if you want my opinion, girl, they've got your card marked – you're down as a troublemaker.'

'But that's not fair. I'm not a troublemaker.'

'You reported a superior for misbehaviour,' her aunt said. 'I warned you how it would be, Jessie. He was one of *them* and they stick together. Always have, always will.'

Jessie felt a sinking sensation. Despite her denials she knew her aunt was right. She could hardly believe this was happening to her. It seemed so unfair. Surely that couldn't be the reason she was finding it so difficult to get a new job? No, she wouldn't believe that, or she really would be ready to jump off Tower Bridge!

'As you said, the situation is difficult all round. A lot of men and women are out of work. I'll find something if I keep looking.'

'You could always work for Archie. He was asking after you yesterday. I told him you couldn't find a job and he said to tell you he could give you a few hours helping out in the shop.'

'I might have to take him up on it yet,' Jessie said and looked rueful. 'But it's a last resort, Auntie. I'm a nurse. I want to use my training if I can.'

'You might have more luck out of London,' her aunt said, looking thoughtful. 'I saw something in a magazine yesterday and meant to show you but I forgot.' She went over to the small oak sideboard and opened the bottom cupboard door, searching amongst the clutter of magazines, balls of knitting wool and other odds and ends that were stored on the shelves inside. 'Ah, here it is. I saved it because there's a knitting pattern I like – but the advertisements are all in the back. Have a look for yourself.'

Jessie took the magazine and sat in one of the deep, slightly shabby armchairs by the fireplace. Her aunt's kitchen was the biggest room in the house, kept warm by the fire that was never allowed to go out and used for cooking as well as heating water and the room itself. They used this room all the time, keeping the tiny parlour neat and shiny for visitors, but it was usually cold in there and nowhere near as welcoming.

She flicked through the magazine, lingering over the picture of a stately house for a moment – what a lovely, lovely house! It must be wonderful to live in a place like that, she thought. She found the list of advertisements right at the back of the magazine and ran her finger down the column. There were several for parlourmaids – servants weren't as easy to come by since the war – two for companions for elderly ladies, and right at the bottom something

11

about a nursery nurse with a few hours devoted to an invalid lady each day. A bell rang in Jessie's memory and she recalled the scrap of paper given her by Nurse Rose. She had left it in her uniform pocket and never looked at it since. It hadn't been worded quite the same, and the telephone number was a London one, though she remembered Mary Rose saying that the job was out of town.

She wouldn't have considered a job like this at the beginning, but now it seemed more interesting, at least as a temporary measure. It might even be a good idea to leave London and get away for a while, give herself time to think and recover from her upset over this whole business.

'Is this a new magazine?' she asked and glanced at the date on the front cover.

'It came the day before yesterday. I have them once a month. I like them because they are so pleasant, the way life ought to be, no rude or nasty articles. Did you see that lovely house? It's just been opened to the public. I suppose the owners are hard up because of the war or something. I thought I might visit one day; it's only a short journey on the train and I like nice houses. Is the advert of any use?'

'It might be,' Jessie said. 'I could telephone and see. I'll pop down to the post office later.'

'Use the phone in the bakery office. I may not run the place now, but it still belongs to me. Tell Eddie I said it was all right.'

'Are you sure? I don't like to take advantage.' She didn't like the man her aunt employed to run the bakery either, but she didn't say that.

'Don't talk daft, girl. Go and do it now. There's bound to be several after those jobs with all the unemployment about.'

'I might have to leave London.'

'What harm can there be in that? There isn't much here for you, Jess. It would be a new beginning. Besides, your home is here. You can come back whenever you like. I'm not throwing you out.'

'I know.' Jessie laughed and jumped to her feet. 'It wasn't what I was looking for, but it might be nice to have a change.'

12

'Go on then.' Elizabeth smiled as the girl went out. She glanced at the magazine and then frowned. Jessie hadn't turned the page. What kind of a job was she looking for? The advert for a hospital wanting two nurses and several doctors in Manchester was at the top of the next page. Elizabeth went to the kitchen door to call her niece back, but she had already crossed the yard and was disappearing inside the bakery at the far end. Oh well, she thought, what did one phone call matter? She would show Jessie the right advert when she came back.

Jessie gave the number to the operator and waited as it rang several times before being answered by a man who spoke as though he had a toffee in his mouth.

'The Kendle residence,' he said. 'To whom did you wish to speak, please?'

'Mrs Mary Kendle,' she said. 'It's about the advertisement in the magazine.'

'I see . . .' The faceless one with the odd-sounding voice seemed to hesitate, then said, 'I will see if Madam is available to speak to you. Please wait.'

'As long as it doesn't take too . . .' Jessie held the receiver away from her ear as she realized she was talking to air, feeling put out. The voice had sounded disapproving and she wondered if that was why the post hadn't been filled before this. His manner would discourage most people for a start!

Jessie was on the verge of hanging up when she heard a little clicking sound and then a rather breathless voice asked, 'Hello . . . are you there?'

'Yes. I wanted to speak to Mrs Mary Kendle please.'

'Is it about the position looking after Lady Kendle and the children?'

'If that's the one in the magazine, then yes.'

'Mrs Kendle isn't here. She lives in Devon and only comes up to London every few weeks, but she asked me to interview anyone who rang if she wasn't here. I'm Mrs Carmichael, the housekeeper here at Sir Joshua's town house. Would it be convenient for you to call this afternoon, miss? I'm sorry, Carmichael didn't give me your name.'

13

'Its Jessie Hale. I'm a trained nurse but I've just lost my job and I'm looking for something different.'

'Oh . . .' The housekeeper sounded hesitant. 'Why did you lose your job, miss, if you don't mind my asking?'

Jessie thought it would be all the same if she did; they all asked and she thought it was best to get it out at the start, then she needn't waste time going round for an interview if they thought she wasn't suitable.

'I reported a doctor for fumbling a young nurse in the linen cupboard and he made out it was just a mistake; they took his side instead of mine.'

'Yes, they would,' Mrs Carmichael said and chuckled. 'Sorry, Miss Hale, but I know how that feels, you see. It happened to me once when I was a young parlourmaid and the master caught me in a similar way. I went to the mistress. She didn't believe me but gave me a reference when I left – so perhaps she did believe me after all, though she wouldn't admit it.'

'I should've kept my mouth shut, but it's done now,' Jessie said. 'Do you still want me to come round for that interview this afternoon?'

'You sound like an honest girl to me,' the woman replied. 'Come at three, please. I'll have time to sit and talk to you then. To tell you the truth we're having a bit of a problem filling this place. It's in Devon, see – does that put you off?'

'No, it doesn't,' Jessie replied. 'I knew that before I rang. Another girl told me about it some weeks ago, but I'd forgotten until I saw it advertised again.'

'Mrs Kendle thought she had the post filled, but she was let down at the last minute – the girl lied about her references. She'd lost her place for stealing, you see. You've got a reference, I hope?'

'Yes, one from Matron. She said it was a good one, but I haven't looked; no one has asked for it yet. I promise you I've never stolen anything in my life, but I think I've been marked as a troublemaker.'

'Shouldn't wonder at it,' Mrs Carmichael said and laughed again. Jessie thought she sounded rather nice. 'Well, come and see me this afternoon. You might be the answer to a prayer, Miss Hale.'

Jessie replaced the earpiece and turned to discover that she was being watched by Eddie Robinson, the man who now ran the bakery for her aunt. He was a big man, florid-faced, slightly balding, and usually smelled of sweat. He couldn't help it, of course – the work was hard and often in over-poweringly hot conditions – but she didn't like him and she didn't like the way he looked at her. She wished now that she'd gone to the post office as she'd wanted, or used Archie's phone. He wouldn't have minded and he wouldn't have made her feel uncomfortable.

'Still not found a job then, Jessie?'

She hated it that he called her Jessie, but she couldn't say anything. Aunt Elizabeth relied on him to run this place, and he was hard-working and honest, which wasn't always the case. She knew her aunt had sacked the two previous bakers for cheating her. She couldn't make trouble for her aunt; it was best just to keep out of Eddie's way.

'It looks as if my luck is about to change,' she said. 'Excuse me, Eddie, I have to get back.'

He didn't move out of her way, which meant she had to squeeze past him to get through the office door. From the leer on his face, Jessie knew he enjoyed baiting her, but short of asking her aunt to sack him there was nothing she could do but put up with his behaviour. Perhaps it was Eddie's treat-ment of her that had made her blow the whistle on Doctor Acrington. It seemed that most men thought they had the right to do whatever they liked with women who crossed their paths. Whether they were high or low born; there wasn't much to choose between them.

But Robbie hadn't been like that, Jessie remembered as she went out into the cold of the yard. He hadn't taken advantage of her that last night, though sometimes now she wished he had. At least she would have known what it was like to be loved by him in that way, and she might even have had his baby. She would have had something to love then, even if she'd been seen as a fallen woman because of it.

She shivered as she ran across the cobbles that led to the kitchen door. It always seemed colder when you came out of the bakery, because of the extreme heat in there. If she worked there perhaps she would become warped like Eddie in time, she thought, and then changed her mind. He was just made that way.

Her aunt was baking when she went into the kitchen. She made all her own cakes, even though she could have had them delivered straight from the bakery, piping hot from the ovens. But then they wouldn't be truly home-made, would they? Elizabeth Pottersby had a light hand with all kinds of pastries. Besides, she wouldn't have known what to do with herself if she didn't keep busy in the kitchen three-quarters of the day.

'How did you get on?' she asked. 'Get through all right?'

'I'm going for an interview this afternoon.'

'To Manchester?' Aunt Elizabeth pointed to the advertisement she had ringed in pencil. 'That's what I was talking about, Jess.'

'I didn't turn the page,' Jessie said and frowned. 'I've rung somewhere else now. I can't let them down. I'll have to go.'

'Well, I suppose you ought to,' her aunt said. 'But you can always say no. You've got to write a letter to this address, not phone, but you could post it when you go out this afternoon. Might as well have two irons in the fire.'

'No, I shan't do that,' Jessie said. 'If I don't think this will suit I'll tell them, then I'll write to Manchester – but I won't string these people along. Mrs Carmichael said her employer had been let down once. I shall be honest with them and say if I don't like the sound of it.'

'Too honest for your own good, that's you, Jess,' her aunt said, but she said it with a smile of approval. 'Well, you please yourself. Nothing is for ever, girl. If you remember that, you won't go far wrong in life, believe me.'

'I shall,' Jess replied and smiled at her. 'Are you making apple pie for dinner this evening?'

'It's your favourite,' her aunt said. 'I always make it at least once a week, and if you're going away . . .' She left the sentence unfinished. She would miss Jessie terribly, but she wasn't going to say. Let the girl decide for herself. Life went on, and she would come home when it suited her. 'There's a pot of thick cream in the pantry on the cold shelf. I think we'll make a treat of it, Jess. Why not?'

Two

Jessie popped into the bookshop on the corner before catching her tram that afternoon. Archie was sitting in his chair behind a table laden with old books, horn-rimmed glasses on the end of his nose, reading, apparently lost to the world. He looked up as the bell rang loudly, a smile of pleasure lighting up his face as he saw her.

'You look smart today. Off somewhere?'

She was wearing her best wool costume of dark blue, with a jaunty little felt hat that had a curling feather across the brim, her one pair of good leather court shoes, and carrying matching gloves and bag.

'I'm going for an interview for a job. Wish me luck?'

'Yes, of course.' He had taken off his glasses and was studying her with his weak, kind eyes. Archie was a thin man, pale and intelligent but not robust. Jessie liked him and she knew his feelings for her were more than friendship, though he never presumed or looked at her in a way that made her uncomfortable. 'Pop in and tell me how you got on when you come back.'

'Yes, all right. See you later then.'

Jessie left him to continue reading. She sometimes wondered how he managed to make a living out of his books. None of them were new and a musty smell clung to some of them, which made her nose tickle. She knew he bought them from auctions and house sales and supposed he must sell them occasionally, though she hadn't seen many customers.

She stopped to buy a newspaper, frowning as she saw that every mine-worker in the country was now on strike and the government was bringing in stringent measures because of the emergency. It seemed such nonsense that one group of workers

18

should go on strike when so many men were desperate for a job, though she knew conditions and pay in the mines were poor.

Her tram arrived just as she reached the stop. Jessie paid her fare and took a seat near the door so that she could get off quickly when they reached her stop. A man had jumped on at the last minute and sat down next to her, forcing her to shift up a bit, even though there were several empty seats elsewhere. Jessie's brow wrinkled as she ventured a glance at his profile. He was about her own age, with short, dark hair and a severe look about him, his mouth set hard in a grim line.

'I'll be getting off in a few stops,' Jessie said, meaning to warn him that she would have to ask him to move.

He turned his head to look at her, his eyes the colour of wood smoke as they surveyed her critically. 'Are you suggesting I should sit somewhere else?' he asked in what could only be called an aggressive manner.

Jessie coloured. She hadn't meant it in quite that way, though she had been a bit annoyed that he'd chosen to sit next to her when there were so many empty seats he could have chosen.

'It's just that you'll have to move when I get to my stop.'

'I can move now if you feel like that.'

How rude he was! Jessie's temper flared but she held it in check. She must have upset him. 'I'm sorry. Of course I didn't mean it that way.'

He made no answer, staring straight ahead as if he hadn't heard her, but he didn't move. He was obviously caught up in his own thoughts and very angry. She felt rather uncomfortable, wishing that she hadn't spoken at all. Should she try to make conversation? Glancing at his face again she thought it was probably best not. He was clearly very upset about something.

The tram stopped six times before she had to ask him to move. He did so without comment, sitting down again as soon as she was out of her seat and into the aisle. Jessie felt relieved when she was off the tram. What a very prickly young man he was.

He had been dressed in a brown suit that looked as if it had seen better days, but there had been nothing rough or uncultured in his speech, and though he had been rude she thought he might have been used to working in an office and not with his hands. She had noticed that his nails were clean, as if he had scrubbed them, his fingers long and slender. Not the hands of a manual labourer.

Why was she giving him a second thought? He was just a rather unfriendly man she had sat next to on a tram and would never see again. Jessie dismissed him from her thoughts as she crossed the main road to the quiet square she sought.

All the houses in the square had been built in the late eighteenth century and were tall, narrow buildings with long sash windows and imposing front doors. These were the houses of families who had once been rich, keeping their London home just for occasional visits and spending much of their time at their country estates. Grouped around a small garden area, they had an air of fading grandeur as if their time had passed, and some of the houses had been converted into apartments that sheltered more than one family these days.

She ran up the three steps to the front door of number eight and pulled the black bell, which made a loud clanging sound within the house. The door was opened promptly by a man dressed all in black, apart from a grey striped waistcoat, who looked down his long nose at her. His expression was one of distaste, as though he wondered what she was doing on the doorstep, but when she gave her name, he nodded and invited her into the hall.

'If you will just wait here, miss,' he said in a voice she instantly recognized. 'I shall inquire if Mrs Carmichael is ready to see you.'

'Yes, Mr Carmichael,' she said, finding it difficult not to laugh at his pompous manner. Just who did he think he was? She had come for a job, not to beg for charity! 'I am five minutes early, but better early than late, don't you think?'

He gave her a look that spoke volumes and went off towards a door at the far end of the hall. Jessie looked about her with interest. The stairs were rather grand, curling to the left as they went up, the banister ending in wide scrolls of shining mahogany that looked as if it had been polished every day of its life, so deep was the gloss. The hall itself was spacious, the floor tiled in black and white marble, which was a bit cold and impersonal, and the furniture clearly old and probably valuable. There was a picture of a horse and dogs with a woman in the costume of the eighteenth century standing by a stream, and Jessie was studying it with interest when she heard a voice behind her.

'Do you like pictures, Miss Hale?'

She turned to see a plump, smiling woman in her middle years. Her hair was a soft brown and rolled neatly away from her face, though she did not wear a cap. Her dress was a serviceable grey but well cut and she had a white lace collar and cuffs and a small cameo brooch fastened at her neck. Her eyes were bright and seemed to light up her face, making Jessie think that she must have been very pretty when she was young.

'I like this one,' Jessie said. 'I haven't come across many as good as this, though my aunt has a few prints in her front parlour.'

'Sir Joshua has many fine pictures, most of which are down at Kendlebury Hall,' Mrs Carmichael said. 'His father was a great collector, but that was when the family was in its heyday. The Kendles aren't as rich as they used to be. Sir Joshua's father was an MP, you know, and his grandfather made a fortune from importing tea, but the money isn't as plentiful now as it was. They're not short of a few bob, of course, but not as rich as they once were.'

Jessie nodded, making no comment. She thought it a little strange that the housekeeper should discuss the family fortunes with a complete stranger, but Mrs Carmichael clearly liked to talk about her employers and went on as she led the way through the hall to the back stairs, then down to a comfortable parlour behind the large kitchen.

'Captain Kendle was in the army during the war,' she said as she motioned Jessie to a large wing chair next to the fire. It was an extremely comfortable room, and Jessie thought the Kendles were clearly generous towards their employees. 'It's his wife that needs the help with her mother-in-law and the children. They have Nanny, poor dear, but she is getting old and poor Mrs Kendle doesn't feel she's up to the job these days – though they couldn't turn her out, of course. Not Nanny.

21

She was Captain Kendle's nanny first and naturally expects to care for his children. You might find a bit of resistance from her at first, but she's not a bad soul – not like some of them. I was at a house before I came here where the nanny was a tartar. Our nanny isn't like that, but she might come it for a while, just until she gets used to the idea of having a helper.'

'I see,' Jessie said and looked at her hesitantly. 'Is it a big house – lots of people working there?'

'The house isn't as big as some I've worked in,' she said. 'Carmichael and me only came to the family a few months before the start of the war, and we run this house with just one maid and Cook, but there are more on the staff at Kendlebury. I've been down to the estate a couple of times to help out when they've had big parties on – Captain and Mrs Kendle were married a year or so before the war started. That's when they opened this house up again see, for Mrs Kendle. She likes to spend a bit of time in town with friends; there's not much for a lady like her to do in the country. Lady Kendle has been an invalid for years, so she doesn't come to town these days, and Sir Joshua closed the house for a while – after his eldest son was killed in an accident, I think. Not that I know much about that; they don't talk about Mr Jonathan. Sir Joshua hasn't been here for years, but Captain and Mrs Kendle come up together sometimes and she visits every few weeks. Got a lot of friends, Mrs Kendle, likes to go out often to the theatre and dinner parties – that's why she needs someone reliable with the children.'

'Yes, I see.' Jessie wasn't sure she altogether approved of the picture Mrs Carmichael was painting of her future employer, but then she didn't have to approve of her employer's way of life, did she? 'What are the children like?'

'Little lambs,' the housekeeper said and smiled. 'Never had children myself – wasn't meant to be for Carmichael and me – but I'm fond of them. Are you fond of children, Miss Hale?'

'Yes, I think so,' Jessie replied. 'I haven't had much to do with them really. I've been working on a general ward at St Joseph's for the last two years since I left the VADs. Before that I worked in a teashop for a year or two after I left school.

22

I live with my aunt, who has no children, but she does have friends who bring their children to visit sometimes. I've always found it easy to get on with them – and I had hoped to have some of my own.'

'You're not married,' the housekeeper said, looking thoughtful. 'I hope you won't be offended, Miss Hale, but you're not a young girl – not old, of course, but not young.'

'I'm twenty-six,' Jessie said. 'I was to be married, but . . . he was killed.' She blinked hard because it still hurt to tell anyone that.

'Oh, I am so sorry,' Mrs Carmichael said. 'It would have been the war, of course. It happened to so many. I didn't mean to upset you, but I have to ask, because Mrs Kendle will want to know all about you.'

'You haven't upset me. If you're wondering whether I'm likely to get married, the answer is no. I had made up my mind to dedicate the rest of my life to nursing, and to be honest if I had found the job I wanted I shouldn't have telephoned you.'

'It was a bit of luck for us you did. I think you are just what Mrs Kendle is looking for, miss. I hope you will consider taking the post. It's eight pounds a month, with uniforms and your keep. You get every other Sunday off and a half-day every week – and because the house is a bit isolated, there's the use of a family car to take you into Torquay on your free afternoon.'

'That's generous,' Jessie said. 'I didn't think nursemaids earned that much.'

'They don't, often,' Mrs Carmichael replied with a smile. 'But there's Lady Kendle as well, and it isn't easy to find a young woman with nursing training – someone who is willing to do both jobs.'

'Why don't they employ two people?'

'Because Lady Kendle won't have a nurse. Nanny used to help her, but she can't lift her now so one of the maids has to do it, and that isn't suitable. Mrs Kendle thought that if she employed a nursery nurse for the children who could also look after her mother-in-law . . .'

'Yes, I see.' Jessie was thoughtful. It sounded as if Mrs Kendle expected a lot from whoever took on the job, but it was more money than Jessie had earned at St Joseph's and would allow her to save. If she wasn't happy working for the family she could always give in her notice after six months or so and come back to London. She might be able to find a job she really wanted by then. 'If I say I am interested, what happens next?'

'I shall telephone Mrs Kendle and tell her about you,' Mrs Carmichael said, looking pleased. 'She says she will trust my judgement but I'll talk to her first and then I could telephone you tomorrow, perhaps.'

'Would it be all right if I rang you? My aunt doesn't have a telephone in the house, and I'll go to a friend's house and use his if I may.'

'You ring me at eleven o'clock tomorrow morning,' Mrs Carmichael agreed with a smile. 'I'm sure the answer will be yes – so don't go changing your mind, will you?'

'No, I shan't do that,' Jessie said and took Matron's reference from her pocket. 'Would you like to see this?'

'Your reference?' The housekeeper turned it over in her hand. 'I don't think I need to, Jessie – may I call you that?' She smiled as Jessie nodded. 'You keep it for Mrs Kendle if she asks, but I shan't bother. I think I know a decent lass when I see one.'

'Thank you.' Jessie got to her feet. 'I'd better not keep you any longer. I expect you are very busy.'

'I keep the house ready in case one of the family—' She broke off as someone knocked at the door. 'Come in.'

A young maid entered and looked at her awkwardly. 'I'm sorry to interrupt, Mrs Carmichael, but Captain Kendle has just arrived. He says he's come for a couple of days.'

'There you are,' the housekeeper said and shook her head. 'Never a word to say to expect him, but that's the gentry all over. I'd better go up and see him. Would you mind waiting for a moment, Jessie? I'll ask him if he wants to see you himself. If he says yes I'll send Millie to you, otherwise I'll come back myself and show you out.'

'Oh . . .' Jessie was surprised by the sudden turn of events. 'All right, if that's what you want – but I could wait in the hall if that makes things easier.'

'Come on then,' Mrs Carmichael said. 'Is the captain in the upstairs parlour, Millie?'

'I'm not sure. Captain Kendle was talking to Mr Carmichael and he sent me to fetch you.'

'Come along then, mustn't keep him waiting.' Mrs Carmichael beckoned to Jessie and she followed in her wake, wondering if she would see her future employer.

As they went into the hall, Jessie saw that it was empty and breathed a sigh of relief, but it was short-lived. The next moment a gentleman emerged from the downstairs parlour carrying a sheaf of letters and papers in his hand. He glanced towards the little group coming towards him without really noticing, seeming uninterested as Mrs Carmichael began to exclaim that it was nice to see him again.

'It is just a short visit,' he replied. 'Business.' He looked up from his letters as he spoke and Jessie saw his face properly for the first time. He was attractive rather than handsome but there was something about him that made her want to stare and keep on staring at him, and it wasn't just the tiny scar on his right temple. She wasn't sure what held her, except that she sensed suffering and saw it in his eyes – the eyes of an old soul, as Ma would have said. 'Did you want something?' There was a hint of impatience in his voice and Jessie blushed, aware that she had been staring rudely.

'This is Miss Jessie Hale,' Mrs Carmichael said, glancing at her and then back at him. 'She's come about the job for Lady Kendle and the children, sir. I've just been interviewing her. I wondered if you would like to talk to her yourself now you're here?'

'Good lord, no,' he said and seemed to glare at her. 'I leave that sort of thing to you and my wife. Excuse me, I must read these letters.' He went past them and up the stairs, not looking at either of them again.

Jessie felt as if she'd been slapped. She was almost sorry that she had practically said she would take the job. Captain Kendle certainly wasn't the kind to make a new employee feel welcome, though perhaps it had been partly her own fault for staring at him.

'Don't let that put you off,' Mrs Carmichael whispered as

he disappeared round the bend at the top of the stairs. 'He's been a bit that way since he came home – the war, you know, it affects some of them up here.' She tapped the left side of her head. 'He was ill for a long time and he never was much of a one for talking, quiet like, Captain Kendle, keeps his thoughts to himself.'

'Yes, I thought he might have been ill,' Jessie said. She wondered why she should feel that stabbing pain in her chest, and then realized that something about him had reminded her of Robbie – Robbie as he had been that last time on leave. Sort of intense, edgy, as though he couldn't bear to let himself think of what he'd seen and done in the trenches, as though he was trying to block out all the things that hurt him, to get through as best he could. 'No, I shan't let it put me off.' In a way it had helped her to make up her mind, because she felt sympathy for Mrs Kendle. It must be very difficult for her with two young children, an invalid mother and a husband who . . . wasn't the same man he had once been. 'I hope I shall be given the job, Mrs Carmichael. You'll put in a good word for me, won't you?'

'Yes, I shall. You can rely on that,' the housekeeper said, beaming as she let her out of the house. 'Don't you worry, miss, that job is as good as yours.'

'Thank you. You've been very kind. Please tell Mrs Kendle that I'm looking forward to being of help to her.'

It had been quite warm for November when Jessie arrived earlier that afternoon, but the sky had become grey and over-cast since then and she shivered as she stepped out into the chill wind. She was trying to remember what Ma had said to her about people with eyes like Captain Kendle's – something about carrying their suffering on from a past life.

'It's in them, Jessie girl,' she'd told her once when they were drinking tea at the old scrubbed pine table in the kitchen. 'Destined to suffer in this life for what they did in a past time, that's what they say about old souls. I don't know if it's true or if they're just sad folk what have the suffering in them, but I've seen it more than once – it were in your father. He used to brood something proper at times, then at others he'd be like a cricket, merry and chirpy all day. Died in an accident at his work on the docks, he did, and me left alone with a babe hardly off the breast. They told me he saw the bale falling but never tried to get out of the way . . . almost as though he thought it was meant for him.'

'You can't believe that, Ma?' Jessie had asked. 'He wouldn't have wanted to leave you. Surely he wouldn't.'

'Maybe he did and maybe he didn't,' Nell Hale had said with a shrug. 'But if one of his moods was on him . . .'

Jessie had found that hard to believe. Surely no one would want to die if they could avoid it. If her father hadn't moved to avoid the heavy bale, he must have been shocked, like a rabbit caught in the light from a poacher's torch, turned to stone by fear. Or maybe it had just been too quick for him to realize what was happening.

And maybe she was imagining things about the man she had seen so briefly at the foot of the stairs. He had glanced at her for one second, and he had been annoyed to find her staring at him; that's what the expression in his eyes meant, nothing more. She would do better to put him out of her mind and think about what she had taken on – if she got the job, that was. The easy bit would be caring for the invalid Lady Kendle; looking after two children would be more difficult because it would be a new experience for her. Yet it was one she felt instinctively she would enjoy. Yes, now she was getting used to the idea, she realized that she was beginning to look forward to making a change.

Jessie popped into Thistles Bookshop to say hello to Archie. She was a little surprised to see that he had two customers, both of whom were buying books from him, which he was carefully wrapping in strong brown paper and string. She waited until they had gone, browsing amongst the books on the shelves and lying in heaps on tables. Archie had placed chairs by the tables so that people could sit down and read for a few minutes before making their choice, which, now she thought about it, she realized was a good idea. She was reading a little book by Oliver Goldsmith entitled the *Vicar of Wakefield* when Archie came up to her.

'Would you like to take that home?' he asked. 'You can read it and bring it back when you like.'

'Can I really?' Jessie was surprised. 'It's quite old, isn't it?'

'Probably about sixty years or so I should think, judging by the cover. It was first published in the eighteenth century, but that isn't a first edition. I picked it up with a load of others at a house sale some months ago. You are the first person to have looked at it.'

'You had two customers this afternoon.'

'Yes – both regulars, collectors,' he said and smiled. 'They come to me for rare books and special editions. I know what they want and keep them in the back room until they come in. If I relied on passing trade I wouldn't earn enough to feed a fly.'

'I had wondered how you managed to keep going.'

Archie laughed, looking younger than he usually did, and she thought she might have misjudged him when she'd told her aunt he was fifty; he probably wasn't much over forty. She just hadn't looked that close, but this seemed to be her day for taking notice of things. Archie had a really nice smile.

'So, did you get the job then, Jessie?'

'I think I may have,' she replied, her face lighting up with pleasure. 'Mrs Carmichael says I'm just right for the job, but she has to speak to Mrs Kendle first – and she's in Devon. I've got to telephone Mrs Carmichael in the morning and see if I suit.'

'You can phone from here if you like,' Archie offered. He had taken off his glasses and rubbed at the bridge of his nose, where they had made a tiny red mark. 'What kind of a job is it? It doesn't sound like nursing.'

'It is of a sort,' Jessie said and explained. 'It isn't what I've been doing, but it will make a change – and I can always give my notice in after a few months if I don't like it there.'

'Yes . . .' He looked at her doubtfully. 'It will be different in the country, Jessie. Do you think you will like it?'

'I'm not sure. You don't know if you don't try, do you?'

'No, that's true enough. Still, as you said, you can always come back. Mrs Pottersby will miss you. I shall, too . . .' A slight colour came into his cheeks as he said that and she smiled at him.

'You're a good friend to me, Archie. I shall miss popping in here to see you, but I shan't forget you. I could write now and then, if you like.' She wasn't sure why she had offered such a thing but his eyes lit up immediately and she could not regret it. After all, there was no harm in writing a letter to a friend.

'I should like that very much, if you have the time,' he said. 'It would be nice to hear how you're settling in, Jessie.'

'Well, I'd better get home and tell my aunt the news,' she said. 'Are you sure I can borrow the book?'

'Of course, for as long as you like. Come in and select a few more to take with you. The books on the tables are worth very little; it wouldn't bother me however long you kept them.'

'I like to read in bed sometimes,' Jessie told him. 'I might take a few with me if that is all right, Archie. If you're sure it doesn't matter when you get them back?'

'Any of these on the tables,' he repeated. 'And don't forget to write to me, Jessie.'

She promised she wouldn't and with the book in her hand started towards the door, but before she could reach it the bell clanged loudly as someone came in. Jessie felt an odd tingling sensation as she realized it was the young man who had sat next to her on the tram earlier that afternoon. He frowned as he looked at her, but she wasn't sure whether he recognized her or not because he walked straight past and went up to the counter to Archie.

'I've decided I'll take the book,' he said. 'If you've still got it.'

'I promised to keep it for you . . .'

Jessie went out, closing the door behind her. The angry young man didn't look like the sort who read many books, but that just showed how wrong you could be.

She tucked her own book into her pocket, turned up her suit collar and started to run as she felt the first spots of rain begin to fall. The sky was very grey now and it felt as if it was getting colder again; she wouldn't be surprised if it turned out to be a wet night.

*   *   *

29

'So you think you've got the job then,' Aunt Elizabeth said as Jessie came down after taking off her best costume and hanging it up to dry so that it didn't lose its shape. 'What was she like, this Mrs Carmichael?'

'Very nice,' Jessie said and went to warm her hands at the fire. She could smell the apple pie in the oven and it made her hungry. 'Yes, I liked her. I shan't be working with her, of course, because she takes care of the London house, and Kendlebury Hall is in Devon. She said the family had a nanny, who was a bit difficult but not really a tartar the way some of them are, but we shall see. I don't have to stay long if I don't like it there.'

'No, of course not,' her aunt agreed. 'They say that change broadens the mind, and it will certainly be a change. I was in service for a year or two before I met Harold, employed as a kitchen help to the cook, I was. I got on with her all right, but I didn't care for the family much – not that I saw them often, but the maids used to grumble about them all the time.'

'In what way?' Jessie asked. She known her aunt had worked in a kitchen – that was where she had learned to cook so well – but she'd never mentioned the family before. 'Were they rude, or demanding, or what?'

'All of that,' Elizabeth said and frowned at the memory. 'Expected the maids to stay up till all hours, never a please or thank you – mind you, they weren't real gentry. Jumped-up jacks, Cook called them, made a fortune out of trade. They say the gentry are much better, nicer altogether. I dare say you'll get on all right, Jess.'

'Yes, I expect so.'

Jessie was thoughtful as she went to bed that night, wondering if she'd made the right decision. Perhaps she ought to have waited a bit longer, written to that address in Manchester. Mrs Carmichael was pleasant, but she wasn't her employer, and the brief glimpse she'd had of Captain Kendle hadn't been encouraging.

She took the book Archie had loaned her to bed and read for an hour or so before putting out her light. It was a while before she settled to sleep and then she began to dream. She dreamed about Robbie calling to her as he lay in the mud of the trenches and she could feel his pain.

In the dream she was there with him, the guns booming, shells exploding into the damp earth, and she could hear the screams of the men who lay wounded and dying. She knew she had to reach Robbie but the mud was so thick it was squelching round her ankles, dragging her down as she tried to get to where Robbie lay. She was panting, her chest hurting as she fought her way to his side. He was face down in the mud and she took hold of his shoulders, struggling to turn him over so that she could see his face, and then suddenly he was on his back, staring up at her, but it wasn't Robbie after all.

Jessie woke with a start from the nightmare. She was hot and sweating and her heart was racing with fear as she recalled the dream, still so vivid in her mind. The eyes staring up at her had been those of a dead man, but it wasn't Robbie – it was Captain Kendle.

Shivering, Jessie got out of bed and pulled on her warm dressing robe. What on earth had made her dream such a terrible thing? She'd had her usual supper of warm cocoa and a couple of biscuits, nothing that should have brought on a nightmare.

Glancing out through the curtains she saw that it was still dark outside, though there was a light on in the bakery at the end of the yard. They started work early there, but she usually slept until much later.

She wouldn't go back to sleep if she returned to bed, not after that nightmare. She would go downstairs and make a cup of tea, she decided, and gave a little shudder. Anything to get that awful picture out of her mind.

'I spoke to Mrs Kendle last night,' Mrs Carmichael said when Jessie rang later that morning. 'She is absolutely delighted that you are interested in taking the position. She knows someone at the hospital where you worked and she is going to be ringing there today to ask about you, Jessie, but she said to consider the job yours if you left for the reasons you told me. She thinks you were quite within your rights to report that doctor. In fact, she said it took courage to do what you did, miss.'

'I was angry,' Jessie said truthfully. 'If I had thought about it a bit more I might not have done it. Are you sure the job is mine?'

'They want you to start as soon as possible, Jessie.'

'I could travel tomorrow if that's suitable,' Jessie said. 'I expect there's a train to take me as far as Torquay, isn't there?'

'Yes, though I think you may have to change somewhere, take the branch line, otherwise you have to come back from Torquay on a branch line. It's only a small place and not all the mainline trains stop there – but ask at the ticket office, they'll tell you.'

'What do I do when I get to Kendlebury?'

'I'll give you a telephone number to ring from the station office. Someone will come out and fetch you if you let them know you've arrived. But I'll tell them you're coming in the morning and they will expect you.'

'Thank you. I shall go home and pack a couple of cases.'

'You do that, Jessie – and good luck.'

Jessie thanked her again, then turned as Archie came into his little back room as she hung up. He looked at her expectantly.

'Everything all right?'

'Yes, fine, thanks,' she told him. 'I'm going down tomorrow.'

'That's good,' he said. 'Would you like to go out for a meal this evening to celebrate? It will be the last time I shall see you for a while.'

Jessie hesitated for a moment, but then made up her mind. It would be nice to go somewhere special for a change, and why shouldn't she go with him?

'Yes, thank you,' she said. 'I think I should like that, Archie. As you said, it may be months before I'm in town again.'

Was it her imagination or did she see a shadow of pain cross his face? She wondered if it had been wise to agree after all, because she didn't want him getting too fond of her, didn't want to hurt him, but she couldn't change her mind now.

*   *   *

32

Jessie glanced at herself in the mirror. She was wearing a dress she hadn't worn since Robbie's last leave and she'd done her hair in a softer style. It was the first time she'd been out with a man for ages and she was nervous. She wasn't even sure why she'd agreed to go.

She liked Archie, of course she did, but as a friend. It wouldn't be fair to let him think there could ever be anything else between them, but that didn't stop them being friends.

'You look nice, Jess,' her aunt said as she went downstairs. 'Going somewhere special?'

'Archie asked me to go with him for a meal as it was the last time I would see him for a while.'

Elizabeth nodded. 'Well enjoy yourselves . . .' She hesitated, then, 'Don't hurt him, love. He's a good bloke. I think he's been hurt before.'

'What do you mean? How was he hurt?'

'It's just a feeling.' Elizabeth smiled. 'I spoke out of turn. I know you wouldn't hurt him deliberately, Jess. As long as he understands it's just friends.'

'Yes, of course he does,' Jessie said, but felt a little guilty. She wouldn't want Archie to get the wrong idea.

Jessie brushed her long hair before going to bed. The light of her lamp picked out the hint of red and made it shine like darkly burnished copper. Her face was a little pale, her eyes wide as she thought about the evening she had just spent with Archie. He was a nice, kind man and a pleasant companion, but his sudden proposal of marriage had shocked her. She had just never thought he would really ask, though her aunt had often said she thought he was interested.

'I know it must be a bit of a shock, Jessie,' Archie had said, looking awkward. 'But with you going away . . . I just wanted you to know how I feel. I've admired you for a long time, but I never thought there was a chance.'

'I really don't know what to say, Archie – except that I'm sorry. I don't want to get married, not at this moment. I am not sure that I ever shall. I haven't really got over Robbie yet.'

Archie had accepted her refusal like the gentleman he was,

not making a fuss or trying to persuade her, but she'd felt awful for letting him down.

'You will still write to me?' he'd asked anxiously. 'We can still be friends?'

'Yes, of course we can,' Jessie had said. 'I like you very much, Archie – I just don't want to get married.'

Jessie sighed and put down her hairbrush. It was getting late and she had to be up early in the morning.

Three

Jessie had plenty of time to think on the train the next morning. She had a packed lunch that her aunt had made for her, a book to read and a magazine she'd bought at the station. She flicked through the pages, reading an article about a clinic that had opened in London earlier in the year to give free advice and cheap contraceptives to women, especially the poor, who were so often worn out by excessive childbearing, which added to their burdens of poverty and neglect.

It made her feel sad and a little angry when she read about the protests by churchmen and others, who should by rights have been all for helping those poor women. They were supposed to care, but all they ever seemed to do was preach at people rather than help them, and condemn Doctor Marie Stopes for trying to help.

She laid the newspaper aside, her thoughts reverting to what was really bothering her as she gazed out of the window at the countryside, through which they were passing at what seemed a terrific speed to someone who had only been on a train a few times in her life. The shock of Archie asking her to marry him still hadn't worn off and she kept going over it in her mind.

'I'm not much of a catch for a girl like you, Jessie. Your Robbie was a fine young man, handsome and strong, the sort who would have worked hard and given you a good life. I liked him a lot and I was sorry when you lost him. I know you still think about him and you haven't found anyone you can love in the same way, but I wanted you to know I was there if you ever needed me. I'm not going to pester you. I just want you to know I care for you, Jessie.'

She'd refused him immediately, of course, but he'd been

so nice about it that she'd been touched and had reached across the table to touch his hand. 'Thank you, Archie. You're a good friend. If I change my mind I'll let you know – but I don't know what else to say at this moment.'

'You don't have to. I know how you feel. I would marry you for companionship, to take care of you, but if all I can be is your friend then I'll be that.'

Archie's humble proposal, his kindness and his generosity had touched her. She had wanted to cry but she hadn't because it might have embarrassed him. Instead, she told him how much she was enjoying the book he had loaned her and the subject was changed. She'd enjoyed her evening out with him, and he'd walked her to her aunt's front door afterwards. He hadn't tried to kiss her and she'd been grateful. She didn't love Archie in that way and she didn't want to be kissed by him, even though she was fond of him as a friend.

Sighing, Jessie put the whole thing out of her mind. She had been travelling for what seemed like ages and she was beginning to feel hungry. Her aunt had packed sausage rolls, sandwiches and a slice of fruit cake.

'It's a long way, Jess,' she'd said. 'And you never know what sort of food they'll offer you when you get there.'

Jessie had had the carriage to herself for most of the time, the lady and gentleman who had been sitting opposite her at the start getting off about an hour after they left London. Since then no one had got into her carriage. It was only as she opened her lunch tin and started to eat that the carriage door was thrust open and someone came in from the corridor. She looked up, feeling as if she'd been caught doing something impolite, and could hardly keep from gasping as she saw who had entered. He was wearing the same brown suit, but this time he had a battered felt hat over his dark hair. He took his hat off and sat opposite her.

Jessie hesitated. She felt awkward about eating her lunch now. Ma had always said it was rude to eat in public.

'Do you mind?' she asked. 'It's just that I'm hungry . . .'

The man looked up from his paper, which he'd opened as soon as he sat down, and frowned. She wasn't wearing her best costume or a hat and she didn't think he had remembered her. Why should he? He'd hardly looked at her on the tram

36

and she doubted that he'd noticed her in Archie's shop. Then he'd seemed intent on what he was after – presumably a book that Archie had kept for him.

'Why should I mind?' he asked. 'Eat your lunch if you're hungry, lass. If I'd thought to bring something, I'd join you.'

He spoke well but there was a faint burr of the North Country in his voice. She hadn't noticed it on the tram, but his tone was much friendlier today, less harsh and clipped, and his mouth was softened by a faint smile. Clearly he was in a better mood than he had been a day or so earlier.

'Are you hungry?' Jessie asked and offered the tin. 'I've got loads here. My aunt always gives me far too much. The sausage rolls are really good, but I shan't eat them all.'

It was his turn to hesitate now, but instead of snapping her head off as she'd feared he might, he grinned and helped himself to a sausage roll.

'Your aunt *is* a good cook,' he said as he bit into it, wolfing it down in a couple of munches. 'I don't think I've tasted better.'

'Have another – and a sandwich,' Jessie encouraged. 'I don't feel so rude if you're eating too. Ma used to clip my ear if I ate in the street, but it's a long way to Devon and I had my breakfast early.'

'I didn't get time to eat anything,' he said. 'I almost missed the train as it was.' Jessie was offering the tin and after a moment's pause he helped himself to a paste sandwich and another sausage roll. 'My name is Paul Smith. It's very generous of you to share your meal with me, miss.'

'Jessie Hale. I'm glad to have a bit of company. I've been travelling for what seems like forever.'

'I caught the train a few stops back,' he said. 'I'll be getting off again soon.'

'Oh . . .' Jessie wondered if she had made a mistake. Perhaps he wasn't the angry young man from the tram; he certainly wasn't displaying any signs of anger or aggression now. 'I've come from London this morning.'

'I was in London the day before yesterday. I'm travelling light, moving about the country for my work. I shall be some-where else the day after tomorrow.'

'Are you a salesman?' Jessie was curious.

He gave a soft chuckle, and there was amusement in his eyes, as if he were laughing at a secret joke. 'Of a sort, I suppose. Yes, you could say that. I sell ideas, talk to people about things.' Jessie offered the tin again but he shook his head. 'No thanks. It was good of you to share, but keep the rest for later; you might get hungry again.'

Jessie put the tin away. The train was slowing to a halt and she could see several people on the platform waiting to get on. A man and two women came into the carriage and sat down. The young man who had shared her lunch picked up his paper. As the train began to move off again Jessie heard a man's voice in the corridor asking for tickets. He went into the carriage next door and she opened her bag to look for her ticket just as Paul Smith got to his feet and started to leave.

He dropped his paper. Bending down to pick it up, Jessie saw that it was two days old. He frowned as she handed it to him, seeming almost in a hurry to leave and not bothering to say goodbye, which was odd after the friendly way they had talked. It was only a few seconds after he'd closed the carriage door that the ticket inspector opened it again. The thought that perhaps Mr Smith had been trying to avoid him crossed her mind, but she dismissed it almost at once. Surely she was wrong! He couldn't have been travelling without a ticket, could he?

Yet it might fit in with what he'd told her, she realized. He hadn't told her what kind of a job he actually did; only that he was selling something. And just how did you sell ideas? Unless he was an inventor. Yet wouldn't he have been carrying a case with drawings or papers of some kind? All he'd appeared to have with him was the newspaper, though his luggage could be in the guard's van as hers was, of course. Jessie frowned. He'd told her he was travelling light – was he also trying to avoid paying his fare?

Perhaps the reason he hadn't eaten breakfast that morning was because he had no money to buy it. Jessie believed that she might have hit on the truth and was glad she had given him some of her food. If he couldn't pay his fare or buy food he must be out of work.

Then she remembered he had bought a book from Archie and he'd paid his fare on the tram, because she'd seen him. So perhaps her imagination was taking a leap too far.

She glanced at her own paper for a moment, but she couldn't stop thinking about the man who had shared her lunch, wishing she had offered her paper to him. He must have found the old one on the station. Perhaps he'd picked it up hoping to find a job advertised. Perhaps he was travelling in the hope of finding work.

Oh, why was she bothering? It wasn't her business. There were a lot of men out of work. She remembered the match-seller in London. At least he had been trying to earn a few pence honestly. Until the government sorted things out, a lot of people might be tempted to travel without a ticket if they dared.

Glancing out of the window as the train pulled into the next station she caught sight of Paul Smith getting off. He wasn't carrying any luggage, but there was no sign of the inspector, so it looked as if he might have got away with it this time. Now, why did that please her? She ought to have been outraged as a member of the fare-paying public that he had cheated the railway, but she wasn't.

She looked at the station clock. It was nearly twelve and she had another hour or more before she reached her destination. She took out her book and began to read.

The station was a small one with a short platform. There was a small wooden building with a picket fence and a neat garden, which seemed to be the stationmaster's home, but nothing more. Jessie felt a little uncertain as she alighted because it seemed so empty, with no newspaper stands or booths selling hot drinks like there were in London and the larger stations. However, the porter who helped her fetch her cases from the guard's van assured her that she'd come to the right place.

'Where do you want to go, miss?' he asked as he carried both her pieces of luggage to the pretty little cottage and set them down on a green-painted wooden bench outside. 'Would you be the young lady expected up at the Hall?'

'Yes.' She felt a surge of relief, although she was also

surprised that it should be known she was arriving that day. 'Kendlebury Hall. I was told to phone from the office when I got here.'

'No need to do that, miss. Tom Carter's waiting for you in the yard beyond the station with the Daimler. We don't get many visitors here; mostly parcels, crates and livestock in the guard's van. Visitors usually take the mainline to Torquay. Quicker that way, see. Only locals use this line as a rule, and they don't travel often.'

'No, I suppose not,' she said. 'Where did you say the yard was?'

'I'll take you there, miss. Nothing much else for me to do. You were the only one to get off and there's no freight today.'

Jessie thanked him. She felt a bit strange, because it seemed so quiet and isolated, and so very different from the bustle of London. She could see a few houses in the distance, but the station was a bit away from the small village, which was really no more than a hamlet. Jessie thought it was easy to see why the main line didn't serve the outlying areas and wasn't surprised when the porter told her he was also the station-master. The railway couldn't make much of a profit from stations like this, she thought. It was a wonder they didn't close it down, especially when there was a better route to the busy main stations.

She was glad of the friendly porter's help as the yard was quite a distance to walk, especially if she'd been carrying her own luggage. She saw a man wearing a pale grey uniform and a chauffeur's cap leaning against a rather impressive car, but he straightened up as he saw her and came to take the bags from her obliging helper.

'You'll be Miss Hale then,' he said and grinned at her. 'I'm glad you turned up, miss. Cook said you would change your mind at the last minute and I'd be wasting my time comin' to meet you. I bet her two bob you would come. She'll be hoppin' mad when she has to pay up!'

He opened the front passenger door for her. She caught the smell of leather and polish as she slid into the comfortable seat. This was real luxury.

'Might as well sit up front as in the back,' he said with

what she thought might be a flirtatious look. 'I'm Carter – chauffeur and handyman up at the Hall. I keep the cars in going order, chop wood or anything else I'm asked to do – within reason. If you want to go into Torquay on your afternoon off, it's me who'll be taking you and fetching you off the train when you come back. You could walk from the station of course; it's a tidy step but manageable when it's fine. But as long as you say when you're coming back I don't mind fetchin' you, miss. I could wait in town for you if you don't want to stay too long.'

'That's very obliging of you, Carter,' she said, glancing at his profile. She caught a glimpse of dark hair slightly streaked with grey beneath his cap, and noticed the laughter lines at the corners of his eyes and mouth. He wasn't a young man by any means, but he had a friendly manner and seemed decent enough. 'Shall we see how things go for a while? I might not even bother to go out much for a start. I shall probably want to get to know my surroundings, and I enjoy walking when I have the time.'

'You don't want to stay here on your free afternoon,' he said. 'If Madam knows you're around she'll find something for you to do. You take my advice and go somewhere on your free days. Employers are all the same – give them an inch and they'll take a mile.'

Jessie laughed. At least there was someone here she could talk to, she thought. 'Tell me what Mrs Kendle is like,' she prompted. 'Is she difficult to work for – very demanding?'

'She's not too bad as long as you don't get on the wrong side of her,' Carter said. 'Sir Joshua can be a bit of a grouch, but the old lady is lovely and the captain . . . he's not so bad underneath. He has his better days, but keep out of his way when he's in a mood.'

'I've met Captain Kendle in London,' Jessie said. 'He wasn't very friendly.'

'The captain doesn't mince his words – and he doesn't take much notice of the ladies, doesn't matter whether they're of his class or servants. He hardly looks at them these days.'

'Surely he looks at his wife?'

'He's polite to her but that's as far as it goes, I'd say,'

Carter replied. 'The little girl is two now – the captain and his wife got on all right until that last time . . .' He paused thoughtfully. 'Cook says it was his wound that changed him, but I ain't so sure.'

'What do you mean?' Jessie looked at him in surprise. 'I know Captain Kendle was ill, but where was he wounded? You're not suggesting that he isn't . . . that he can't . . .'

'That he isn't a proper man anymore? No, at least not for any physical reason,' Carter said and frowned. 'It could be a mental problem, of course, but he was wounded in the arm and chest – nothing that prevents him from doing his duty, as you might say. He just doesn't seem interested, that's all.'

'You don't know that,' Jessie said. She was slightly shocked at this turn of conversation; they ought not to be discussing their employers like this! 'You can't know what goes on in the privacy of their bedroom.'

'They have separate rooms, and he never visits her in hers – at least that's what Alice says, and she should know. She makes their beds and cleans the rooms. She told Cook that the second pillow never gets used.'

'Not conclusive,' Jessie said with a little frown. She wasn't sure why she was taking this stand, but it seemed wrong to write someone off that way, and she was uncomfortable with discussing details of things she felt should be private. 'I'm not sure we ought to be talking about such things, Carter. It isn't really any of our business, is it?'

'No, but it's natural, see. They're our family and we like to know they're all right. Lady Kendle is worried about them, I know that much.' He pulled a wry face at her. 'I'm the one what carries her about, see. She can't walk, can't hardly get out of bed, but she likes to look at the garden. I carry her down and push her about in the bath chair when it's fine. She always thanks me and she talks to me, just little things, that's how I know she's worried about her son and his wife. She often talks to me about the old days, her memories, the early days of her marriage, and I think she is unhappy about the way things are since the war. I heard Sir Joshua tell his wife that the captain must have a lady friend he visits, but I don't think that's right. You can always tell when that sort

42

of thing is going on, see, and it ain't – not to my way of thinking.'

Jessie found herself sympathizing with Captain Kendle suddenly. It must be irritating for a private man – which by all accounts, he was – to have everyone so interested in his every movement.

But she soon forgot about the captain and his troubles as the car swept round a bend and entered the estate through a pair of tall iron gates that were opened wide and wedged back by tufts of grass and debris that had accumulated over time. There was a small red-brick gatehouse, but the windows were thick with cobwebs on the inside and it was clear it hadn't been used for a while. They drove for some minutes between dense trees, some of which had grown over into an arch in parts. It was dark through the trees and when they emerged into the open once more she saw that there was a gravel drive leading up to the house – but what a house! Jessie craned forward to catch a better sight of the building as they crunched their way towards it.

Her first thought was that it was beautiful, golden and lovely, built of a honey-coloured stone with white pillars forming a sort of portico at the front entrance and steps leading up to the veranda that ran along the front and the side of the house. The windows were long and narrow with small squared panes of glass, the door massive and made of a dark oak that time had turned almost black. Lawns surrounded it on all sides and there were rose beds under the verandas, the trailing varieties curling up over the balustrades, mixing with jasmine and honeysuckle. At one end there was an annexe leading into what seemed to be a kind of gallery with long glass windows and a domed roof, though she only caught a glimpse as they swept round the side to the back of the house. She asked Carter what they had just passed and he told her it was called the Orangery, though no one bothered with it these days, which was rather a waste, Jessie thought.

She imagined the house would look wonderful in summer when the roses hung there in clusters, and the scent in the house through the open windows must be marvellous at times. The gardens themselves were extensive and quite beautiful.

Some little distance from the house she could just see a small lake shimmering in the winter sunshine, and there were a couple of tiny buildings that must be summerhouses but which looked like temples from the fables she had read as a child.

It wasn't a huge house by country house standards, for Jessie had seen and admired pictures of some of the great English country houses, though she had never actually visited one. Aunt Elizabeth had told her that some of them were open to the public at certain times of the year and they'd often spoken of visiting one day, but somehow they'd never got round to it, perhaps because of the war.

She thought that this house looked as if it was a family home, used and loved rather than for show. She saw a gardener with a wheelbarrow and a rake; he seemed to be clearing up debris, bits of wood that had fallen from the trees that bordered the lawns, a few weeds and stones tossed in his barrow. He was leaning on his brush handle, smoking a cigarette, taking his time to look about him and enjoy his work rather than rush at it, and she thought that he was quite elderly.

'How many gardeners does Sir Joshua employ?' she asked Carter as he drew the car to a halt in the courtyard at the rear of the house. 'It must take several to look after this place.'

'There's just Fred Dobson, his son Ned, and Jethro Wylie's boy on a regular basis these days,' he replied as he switched off the engine. 'The captain does some of the tree work himself sometimes, and when they are slack on the farm he gets some of the men to come in and do the heavy jobs. Fred is really only up to the titivating these days, though he keeps the kitchen garden a treat, always plenty of vegetables for the table. There used to be nearer a dozen outside men once upon a time; the gates were always kept shut in them days with a man to open and close them every time, and there were several grooms and all.'

Jessie remembered what Mrs Carmichael had said about the family not being as well off as it had been once, but she didn't comment. Carter was getting out of the car. He took her bags from the boot and motioned for her to follow him towards what looked like the kitchen door, but was actually a sort of back lobby. The kitchen was to the left, just inside a small dark hall, and Carter waved an arm towards it.

'I'll take these bags to your room, miss,' he said. 'Go into the kitchen and Cook will give you a cup of tea. She'll send someone to let Mrs Pearson know you're here, and she'll show you the ropes. Mrs Kendle is out this afternoon, but she'll be back later. She drove herself in the roadster; it's the captain's two-seater, but Madam uses it when he's in town because she prefers it to being driven in the Daimler.'

Jessie thanked him and went into the kitchen, which was big enough to have dropped Aunt Elizabeth's whole downstairs into and still left room over. The floor was of soft brown tiles that Jessie knew would look red when wet, worn smooth in places by the passage of many feet over the years. Under the windows were three deep sinks with wooden draining boards between them and at one end a huge black iron range for cooking; there was an old-fashioned spit hanging above it and large ovens to either side of the hob. Jessie's aunt cooked on a similar, though much smaller range. A long scrubbed pine table ran down the middle of the room and there were various dressers against the walls, set with blue and white china and a medley of cooking utensils. The room smelled of herbs and baking and there was a small open fire opposite the window, with a wooden grandfather chair placed at either side.

At the sink furthest from Jessie a young girl of about sixteen was standing with her arms up to her elbows in suds, scrubbing pans. An older woman with a large white apron pinned over her ample middle was at the kitchen table, setting out the cakes that had made the room smell so delicious on a wire tray for cooling. She turned as Jessie coughed politely to let her know she was there, the surprise in her face a picture to see.

'Well, bless my soul,' she said. 'Carter was right after all. You must be Jessie Hale. I was sure you wouldn't come. Stands to reason in my opinion, a young woman trained as a nurse wouldn't waste her time coming here – and all the way from London, too.'

'I'm sorry you lost your bet,' Jessie said. 'I believe I've cost you two shillings.'

Cook's belly shook as she laughed. 'Lord love you, lass, it would have been cheap at twice the price to get you here. We've been that muddled since the last girl left us that we haven't known whether we're comin' or goin' – have we, Maggie?'

'Why did she leave?'

'Too much work,' Cook answered. 'I shouldn't be tellin' you that, miss, or you'll be off on the next train home, I shouldn't wonder.'

'I don't mind work. We had to work hard in the VADs – and in horrible conditions, too. If you can get through that you can get through most things.'

'In the VADs, was you?' Maggie was drying her arms on a bit of towel and came towards the table, looking interested. She was a pretty girl, thin and pale but with dark curly hair. 'My sister Peggy was, too. She married one of the soldiers she helped to nurse. They live in Manchester now. She keeps inviting me to go up there, says I'd find a job that pays better than this one in a shop. I wouldn't mind trying it, but me ma won't let me until I'm older.'

'Work isn't that easy to find at the moment,' Jessie said. 'There are a lot of men who can't find a decent job. You're probably better off where you are, Maggie. May I call you that? And my name is Jessie.'

'It's nice to have you here, Jessie,' the younger girl said and smiled. 'There ain't many young folk here now; they've all gone off to the city, so Ma says.'

'It was the war,' Cook said, nodding her head so that her chins wobbled. 'They took the men for the army and then the lasses went off to find work in the munitions and factories, or nursing like you. You can't expect them to come back to a place like this, can you? Stands to reason there's more life in the towns for young ones. Maggie will be off as soon as she can, and then what shall I do? I can't manage everything myself.'

'You'll find someone to take my place,' Maggie said. 'Maybe I shan't go if I find myself a feller.' She grinned wickedly at Jessie. 'Have you got a feller, Jessie?'

'No, I haven't,' Jessie said. She didn't think it necessary to elaborate for the moment. 'Have you?'

46

'I've got my eye on a lad, works on the farm,' Maggie said and giggled. 'But don't tell Ma I said so or she'll have my guts for garters!'

Jessie promised she wouldn't and was invited to sit down and have a cup of tea with them. 'We were just about to have five minutes, weren't we, Cook? If you're good, Jessie, you might get one of them buns.' Maggie eyed them hungrily.

'That girl's got worms,' Cook exclaimed as she saw Maggie's eyes on her baking. 'Go on then, lass. I ain't one to starve the young, though you'll be havin' your dinner before long.'

'Can't wait,' Maggie said and snatched one of the rock cakes before Cook could change her mind. It was still hot and burned her mouth as she bit into it but she just fanned her mouth and grinned as she wolfed it down. 'You want to try one, Jessie, they're good.'

'Thank you, but I ate my lunch on the train and I'm not hungry yet – maybe later, at supper, if I may. They do look good.'

Before Cook could answer a woman came bustling into the kitchen. She was a woman of middle years, slimmer than Cook and dressed in a neat dark grey dress with a white collar pinned with a silver brooch at the neck.

'I'm Mrs Pearson, the housekeeper here,' she said, offering her hand to Jessie. 'And you will be Miss Hale. I am very pleased to meet you and glad you have joined the staff. I see Cook has poured you a cup of tea, so I'll let you drink that and then I'll take you up to your room and show you how to find your way about.'

'Will you have a cup of tea with us, Mrs Pearson?' Cook asked.

'I'll have mine later, when I take a tray up to her ladyship. She likes a bit of company and I'll sit with her for a few minutes. Alice hasn't had time to see to her this afternoon because she's been looking after the children. Nanny had one of her little turns just after Mrs Kendle left . . . doesn't she always these days?'

Cook shook her head over it. 'Nanny is getting past it,' she said. 'By rights she should be pensioned off, but she won't

47

hear of it – and Mrs Kendle says she couldn't manage without her.'

The housekeeper pulled a face that spoke volumes but no one added anything to Cook's statement.

'I suppose I'll have to take Nanny's tea up then,' Maggie said. 'She don't like me doin' it, says I'm not supposed to be above stairs.'

'She's right,' Cook said and pulled a face at her. 'I can't spare you to run errands for Nanny.'

'Perhaps I could take it later,' Jessie offered and they all looked at her in surprise. 'Once I've taken my coat off and made myself tidy. If you could show me where her room is, Mrs Pearson, I should like to start making myself useful as soon as possible. And if Nanny isn't well I might be able to help her.'

'It's just her age,' Cook said. 'But it would help me if you wouldn't mind doin' it when Alice has her hands full – mind it will be your job to look after the children now, so she'll have a bit more time to do her own work. There's only the four of us now, see, plus Nanny. She does a bit when she's up to it, but only for the children.'

'That must make a lot of work for all of you,' Jessie said. 'This is a big house to look after. You must tell me what my duties are, Mrs Pearson. I know I shall be looking after the children and helping with Lady Kendle, but if I can do anything else to help, perhaps when the children are having a nap . . .'

'Well, isn't that nice?' Cook said and beamed at her. 'Bless you, Jessie love. If you look after those children and help with Lady Kendle, the rest of us will manage just fine. Off you go with Mrs Pearson now. You can take the tray to Nanny this evening, because she'll want to meet you, but Alice usually does it and that's how it should be.'

Jessie had finished her tea and she stood up, following Mrs Pearson out of the kitchen and along the hall to a door at the end. When opened the door revealed a set of stairs that led up to the first floor.

'If you're going to the main rooms, this is the way,' Mrs Pearson told her. 'But the bedrooms are up this next staircase, and the staff bedrooms are on the floor above. Some of them were actually attics in the old days, but we don't use those now. We had more staff years ago, you see, but now there aren't so many so Lady Kendle told us to make use of the best rooms and shut the attics off. Nanny's room is that one, right at the end because it leads into the nursery, which is on the same floor as us, but at the front of the house.'

Jessie was following her up a third flight of stairs, which led to a long, narrow hall. The other two floors had been furnished rather better than this one, but there was still a plain brown carpet on the floor and the walls were covered in a bright floral paper to make them look more cheerful. The room to which Jessie was shown was comfortable, with a single bed, a wardrobe, and a large chest of drawers with a mirror on a stand, and there was a chair and a table by the window. Someone had placed a tiny vase of chrysanthemum buds on the table and there was also a pen tray and inkwell with a leather-covered blotter.

'Oh, they smell lovely,' Jessie said, catching the scent of the flowers as she went over to look out of the tiny window. 'I can see the park from here and some buildings – is that the farm Carter mentioned?'

'No, it's the old stables,' Mrs Pearson told her. 'There's only a couple of horses now and they are kept at the farm stables. Carter uses one of those buildings for his workshop and others have been knocked into one to make a garage for the cars. There used to be ten or fifteen horses there once.' She gave a little sniff of disapproval. 'Do you think you will be comfortable here, Miss Hale?'

'Please do call me Jessie. Yes, I am sure I shall, Mrs Pearson. Once I settle in I shall be quite happy.' She took off her coat and hung it in the wardrobe, which had plenty of hooks and half a dozen hangers for her use. 'Now, if I look tidy enough, I'll go down and fetch Nanny's tray. I believe you said she was at the far end of the hall, didn't you?'

'I'll take you and introduce you if you're sure you're ready. You don't want to have a few minutes to yourself to unpack your things?'

'I can do that before I go to bed,' Jessie said. 'I would

prefer to make myself useful if that is all right. Shall we go now?'

'Yes, come along then.' Mrs Pearson looked at her with approval. 'I must say you are a big improvement on the last girl Mrs Kendle employed. Gave herself airs that one, wouldn't mix with the rest of us or do anything other than strictly what she was employed to do.'

'Silly girl,' was the only comment Jessie allowed herself as she followed Mrs Pearson to the door at the far end of the hall. The housekeeper knocked and then went in, even though there was no answer. She stopped abruptly and gave a gasp of dismay at the sight that met her eyes. Looking beyond her, Jessie saw that Nanny had slumped on the floor next to the bed and was lying face down. 'It looks as if she's more seriously ill than you thought.' Stepping into the room past the stunned housekeeper, Jessie knelt on the floor and took hold of Nanny's wrist, giving a little sigh of relief as she felt a faint pulse. 'It's all right, she isn't dead. I think by the look of her that she may have had a stroke. I'll get her to bed and perhaps you could ask Carter to fetch a doctor?'

'Yes, Miss – I mean Jessie. Do you think you can manage her on your own?'

'Yes, I am sure I can,' Jessie said. 'You go and find Carter and I'll get her comfortable. I'm used to this sort of thing; it's my job.'

Jessie lifted the old lady into a sitting position and was pleased to hear a faint moan as her eyes flickered. She managed to open them for a moment and look at her, though they closed again almost at once. Jessie lifted her and then took the weight on to her shoulder as she had been taught. Nanny was much lighter than most of the patients she had been dealing with at the hospital and felt little more than skin and bones. Clearly she hadn't been eating properly for a long time; she had probably been feeling ill but worried about making a fuss in case she was turned out.

'It's all right,' she said as the old lady's eyelids flickered and her eyes seemed to focus on her for a few moments. 'You've had a little turn, Nanny, but I don't think it's too serious. A few days in bed and you're going to be as right as rain again, if you do what the nurse tells you and take a little more care of yourself.'

'Nothing wrong . . .' Nanny mumbled but couldn't get any further as she was gently deposited on the bed and covered with a thick eiderdown.

'Nothing wrong that a little care won't cure,' Jessie agreed. 'You just rest now and the doctor will be here soon.'

She sat on the edge of the bed and stroked Nanny's face and then her hands, knowing that gentle contact helped to reassure patients in this condition, for whom fear was a major source of discomfort. 'You'll soon be up and looking after the children again, Nanny. Don't you worry about anything. I'm here now and things are going to be much easier for you. You shouldn't have to do so much and now you won't have to.'

Jessie saw a tear slip from the corner of her patient's eye and knew that she was getting through to her, even though she was giving no sign of having heard her.

'Just rest and sleep now, and then in the morning you are going to feel much better.'

She smiled as she felt Nanny's hand move slightly in hers. It had been a stroke, she was sure of it, but fortunately it had not been a massive one and with luck and the proper care the old lady might soon be up and about again.

It was just as well that she had come, Jessie thought. Nanny was already considered troublesome by most of the household and if there had been no one to nurse her she would probably have been on her way to the infirmary before long.

She left the bed and went over to the dressing table, finding a little flask of lavender water. There was a handkerchief next to the cologne and she shook a few drops on to it, taking it back to soothe Nanny's forehead. It was as she was doing this that the door opened behind her and she spoke without glancing round.

'Has Carter gone for the doctor? I think she will be all right, but I should prefer another opinion. He can't do much for her except advise rest and care, and I'll see she gets that, but it's best to be safe.'

'I quite agree with you,' a voice said, making her look round sharply. 'Thank you for taking charge so efficiently, and for caring. I am sorry I don't remember your name, though someone did tell me.'

'Captain Kendle!' Jessie said, startled. 'I'm Jessie Hale. I've come to help with the children and Lady Kendle. Forgive me, I didn't know it was you. I thought Mrs Pearson had come back. I had asked her to send for the doctor.' She bit her lip as she felt his dark gaze on her. 'It was habit, I'm afraid, working at the hospital. I suppose I should have asked permission from someone first.'

'Oh no,' he said and his smile made her heart miss a beat because it was so unexpected. 'In this case you did exactly as you ought – and I can't thank you enough. Nanny may be a bit troublesome these days, but she is very precious to me. I should not want to lose her.'

'I don't think you need worry just yet,' Jessie said. 'She's very tired at the moment because she's had a little stroke, but she understands what I've been saying to her and she can move her hand. We shall have to hope that nothing further develops, but for the moment we've been lucky.'

'Yes,' he said and his voice and face both registered approval. 'I think we have been very lucky, Miss Hale.' Somehow she didn't think he was talking about Nanny at all.

Four

'I understand we had a crisis while I was out this afternoon. My husband tells me you dealt with it most efficiently, Jessie.'

Mary Kendle was dressed for the evening in a long blue gown, which clung lovingly to her slender figure. Her fair hair was cut short in a very modern style and she was wearing red lip rouge. Ma would have called her 'fast', Jessie reflected and blushed at her own thoughts. She had no right to criticize her employer, even to herself.

'It was just as well we went in when we did,' she replied as Mary Kendle's gaze narrowed. She was staring again! It was a bad habit and she must learn to curb it. 'Nanny could have been very ill if she'd lain there long.'

'I hear the doctor visited. What was his opinion?'

'He thinks she's been lucky. The seizure was slight and she should recover as long as she stays in bed for a while.'

'That is going to be difficult. We really don't need another invalid in this house.'

Her tone implied that one was enough and Jessie was shocked. She had not yet been taken to see Lady Kendle but by all accounts she was a lovely person and tried not to be a trouble to anyone.

'I don't mind helping to look after her, Mrs Kendle,' Jessie said. 'I can see to her first thing, before I get the children up, and I understand Lady Kendle doesn't require me until after she's had her breakfast.'

'But what happens to the children while you are attending to Mother?' Mary Kendle sighed and looked annoyed. 'Why did it have to happen now? Just when I thought we were getting things settled.'

'It will only be for an hour or so. Perhaps Mrs Pearson or Alice could help. And Nanny should be able to sit quietly with the children in a few weeks' time – if she makes a good recovery, of course.'

'Well, I suppose we are obliged to keep her here for the time being.' Clearly Mary Kendle wasn't happy about the situation, but it seemed that Nanny was safe for the moment. 'I do hope you won't leave us in the lurch, Jessie. It is so difficult to find anyone suitable these days.'

'I shan't leave without good reason, Mrs Kendle. I'm looking forward to making myself useful.'

'What a relief,' Mary replied and smiled for the first time since the interview began. She was rather lovely and quite young, Jessie thought, about the same age as herself, or younger. And it took a lot of effort to run a house like this and look after a family. 'I shall take you in to see Mother before dinner. Mrs Pearson has her meals in her own room. You will naturally have your lunch in the nursery with the children, but in the evening you could fetch a tray to your own room, I suppose. Maggie is too busy to carry it up, I'm afraid.'

'I would rather eat with Cook and Maggie if you don't mind, Mrs Kendle.'

'What an obliging young woman you are, Jessie. Thank you. Shall we go up to Mother now?'

It wasn't a question. Mary was used to having her word stand as law in this house. Jessie had mixed feelings as she followed her from the room. Mary Kendle obviously had a lot on her mind. This house must be difficult to run, especially with a shortage of staff, and life couldn't be all roses for her, but there was something about her that Jessie didn't quite like. She thought her employer might be impossible to please, and there was a hard edge about her manner when she was put out.

Lady Kendle was quite another matter, Jessie decided five minutes after being introduced to the fragile old lady. Her hair was silvery-white, long and pulled neatly into a loop at the back of her head. Her face was deeply lined by the ravages of ill health, but her eyes were bright, inquisitive and kind.

She was very concerned about Nanny and wanted to hear all the details.

'Poor, poor Nanny,' she said as Jessie told her how she had found her. 'I thought she was looking a little unwell this morning when she came in to bring me the papers and talk to me for a few minutes. We've all expected too much of her. She is eighteen years older than I am, you know, and she's worked hard all her life. She worked in a laundry for some years when she was just a child, somewhere up north. She started first as a nursery maid with my husband's parents and then became Nanny when the old nanny retired.'

'The doctor says she will recover given rest, so we must hope for the best,' Mary said and frowned as if she didn't want to talk about the children's nurse.

'What do you think, Jessie?' Lady Kendle asked, looking at her. 'You're a nurse, so I've been told.'

'Yes, my lady, Jessie replied wondering if she should curtsey. She'd never met a real lady before. 'I was in the VADs and then at St Joseph's hospital for two years. We had several patients like Nanny there. It was a church hospital and three of our wards were kept for the poor and elderly. I think bed rest should help. She may have been neglecting herself. If she can be persuaded to rest and eat she should do well.'

'You've had good experience then.' Lady Kendle's gaze was intent. 'Will you find your duties here too much, Jessie? You will have two elderly patients now, as well as the children.'

Jessie smiled at the idea. 'We often had twenty or more patients on the ward. I've been used to being busy, my lady. I don't mind hard work.'

'Call me ma'am – or Anne, if you like,' Lady Kendle said, smiling at her. 'We don't use the title unless it's a formal occasion. I'm very glad you've come and I hope you will be happy with us. Mary needs someone like you to help her. She has too much to do, as have the rest of you, I'm afraid.'

'Thank you, ma'am. Is there anything I can do for you now?'

'No, thank you. Mrs Pearson did my pillows earlier. She will bring me my evening meal on a tray when she is ready.

I don't require much these days. But you may come and see me before you retire, if you will. I should like to talk to you again.'

'Yes, of course, ma'am.'

Jessie had intended to do that anyway. A warm drink of milk and a biscuit often helped patients to settle for the night and it would be no trouble once she'd seen that Nanny was peaceful.

Mrs Pearson arrived with the tray for Lady Kendle. It was beautifully laid out with an embroidered cloth and silver covers over the plates, but Jessie wondered what was under them. She hoped it was something tempting to an invalid's palate. Lady Kendle looked thin and pale, as if she ate too little.

'Well, I shall leave you to find your own way down,' Mary said as they left her mother-in-law's room. 'I hope Mrs Pearson made sure you know your way around.'

'Yes, thank you.' Jessie hesitated. 'Should I call you by your name, Mrs Kendle?'

'The domestic staff call me ma'am,' Mary replied. 'But you are rather different, Jessie. You have been properly educated, I think. Use my name if you prefer. As my mother-in-law said, we want you to be happy with us.'

'Thank you, Mrs Kendle.' Jessie nodded, turning in the opposite direction. She wanted to look in on Nanny again before she went down to supper.

The doctor had given Nanny a sedative and she was sleeping peacefully, her breathing normal and not laboured. Jessie checked and smiled as she found her skin dry and cool. No sign of a fever or sweating. With any luck she would be feeling better when she woke, though she was bound to be an invalid for a while. Jessie wondered what might have happened to the old woman if she had not answered that advert.

Leaving Nanny's room, she went downstairs to find Maggie setting the table in the servants' hall, which was a grand name for a rather small room just off the kitchen.

'In the old days the servants took it in turns to eat in here,' Maggie told her as she helped place the last few items on the table. 'Once the main course has gone upstairs we have ours in here. Cook sent the soup up ten minutes ago. She's putting the roast under covers now so I'll be bringing ours through soon.'

'Do we all eat in here?'

'Mrs Pearson fetches hers on a tray and takes it to her room – it's down the hall from us. Alice and Carter are upstairs serving the family. Carter is a jack of all trades, so Cook says. He was Sir Joshua's man at the start. Now he drives the car and does anything else they ask him. It wouldn't have done once, I can tell you, but we've had to manage because of the war. Alice complains there's too much work, but she won't leave. She's got her eye on a local lad. Besides, they're always looking for more help. Not their fault if they can't find it.'

Jessie followed the informative maid into the kitchen and discovered that Cook was dishing up vegetables and crisply roasted potatoes on to silver dishes. Everything was placed under matching covers and sent upstairs in a serving hatch that operated by way of a pulley.

'Captain Kendle had this put in just before the war. The food keeps better for them since he persuaded his father to have it done,' Cook told her. 'Must've gone cold in the old days before they got it. 'Sides, it saves Carter and Alice running up and down them stairs. They'd never manage fetching it all that way.'

'Shall I get ours?' Maggie asked her.

'Help me send this lot up first.'

Maggie carried the heavily loaded trays to the hatch, putting them inside and pulling the rope that let Carter know they were ready.

'What about Carter and Alice?' Jessie asked. 'When do they eat?'

'Alice will pop down when they're all served up there,' Cook said. 'Carter stays until they've finished, then Mrs Pearson goes up to serve the puddings and he comes down to have his. We used to do it in more style once. Things 'ave been let go since the war. We thought it would get better when the captain came home; he used to be full of ideas – bit of a designer himself he was, always on the go, wanting to

57

modernize us all. He don't seem interested in the house these days. Still, I dare say he's got more than enough to do.'

'Surely the house is Mrs Kendle's responsibility.'

'Well, least said, soonest mended on that score,' Cook said and set some dishes on a tray just as Mrs Pearson came in carrying what looked liked Lady Kendle's tray. Jessie lifted the covers and saw that the food had been hardly touched, though she couldn't fault the poached fish that had been sent up. 'Here you are then, Eve. It's a bit of poached fish as you asked, same as her ladyship.'

'Thank you, Kate,' the housekeeper said. She looked at Jessie for a moment, hesitated, then picked up her tray and went out without a word.

'She probably thought of asking you to eat with her,' Cook said. 'Must get lonely on her own sometimes, but she won't eat with us. Got to keep up some sort of standard, I suppose.'

Jessie nodded. The nurses at St Joseph's had eaten in a separate dining room from Matron and the doctors. She pitied Mrs Pearson in her lonely state but she wasn't going to join her. She liked being with Cook and Maggie, and she was looking forward to meeting Alice.

'What happened to Mr Pearson?' she asked. 'Or is he about somewhere?'

'He used to be the butler here,' Cook said. 'Died of a lung fever a few years back. Things were different here when he was in charge, I can tell you. We had lots of parties and people staying then, and plenty of servants to look after them.'

'Come on,' Maggie said. 'I've got our dinner ready. I'm starvin'!'

'What did I tell you? That girl's got worms,' Cook said, but she smiled and picked up one of the loaded trays as Maggie led the way towards their dining room.

The parlourmaid came down for her dinner just as Maggie had finished setting everything on the table. She was a bright, pretty girl with fair hair and lovely clear grey eyes. She smiled at Jessie, said she was glad she had come and flopped down in her chair.

'I've hardly had a minute all day,' she said. 'And I've just heard they're havin' a dinner party this weekend. There'll be guests overnight, too, which means more work for all of us.'

'Will your ma come in, Alice – and yours, Maggie? Goodness knows how Madam thinks we manage when she has her posh friends to stay!' Cook said and pulled a face. 'You say you haven't had a minute, Alice – what about me? My feet are killing me!'

'I was wondering how you would cope with guests,' Jessie said.

'We get extra help in when we need it,' Cook told her. 'I suppose if I put my foot down Madam would have to find another girl or two on a permanent basis, but I'm comfortable here and we manage most of the time.'

'Can we start?' Maggie asked. 'My stomach is rumbling and they'll be ringing for their pudding before we know it.'

Silence reigned as they ate. It was steak and kidney pudding with roast potatoes, cabbage and butter beans. Jessie cleared her plate with relish. Cook certainly knew her job and the suet pudding melted on the tongue. They had barely finished eating when a bell rang. Cook and Maggie got up together and went through to the kitchen.

'Dirty dishes down, puddings up,' Alice said and reached into a pocket beneath her starched apron. 'I'm dying for a ciggie. Cook hates it if I smoke while we eat. You don't mind, I hope?'

'It doesn't bother me.'

'Want one?'

'No thanks, I don't,' Jessie said. 'Should I carry these plates through, do you think?'

'Up to you.' Alice shrugged. 'I've finished for the day, barring emergencies. Mrs Pearson and me take it in turns to do the tea tray; hers tonight, thank goodness. I'm worn out. What with me own work and the kids.'

'Well, I'll be taking care of the children now.'

'Yeah, so I've heard.' Alice grinned at her. 'You'll have your hands full with that Jack – a regular tearaway he is and no mistake. Little Cathy's a love, but that boy can be a monster. You haven't met them yet, have you?'

'No. I was told it was too late after I'd seen to Nanny. Mrs Carmichael said the children were little lambs.'

'She would,' Alice said, drawing deeply on her cheap cigarette. 'Doesn't have to look after them, does she? That house is easy to run compared with this.'

Jessie absorbed that one in silence. She hadn't given the children too much thought, imagining that it would be easy enough to look after them. She had expected Nanny would be able to advise, but it seemed she was on her own for the moment.

'I expect I'll cope,' she said and got up, gathering a few dishes to take into the kitchen.

Cook was loading a tray of puddings into the serving hatch. Maggie had piled the dirty dishes into one of the sinks to wash later. She turned and smiled as she saw what Jessie had done.

'You didn't need to do that,' she said. 'I was going to bring our pudding through in a moment. It's treacle tart for us – scrummy!'

Jessie laughed. It seemed her new friend was always hungry, but she was still thin and there was no sign of all that food she put away on her hips.

'I like treacle tart, too,' she said, 'but only a small piece for me please. I'm full up after all that dinner.'

Maggie was about to make some remark when Carter walked in. Jessie noticed that he looked very smart in a black suit and white shirt with a bow tie. Clearly he'd changed uniform for his evening duties.

'Any of that steak and kidney pudding left for me?'

'Course there is, we kept it hot for you. Sit down and I'll fetch it to you. Do you want it here or in the room?'

'I think I shall pop in and take another look at Nanny,' Jessie said. 'I shan't be long.'

She ran up the stairs, going carefully into the sick woman's room to find her sleeping peacefully. Smiling to herself, she left her to sleep. Nanny was very tired and a long rest would do her good. Nursing was what Jessie was used to, but looking after the children was another matter. Alice's comments had made her a little nervous. She hesitated, then turned towards the nursery. The children would no doubt be sleeping, but she was curious and to see them asleep might be a good way of reassuring herself.

She opened the door softly, not wanting to wake them, and then her heart caught. A shaded lamp was burning on a table beside the bed and a man sat on the edge. In the light of the lamp his dark blond hair had taken on a coppery look. He was stroking the child's head and a storybook lay opened on the chest beside the bed. Jessie hesitated, realizing that she was intruding. She was about to leave them when he turned his head and saw her. He put a finger to his lips, then beckoned to her to approach. She did so, careful not to make any noise.

'Jack was having a nightmare,' he whispered. 'I've just managed to get him off.'

She nodded, looking down at the sleeping angel. His fair hair was falling across his forehead, his face pink and soft, his skin like the down of a peach. Jessie's throat tightened. How could anyone call such a beautiful child a monster?

Jack's father pointed to a cot further down the room. Jessie went to investigate. Catherine Kendle was dark-haired, more like her mother, with a sharp, foxy face. A lovely child, of course, but not as beautiful as her brother.

Captain Kendle was beckoning to her again. She saw that he was ready to leave and followed him from the nursery, waiting as he carefully closed the door behind them.

'I just wanted to look at them,' Jessie said, feeling that she needed an excuse.

'Best time to meet them when they're asleep,' their father said and grinned at her. She hadn't seen that look in his eyes before and it gave her a jolt. He was different, seemed younger, happier somehow. 'Catherine isn't much trouble yet, I'm told, but my son is a monster, Miss Hale. If I were you I should run while the going is good.'

'Oh no, I don't think so,' she said, blushing at the teasing note in his voice. This was surely a different man to the one she had seen in the London house. 'It may not be easy without Nanny to advise me, but I expect I shall cope.'

'I am certain you will,' he said. 'Well, I mustn't keep you. I have work to do this evening, and I am sure you want to rest for a while. You've had a long journey and this must all seem strange to you.'

Jessie gave him a faint smile as he turned away. He had

61

withdrawn again, as though a door had closed inside him, shutting her out, but somehow she knew that it wasn't just her he was shutting out; it was his life. She found herself wondering about him as she went down the back stairs. Her first opinion of him had been that he was a cold, hard man, but that wasn't true. He cared about Nanny and it was clear that he loved his son. Yet everyone said that he was a reserved man and Carter had hinted that his marriage wasn't all it might be.

But that wasn't her business! Jessie put her employer's husband from her mind. She was here to help with Lady Kendle and look after the children, not to pry into their private lives. As she approached the kitchen she could hear voices.

'What do you reckon to her then?' Carter was asking. 'Seems an obliging sort of girl.'

'How long do you think she will stay?' Alice asked. 'I wouldn't if it weren't for Walter. If the silly idiot would come I'd be off to London tomorrow.'

'Don't you let Walter Brock hear you call him that,' Cook said. 'He'd give you a black eye, my girl.'

'He'd get one back. I don't stand for that nonsense.'

'I reckon she's all right,' Maggie said. 'I like her and I hope she stays.'

'Well, I think . . .'

What Cook was about to say was lost as Mrs Pearson called to Jessie. She had come down the stairs and was trying to catch up with her.

'Jessie! I'd like a word if you don't mind.'

'Yes, Mrs Pearson,' Jessie said and waited for her. 'Did you want something?'

'Just to talk about Nanny. How long do you think it will be before she's able to get up again?'

'It'll be a few days before she can do more than sit out in a chair,' Jessie replied. 'But if you mean when she'll be herself again, that's something I can't tell you. I think she was lucky and there was no real damage done, no paralysis or loss of mobility. She should make a good recovery but she could have another stroke within hours and that might be another story.'

Mrs Pearson pulled a wry face. 'It's going to make so much

more work – and there's guests this weekend. I really don't know how we're going to manage.'

Mrs Pearson was clearly put out and Jessie felt annoyed. As if extra work mattered when someone was ill. She bit back the angry words that leapt to her tongue. 'I shall be looking after her. You don't need to worry.'

'You can't do everything. You have the children and Lady Kendle to see to and can't be running after Nanny all the time.'

'I can manage most of the time.'

'Mrs Kendle says I have to look after the children for an hour in the mornings until Nanny is better. As if I haven't enough to do as it is! This house doesn't run itself, you know.'

'No, I don't expect it does.'

'Madam leaves everything to me and I'm sure I don't know how she expects me to manage with so few staff. I can't be expected to mind the children as well as my own duties.'

'I'm sorry about that. It's just while I look after Lady Kendle. I'll be as quick as I can, I promise.'

'Well, it's not your fault,' she said. 'Madam should have taken on two new girls, but there's no point in trying to tell her. She won't listen. I suppose we're lucky to have you.'

Jessie felt like having a go but kept her mouth shut. Mrs Pearson was clearly worked up and answering back would only make things worse. She went into the kitchen. Maggie was finishing a huge slice of treacle tart.

'There's a scrap left for you,' she said. 'Do you want hot custard on it?'

'No, just as it is,' Jessie replied. 'Any chance of a cup of tea – or do we have it later?'

'I've come for the upstairs tray,' Mrs Pearson said. 'Then I'm going to my room. I've had enough for one day.'

'What about Lady Kendle's supper drink?' Jessie asked.

'She never has anything after her meal,' Cook said. 'She only ate her soup at dinner. Never touched the fish I sent up.'

'I'll take her some warm milk and biscuits when I go up,' Jessie said. 'She needs something to give her strength.'

'She won't drink it,' Mrs Pearson said and sniffed. 'But suit yourself. When I've seen to the tea I'm not doing another thing.'

'She can be a right misery when she likes,' Maggie muttered as the housekeeper went out. 'She wants to swop places with me and Cook sometimes.'

Jessie smiled but made no comment as she ate her treacle tart and drank the tea Cook had poured into a large blue and white cup. Being in the kitchen with the staff at Kendlebury wasn't much different from being in the hospital canteen. The nurses had moaned about Sister or Matron; here it was Mrs Pearson or Mary Kendle, but it didn't mean very much. It was just letting off steam after a hard day's work.

It was nice being part of a team again, Jessie thought as she listened to their gossip. Alice's young man was taking her to a dance in Torquay on Friday night. She was excited about it, telling Maggie about the new dress her mother had made for her.

'I bought some black satin shoes on my afternoon out,' she said. 'I'm dying to wear them but they pinch a bit. I shall have to stretch them before tomorrow or they'll cripple me.'

'I'll do that for you,' Cook said. 'I'll put damp newspaper into the toes and let it dry; that should do the trick.'

'No you won't!' Alice cried, horrified. 'I've got some proper shoe trees. The woman in the shop said they would stretch.'

'Them salesgirls will say anything,' Carter told her, coming in from outside with a bucket of wood for the fire. 'You let me try them on for you. I'll stretch 'em!'

'You will not!' Alice knew she was being teased but wasn't in the mood for it. 'I'm going to my room. I want to curl my hair in papers.'

'Wish I could,' Maggie called after her. 'I've got this lot to wash yet.'

Jessie looked at the sink piled high with dishes.

'Can I help?' she asked.

'I'm used to it,' Maggie said. 'Don't bother me . . . But you can dry the dishes, I suppose. Not the glasses 'cause we rinse them in cold water and leave them to drain, then polish them when they're dry. Get a better sparkle that way. If you put the dishes on the table Cook will put them where she wants them.'

'Are you going to the dance?' Jessie asked as she followed her to the sink and picked up the drying cloth.

'Fat chance,' Maggie moaned. 'Even if I'd got someone to take me, my Ma wouldn't let me go. Says it is where girls get into trouble – palaces of sin, that's what she calls dance halls.'

'Tell you what, I'll take you to a tea dance on your afternoon off,' Carter said. 'They have them every Thursday, Saturday and Monday in Torquay. Take you next week if you like.'

'Go dancin' with you?' Maggie pulled a face. 'No thanks. I want a young feller.'

'That Billy Wright, I suppose,' Carter said, not in the least bothered by her refusal. 'Can't see him dancin'. You'll be lucky to get him to the music hall. All he wants to do is drink down the pub.'

Maggie stuck her tongue out at him but he only laughed. Jessie smiled at their banter. She thought she was going to like it here.

It was half past nine when Jessie took the tray up to Lady Kendle's room. She knocked softly in case the old lady was sleeping, and was invited to enter. She put her tray carefully on the chest beside the bed.

'It's only warm milk and a biscuit, ma'am. A little snack at this time sometimes helps you to sleep.'

'Did you learn that in nursing, Jessie?'

'My aunt always swears by a warm drink at night,' Jessie said.

'Why did you give up nursing?'

'I lost my job.'

'Would you tell me why?' Jessie did so and Lady Kendle looked sad. 'It is so unfortunate when that sort of thing happens. The doctor was at fault, of course, but they couldn't afford to lose him. I'm afraid you were expendable, my dear. It is very unfair but the way of things.'

'My aunt warned me how it would be, but I had to speak out. The girl was upset and she wasn't the first. I thought it was time he was stopped.'

'I understand why you felt that,' Lady Kendle said. 'But sometimes it's best not to tell what you've seen, better just to pretend you don't know what goes on.' She sighed and the sadness in her became so overpowering that Jessie felt it as a physical ache. 'I discovered that many years ago, but it was a hard lesson for you to learn, Jessie.'

'I was angry at first but I'm over it now.' Jessie wondered what kind of memories had brought that look to Lady Kendle's eyes.

'It was fortunate for us, of course, but I am genuinely sorry, my dear. I believe you must have been a good nurse.'

'I hope I was. I tried to do my work well. Aunt Elizabeth always says "do your best and you can't do more".'

'I am quite sure you did.' The bright eyes dwelt on her face. 'Do you think you will like living here? It is very quiet in the country, you know.'

'It will be different,' Jessie admitted. 'But I've come here to do a job and I expect I shall be busy.'

'Oh yes, you will be busy,' Lady Kendle said. 'We need more staff. It's the plain truth that we haven't enough. My son says we have to be careful with money. Sir Joseph thinks he is too careful already and Mary hates being told she can't spend money, but then most of it is hers, of course. She has a perfect right to do what she likes with her own money.'

Lady Kendle reached for her warm milk and sipped it. Jessie smiled inwardly but said nothing. Lady Kendle obviously wanted someone she could talk to, but it wasn't her place to ask questions; she would listen but not pry.

'Harry changed when he came back, after he was wounded that last time. Captain Kendle, that is,' she said and took another drink. She wasn't sure why she was telling the new girl this, but she couldn't talk to her son these days and she certainly couldn't tell either her daughter-in-law or her husband what was on her mind. 'It's this house – too big for us in these modern times. We should sell it and buy something smaller, something that only needs a few servants to look after it. But we shan't, of course, we shall soldier on somehow and perhaps when I'm gone, Harry might sell one day.' She smiled to herself. 'He told me it would make a good hotel if it was nearer Torquay, but as things are he probably couldn't give it away.'

'It would be a pity if this house were to become a hotel,' Jessie said. 'It is a beautiful family home.'

'For a beautiful family.' Anne Kendle pulled a face. She had thought something of the kind once, but that had been a long, long time ago. She finished her milk and put down the glass. 'That was very nice. Thank you for coming to see me, Jessie, and for the drink. I think I should like to sleep now.'

'Is there anything more you need?'

'No, thank you. Harry will come in later and see if I'm all right, and Sir Joshua sleeps next door. He helps me in the night if I need him. I am very lucky, you know. I often think of others less fortunate and realize how much I have to be thankful for.'

Jessie smiled but made no comment. She had completely fallen under Lady Kendle's spell and thought that her family was lucky to have her. Many women confined to their rooms for most of their lives would complain endlessly, but it was a pleasure to serve this invalid.

Jessie glanced in at Nanny once more before she went to bed. She was still sleeping and there didn't seem to be much point in sitting up. Jessie would be up again by five and look in on her then. Hopefully, Nanny would sleep through the night and be much better for it in the morning.

Jessie unpacked her few bits and pieces, hanging them in the wardrobe before undressing. Sitting in front of the table by the window, she brushed her long hair and glanced at herself in the hand mirror her aunt had given her on her eighteenth birthday. The casing was made of silver and, though old and a little battered, it was Jessie's most prized possession.

'I bought it second-hand down the market,' Aunt Elizabeth had told her. 'But I've had the brushes renewed so they're nice and clean.'

'It's all lovely,' Jessie said and hugged her because it was such a wonderful and unexpected gift. She wondered how her aunt was feeling, whether she felt lonely. She had a lot of friends, Jessie knew, but that wasn't the same as family, was it? Her aunt would feel strange sitting down to supper on her own.

Jessie smiled and took out her smart leather writing case. It had been a present from Robbie when he first went to France.

'So that you've got something to remind you of me,' he'd told her and she always felt a pang when she used the notepaper inside, because it had been bought for writing to Robbie.

But she was going to use it now to write to her aunt, because she knew that she would be feeling a bit odd in that empty house, just as Jessie was feeling rather strange in her new room. It had been fine when she was with the others, but now she couldn't help feeling rather cut off from her friends and she missed her aunt. They'd been so close these past years, sharing everything.

She bent her head to the task, writing several pages before looking up. The moon had come up now, making it quite light outside. She stood up to get a better view and saw a man walking alone. His hands were in his pockets as he walked, head down, and there was something about him that seemed to tell Jessie that she wasn't the only one in this house feeling a little lonely. Captain Kendle was a complex man, a man of moods and not easy to understand, but Jessie thought she liked him better than his sharp-tongued wife.

She watched until he disappeared from view, then sat down to finish her letter to her aunt. Tomorrow she would think about a letter for Archie, but at the moment all she wanted was her bed.

Five

Nanny was awake when Jessie went in at a quarter past five the next morning. She looked at her a bit oddly, then announced that she had wet the bed.

'I'm sorry,' she said. 'I tried to get out but then I went dizzy and peed myself. You'll have to help me get up. I dare say I shall be all right when I've dressed.'

'You can get dressed if you want and sit in your chair,' Jessie agreed. 'I'll put it by the window for you and you can have your breakfast there while I change the sheets.'

'We'll see about that, miss!' Nanny pulled a face. She clearly thought she would be able to walk about once she could get out of bed, but even the effort of putting her feet to the floor exhausted her. She sat there for a few seconds looking grey and frightened, and she let Jessie dress her in a clean nightgown and her old dressing gown, then leaned heavily on the younger woman's arm as they walked slowly and carefully to the chair.

'It's knocked me for six,' she said as she sat down. 'Stupid of me to crock up like this. Good thing you came, Jessie. They would have had to send me to the Infirmary if you hadn't. Might have to as it is if I'm too much trouble.'

'Oh, I'm sure they won't,' Jessie said and smiled at her. 'Captain Kendle is very fond of you, you know. I'm sure he would look after you himself if he had to.'

'He came in to see me before you as it happens,' Nanny said and gave a cackle of laughter at the idea of being looked after by her boy. He would always be a lad to her, of course, whatever he did, including winning medals for bravery on the Somme. 'I couldn't think what had happened, but then he told me – and all about you. How you'd taken charge straight away, and that you were decent and kind.'

69

'So that's how you knew me. I did wonder.' Jessie laughed softly. Nanny had been testing her. 'Would you mind having your breakfast early? It will make things easier if I can finish here before the children are up and about.'

'Not sure I want more than a cup of tea.'

'You must try to eat a little. What do you usually have?'

'A bit of toast and jam.'

'What about a boiled egg and bread and butter soldiers?'

'Think I'm a child, do you?' Nanny glared at her.

'It's what I like for breakfast if I'm lucky enough,' Jessie said. 'And no, I don't think you've gone senile. Strokes have to be very bad to affect your mind as a rule. It's more often one side of your face, an arm or a leg – but yours was very mild, you know. I think you were just worn out. You'll be fine when you've had some rest.'

'Think so, do you?' Nanny's eyes narrowed intently. 'Not humouring me?'

'I'm pretty sure,' Jessie said. She pulled the sheets off the bed and took them with her as she left the room. 'Don't try to do anything, Nanny. I'm going to get your breakfast first and then I'll make the bed – all right?'

Nanny gave her another hard look but didn't say anything. It wasn't easy for her to be waited on after a lifetime in service.

Jessie took the sheets down to the dirty linen room. Maggie's mother came in to do the washing twice a week and there was a pile waiting to be sorted. Another sheet or two wouldn't make much difference.

Maggie came in with a bucket of dirty water as Jessie was about to leave. She glanced at the sheets and then poured the water down the big stone sink.

'Ma does sheets on Mondays and Thursdays, but I'll put these in the copper and boil them. Nanny's, I suppose?'

'A little accident. She couldn't help it.'

'Don't suppose she could, poor old bugger. I've finished scrubbing the kitchen and pantry. Floor will be dry in a minute. Do you know where to find clean linen?'

'Yes, thanks. Mrs Pearson showed me yesterday. I want a boiled egg and soldiers for Nanny. Shall I get them myself or ask Cook?'

'Ask her. She'll only be miffed if you don't.' Maggie grinned. 'Go on in. I've got to help Alice get the downstairs done before anyone is about. She's doin' all the bedrooms today and she'll never get round if I don't give her a hand.'

Jessie nodded and went into the kitchen. Cook had made a pot of tea and she gestured to her that she should have one.

'Thank you,' Jessie said. 'But I mustn't be too long.' She explained what she needed and Cook got up to fetch a pan of water, which she set to boil. 'Can we have the soldiers really thin please? Nanny won't be able to manage much, but we need to tempt her.'

'Of course you can,' Cook said and smiled at her. 'You've a kind heart, Jessie. I suppose that comes from being a nurse.'

'Perhaps,' Jessie said and drank her tea. 'It doesn't always follow though. I've seen nurses be unkind to elderly patients. Patients can be very difficult at times, you know.'

Cook nodded, setting the tray with two plates of bread and butter with the crusts off and cut into fingers and two boiled eggs. She added a small teapot, a jug of milk, sugar bowl and two cups and saucers.

'Can you manage all that?' she asked, slipping a cosy over the pot. 'It's quite a long way.'

'I'll manage,' Jessie said. 'If I sit and eat my egg with Nanny I think she may feel more like attempting her own.'

'Like I said, you've got a good heart, lass.'

Jessie shook her head. She carried the tray upstairs. It wasn't too heavy, which was as well since it was a long way. Nanny looked at her suspiciously as she set it down.

'Are you going to force-feed me? I'll never eat that lot.'

'Some of it is for me. I'm going to keep you company.' Jessie smiled as she saw the older woman's surprise. 'Today I'll take the top off your egg for you. Not because you can't, but it might be an effort.'

Nanny said nothing. She watched as Jessie sliced the tops of both eggs expertly.

'Glad you know the proper way,' she said. 'I hate bits of shell all over.'

'So do I,' Jessie agreed. She fetched the dressing stool to the table and perched on it, dipping her soldier in the perfectly

71

cooked egg and biting into it. Nanny watched as she chewed, laying the rest of the bread finger down as she prepared to pour a cup of tea for them both. 'Milk and sugar?'

'Milk, no sugar – milk after the tea, mind.'

Jessie looked at her. 'We've always had it the other way. Why do you put the milk in last?'

'It's polite, the proper way,' Nanny said. 'Some say as it makes a difference to the taste. They do it that way upstairs.'

'Oh well, I suppose it won't kill us,' Jessie said and laughed. She was pleased to see a flicker of a smile in Nanny's eyes. There was a knock at the door and Alice popped her head round.

'I've brought sheets,' she said. 'I'm making up beds in all the guestrooms, because we've got company coming for the weekend. I'll leave you to it then. Are you feelin' better, Nanny?'

'Yes, thank you, Alice. It was nothing much. I'll be up and about in a day or so.'

'Right then. See you later, Jessie.'

Nanny frowned as she went out, then picked up a thin slice of bread and butter, dipping it in the egg. Her hand trembled slightly but she managed to get the tasty morsel to her mouth and ate slowly.

'Is it all right?' Jessie asked as she dipped again.

'Food for babies,' Nanny grumbled. 'But I've got to eat or I'll be a trouble to everyone.'

'You haven't been eating properly for a while, have you, Nanny?' Jessie gave her a gentle smile. 'I expect you were too tired. You had too much to do.'

'I should have retired years ago,' Nanny said, surprising her. 'Could have gone to live with my sister in Torquay. She's a widow, lives in a cottage her husband left her. She begged me to go but Mrs Kendle asked me to stay, and then there was her ladyship. I didn't want to desert them.' For a moment her eyes looked watery. 'Now that I've become a liability they won't want me here. I'll just be in the way.'

'You really are going to get better,' Jessie told her. 'I know you feel a bit low now and that's natural, but you will improve if you rest and eat. Besides, I need your help. I'm not sure I know how to manage the children. I've looked after sick children, of course, but I understand Jack is a bit of a handful.'

'Master Jack is no better or worse than most lads of his age. Be firm with him, Jessie. Don't threaten or bully. Just give him a straight look if he plays up, and if you have to – but only if he's done something really naughty, mind – give him a sharp tap on his leg. If you're firm you shouldn't need to slap often. Some nannies use a cane or deprive children of their treats. I've never had to do that myself.'

'Thanks, I'll remember that,' Jessie said. She finished her breakfast and got up to make the bed. When she returned Nanny had drunk half a cup of tea and eaten two tiny soldiers. 'Had enough? You've done well. I'll bring you something light at lunch. Would you like to go back to bed now?'

'Let me see if I can do it myself. I don't want to wet the bed again.'

Nanny pushed herself up out of the chair. She stood for a moment and then walked very slowly back to the bed. It exhausted her but she managed it and smiled triumphantly as she hitched herself into position.

'That's better. I told you I'd be all right once I was up.'

'Of course you did,' Jessie said. 'Is there anything you want before I go – something to read, perhaps?'

'I'll just rest and think. Don't worry. I'll be all right.'

'I'll come in when I can.'

Jessie took the tray downstairs. She left it on the draining board for Maggie to see to and then asked Cook about the children's breakfast. Told that Maggie would bring it up to them at half past seven as usual, Jessie went back upstairs to the nursery. The noise coming from inside told her that Jack was awake and already playing some kind of game. As she went in she saw that he was lying on the floor with a tin car and some lead soldiers. His sister was standing at the end of her cot watching him, but making no sound, her grey eyes wide and clear.

'Hello,' Jessie said. 'Are you having fun?'

Jack raised his head and gazed at her solemnly. 'The soldiers are dead,' he announced. 'I've killed them.' He pointed a finger

73

at her. 'Bang! Bang! Bang! I've killed you too. You've got to fall over.'

'I don't think so,' Jessie said. 'Someone has to wash your face and help you to dress. Who's going to do that if I'm killed?'

'Nanny,' he said. 'Nanny gets us dressed. Alice put us to bed last night. I don't like Alice much. She gets cross if I splash her when I'm in the bath.'

'Perhaps she doesn't like getting her clothes wet.'

Jack considered that for a moment then grinned. 'I got wet when I fell in the fishpond. Ned had to come in and pull me out. I smelt terrible and was covered in weed. Everyone screamed and made a lot of fuss. They thought I was dead.'

'You might have been,' Jessie said. 'Think how sad your mother and father would be then.'

'Father would be sad,' Jack agreed. 'Mother wouldn't mind. She says I'm a nuisance and will be glad when I go away to boarding school. What is it like at boarding school?'

'I don't know. I didn't go,' Jessie said. ''Sides, I bet she'll be sad when you go. She'll probably cry.'

'No, she won't. I heard her tell Father she wanted me to go soon. He said she was a heartless bitch.'

Jessie was shocked, but tried not to let him see that he had succeeded in his aim. 'You shouldn't say things like that, Jack. It isn't nice.'

'Why not? It's true. Father says one shouldn't tell lies and I don't – but I can't see why I can't tell the truth.'

'Your father is quite right, but sometimes it is best not to repeat things you've heard – private things.'

Jack looked at her with interest. 'Are you going to smack me? Alice smacks me when I say rude things to her.'

'I might smack you if you are really naughty, but I don't mind what you say to me.' Jessie smiled as she saw the uncertainty in his eyes. 'Sticks and stones may break my bones but names won't hurt me.'

'Nanny says that too. Where is she?'

'Having a rest. If you help me to get you dressed I might take you to see her later for a few minutes. Would you like that?'

74

He considered, then said, 'Nanny loves me. I think I love her. She won't die, will she? She's very old, you know. Even older than you.'

Jessie's lips quivered. He *was* a little monster. Master Jack might only be five years old, but he knew exactly what he was up to and she guessed that he was provoking her, testing her, rather as Nanny had earlier.

'Oh, I'm quite old,' she said. 'Not as old as Nanny, but much older than you – and you're older than Catherine.'

'She's only a baby.' He gave her an old-fashioned look. 'I'm glad you didn't call her Miss Cathy. The servants do and it's not her proper name. You're different.'

'Am I?'

'Yes. Who are you and why are you here?'

'I'm Jessie and I've come to look after you and your grandmother,' Jessie said. 'What would you like to wear today?'

'Can I wear what I like?'

'I don't see why not,' Jessie said. 'Unless your parents want to take you out and then you would have to look very smart.'

'I'm not wearing that soppy sailor suit!'

'Shall we see what you have in the cupboard?'

'It's a wardrobe, silly!'

Jack went skipping ahead of her. It took him several minutes to decide which of many outfits he wanted to wear, most of the others deposited on the floor for someone to pick up again, but in the end he chose a pair of riding breeches and a brown Norfolk jacket. Since he was happy with his choice Jessie assisted where needed, which wasn't often as he could manage most of his buttons himself, but needed a little help to get his boots on. Riding boots, she thought, but made no comment. Once he was more or less ready she left him to play with his toys and went to fetch Catherine, who had been watching in silent wonder from her cot, making hardly a sound except the odd cooing noise now and then.

The little girl was wet and it took Jessie a while to discover how to fix her nappy properly. She was a bit surprised to find the child still in nappies, for she was supposed to be almost three years old, but perhaps it was natural. She wasn't sure about these things.

75

'Oo is oo?' Catherine asked in her baby talk after the nappy was changed, reaching up to pat her face. 'Nice. Nanny come now?'

'I'm Jessie,' she said and kissed the little girl. 'Nanny is resting. You will see her soon.'

She put the dry, contented and fully dressed child on the floor and watched as she crawled towards Jack's soldiers. She began to stand them up one by one, seeming intent on her task. Yet she didn't scream or cry when Jack knocked them down again, simply started the process once more. Jessie frowned. Something seemed not quite right. Was the little girl backward for her age? Or was it just that she didn't have enough experience with children to know these things?

She heard the doorknob rattling and went to open it, letting Maggie in with her loaded tray. She'd brought boiled eggs and soldiers for the children, as well as some toast, jam and two mugs of cold milk. She set the tray on the table, which was large and scarred by generations of children, glanced at Catherine and then at Jessie.

'Little love,' she said. 'Never any trouble. Not like Master Jack here. He's a terrible rogue.'

Jack pulled a face at her but didn't seem to mind. He picked up the car he'd been playing with and came to the table.

'Can I have toast and jam? I don't like egg.'

'What would you like in the morning?' Jessie asked.

'Kippers, like Mother – or just toast and jam.'

'I'll ask Cook for a kipper for you next time she has some if you eat some of your egg.'

'Why can't I have it now?'

'Because the egg is cooked. Some little boys aren't lucky enough to have an egg for their breakfast,' Maggie said. 'They only get bread and dripping or nothing at all. You do what Jessie tells you, Master Jack.'

'Not if he doesn't like egg,' Jessie said and picked Catherine up, sitting her on her lap. 'He can eat what he wants. Catherine wants her egg, don't you, darling?' Catherine's cooing seemed to indicate that she did. She bit into her soldiers with every sign of enjoyment.

'See you later,' Maggie said and went out.

Jessie continued to feed Catherine, letting Jack get on with his own breakfast. When she glanced at him she saw that he had managed to get the top off his egg and was spooning it into his mouth and biting a finger of bread liberally covered with strawberry jam. Jessie was amused at the combination but didn't object. She'd told him he could eat what he liked and he'd taken her at her word.

'What do you want to do after breakfast?' she asked. 'Shall we go for a walk? You could show me the fishpond you fell in if you like.'

'You might fall in and get killed.'

'I shan't if you show me where it is. We could play a game if you've got a ball of some kind.'

'I've got all sorts of balls. I play cricket with father sometimes. And we do sums. He teaches me when he comes to visit after tea. I can read some words, too. I can read a whole book.'

'That's clever of you. When will you go to school?'

'Father says I should have a tutor until I'm seven. He says he's going to get one whatever Mother thinks. What is a tutor, Jessie?'

'A sort of teacher. One who comes to the house instead of you going to the school.'

'Father says . . .' Jack went silent of a sudden and, glancing towards the door, Jessie saw that Captain Kendle was standing on the threshold watching them, a hint of amusement in his eyes.

'How are you doing, Miss Hale? I thought I would look in just in case there were any problems.'

'None at the moment, sir. We are getting on just fine.'

'So it would appear. I'm going to the farm this morning, Jack. Want to come?'

'Yes please!' Jack jumped down from the table. 'Can we go now?'

'You had better ask Jessie if you may be excused, young man.'

Jack turned to look at her, an expression of such longing in his face that she smiled. She had guessed that Captain Kendle was taking his son out of the way to make things

77

easier for her that morning and she was touched by his consideration.

'Yes, of course you may go, but wipe your mouth on the flannel first. You have strawberry jam all over it.'

Jack ran immediately to the sink and scrubbed at his face with the flannel he had used earlier. Jessie glanced at his father uncertainly as she asked, 'Is he dressed correctly? We were just going to play in the garden and he chose his own clothes.'

'He's fine,' Harry Kendle said. 'I would like a little talk – perhaps this evening before dinner, Miss Hale?' He looked down at the eager face of his son. 'Have a pleasant day. Come along, Jack. I might put you up on my horse as you're wearing your breeches.'

The nursery seemed very quiet after they had gone. Jessie found some warm clothing in Catherine's cupboard and dressed her in a pretty velvet coat with a matching bonnet and a wool scarf about her neck. The sun was shining but it would be cool outside.

'Shall we go and play, Catherine?'

'Play!' the child said and smiled, delighted with the suggestion.

She was such a happy child and, as everyone had said, no trouble. For nearly an hour she played ball with Jessie in the garden, toddling after it a little unsteadily and falling often on her bottom or her knees. However, she picked herself up and laughed, seeming to think it was all a part of the fun. There were no tears, only smiles, but Jessie was anxious.

She carried the child as she walked right round the house, wanting to get to know her surroundings better. It really was lovely in the gardens, and they were well kept despite the shortage of men to look after them. She thought how much her aunt would like to see them and wished for a camera so that she could send a photograph to her in London. How wonderful those rose beds must look in summer. It wouldn't be long until Christmas now, of course, and there had been a slight frost overnight.

Mrs Pearson met her when she took the child back into the house.

'Lady Kendle is ready for you now. Give me the child.'

'I think I shall take her to see her grandmother. Jack has gone out with his father and Catherine will sit quietly while I do what's needed. You get on with your work, Mrs Pearson. I know how busy you are today.'

'Well, if you're sure.' The housekeeper was clearly relieved not to be looking after Catherine.

'Yes, I'm sure.'

Lady Kendle was propped up against her pillows, waiting. She looked surprised but pleased when Jessie took the little girl in and sat her down in an armchair by the window.

'Sit there and then you can kiss Grandma in a minute.' Jessie glanced at Lady Kendle. 'I hope you don't mind, ma'am? She won't be any trouble.'

'Catherine never is,' Lady Kendle replied with sadness in her face. 'Have you been told?'

'No one said, but she's a little backward, isn't she?'

'My son took her somewhere. They say it happened when she was born. She may never be quite as she should – but as you say, she's no bother.'

'It's a shame,' Jessie said, pity stirring, not just for the child but her parents, too. 'I know it happens sometimes if there are complications.'

'She was a twin. The boy was born first and seemed perfect, but he died a few hours later. We shall never understand why; the doctors couldn't explain it.'

'I had no idea. It must have been terrible for Captain and Mrs Kendle.'

'Yes, it was. Mary has never accepted it. She . . .' Lady Kendle shook her head. 'Has Jack gone with his father? Harry thought it would help on your first morning, especially with Nanny ill. How is she, by the way? My son thought she seemed to have made a remarkable recovery.'

'It is quite often that way if the stroke is mild, and she is doing very well. We must keep her quiet for a few days but it won't be too long before she can sit with the children for a while, though I shan't let her do anything tiring, of course. I have every hope that she will make a complete recovery, but we must take care of her.'

'That is excellent news. If Carter has time I should like to

79

be taken up to see her later – but only if he can spare a few minutes.'

'I'll tell him, ma'am.'

Jessie helped her patient from the bed, pushing her bath chair to the basin and leaving her to wash while she made the bed tidy. She then fetched the clothes Lady Kendle asked for and helped her to dress. She wheeled the chair to the window so that the elderly lady could look out at the garden, fetched books, a shawl and various other items, measuring out her medicine carefully into a little glass. She finished tidying the room, and when she turned to look saw that Catherine had managed to climb up on to her grandmother's lap and was playing with the necklace she wore quite contentedly.

'I hope she isn't bothering you.'

'Not at all. You can bring her whenever you wish,' Lady Kendle said. 'But Jack is so impatient, always running about and shouting. I can't tolerate more than a few minutes of his company unless his father is there. He always behaves when Harry is around.'

'I'll remember that,' Jessie said. 'But you would like to see him for a few minutes if he is good?'

'If you could perform a small miracle, I should be delighted. Now run along and do whatever you have to do, Jessie. I shall be quite all right until lunch. My husband will bring the newspaper in soon and then we shall talk. I shall not be neglected, so you need not worry about me.'

'Yes, ma'am.'

Jessie took Catherine from her. The child chortled with pleasure, patting her face as she was carried from the room. She didn't say any words, though she did make cooing noises. Jessie wondered if she was just lazy. She seemed perfectly capable of making herself understood, which meant she must understand most of what went on around her.

Taking Catherine with her, she went to see Nanny and discovered that she was awake. She was pleased to see them, and smiled with pleasure as Jessie let the child kiss her.

'Poor little lamb,' Nanny said. 'They don't love her, Jessie. Her father is kind to her, but even he doesn't really love her.'

'Oh, surely they must!' Jessie said. 'Lady Kendle was pleased to see her just now.'

'You never took her in there?'

'She sat quietly all the while, watching the way she does. Her ladyship said I could take her any time, but not Jack unless I could make him be quiet.'

'He's only quiet for his father,' Nanny said. 'Well, miss, you've done more than I've dared. It's good for Catherine that you've come. At least you'll be kind to her.'

'You can be sure of that,' Jessie said. 'I adore her already. Now, is there anything you want?'

'I used the pot under the bed,' Nanny said. 'It needs emptying – but Maggie will do it later.'

'I'll take it to the bathroom along the hall,' Jessie said. 'You don't want that left here all day. Can I leave Catherine with you for a moment?'

'Yes, of course. Just sit her next to me.'

Jessie performed the necessary service, thinking it a good thing that Captain Kendle had considered it worthwhile to have modern plumbing for his staff as well as himself. She wouldn't have fancied carrying the pot all the way out to a midden as they would have had to do once upon a time.

Catherine had curled up as if ready to sleep when Jessie got back, and Nanny seemed content to have her there.

'If you can cope with her for a little longer I could organize your lunch,' she said. 'But if you would rather I took her with me, I will.'

'She's fast asleep, bless her,' Nanny said. 'As long as you're not too long. I can't run after her if she decides to get off the bed.'

'Perhaps I'd better take her,' Jessie said and lifted the sleeping child. Catherine didn't stir. 'I'll ask Cook if Maggie can bring your tray up, but I want to make sure they are sending you something you can eat.'

She smiled at Nanny and went out, leaving the door slightly ajar. Catherine slept soundly as she carried her down the back stairs, but she stirred as they went into the kitchen, opening her eyes to look about her curiously.

'Well, bless my soul,' Cook said, looking very surprised. 'Who have you brought to see us?'

'This is Miss Catherine Kendle,' Jessie said. 'I wanted to ask what you were giving Nanny for lunch.'

'I thought some chicken soup and bread and butter,' Cook said and came to have a closer look at Catherine. 'I don't often get the chance to see her. This is the first time she's been to the kitchen – isn't it, my lovely?'

'She might have slept if I'd left her with Nanny, but I didn't want to chance it so I brought her here. Will Maggie take Nanny's tray up? Once she's well enough to keep an eye on Catherine I'll do it, but it's awkward at the moment.' She deposited Catherine in one of the grandfather chairs. 'Can I have some milk for her?'

'O'course you can,' Cook said and went to fetch it from the cold pantry herself. She brought a mug back half filled with fresh milk. 'There you are, my precious.' She glanced at Jessie. 'Will you have a cup of tea yourself?'

'Yes, why not?' Jessie said. 'If I'm not in your way.'

'Mrs Kendle is out to lunch today,' Cook said. 'Captain Kendle and Sir Joshua only require some cold chicken and mashed potatoes. Alice will ring when they're ready. It's just as well really, because I've got ahead with some of my work for the weekend. I like to prepare something fancy for them; they expect it.'

'It's a relief to you to get ahead, I'm sure,' Jessie said and smiled as Cook poured them both a cup of tea.

Catherine was drinking her milk, looking about her with interest at all the things she had never seen before. She waved her free hand and chortled as Maggie came in, but didn't say anything.

'Yes, that's Maggie,' Jessie said, taking the empty mug from her hands. 'You like Maggie, don't you, Catherine? Can you say her name for me?'

Magg–i,' Catherine said and chuckled at her own success.

'Very good,' Jessie said. 'We shall have to see what more you can say if you try.' She picked the child up again and looked at Cook.

'Master Jack would like a kipper for breakfast tomorrow if you have one, please, and we would like cold chicken and mashed potatoes for lunch in the nursery if there's enough to spare.'

'Will Miss Cathy eat it? She usually just has bread and jam or an egg. Nanny sometimes does her a little stewed fruit or mince.'

'Then it's time she tried something different,' Jessie said. 'We'll all have the same and see how we get on, please.'

'There's plenty of chicken,' Cook said. 'I'll send it up – but you'd better have some bread and butter too, just in case.'

Jessie took Catherine back to the nursery and changed her nappy, which had become wet while she was in the kitchen. She was just showing Catherine a storybook and telling her what all the pictures meant when Jack came in and stared at them.

'That's my book,' he said. 'Why are you showing it to Catherine?'

'Because she likes it,' Jessie said. 'Do you mind sharing it with her? I couldn't find a girls' storybook.'

'She hasn't got any, only dolls,' Jack said and shrugged. 'I'm too old for that now. She can have it if she likes.'

'Thank you, that is very generous of you.'

'When can we see Nanny? You said we could.'

'I'll take you after you've had your lunch,' Jessie said. 'Did you have a lovely time on the farm?'

'Father took me on his horse,' Jack said, his face glowing. 'He was in the war, you know, and very brave, so Nanny says. I'm going to be brave when I grow up.'

'I think you were brave to ride a horse,' Jessie said. 'That must be very frightening.'

'It isn't, it's exciting,' Jack said and then turned to look as Maggie brought their lunch in on a tray. 'I'm not eating egg or mince.'

'I ordered chicken and mashed potatoes,' Jessie said. 'Do you like chicken, Jack?'

'As long as it isn't all messed up in a mince with gravy,' he said. 'I don't like gravy, but chicken is nice like this.' He took a piece and ate it with his fingers, looking at her as if he expected to be reprimanded.

'That's good,' Jessie said. 'I like it very much. Shall we see if Catherine does, too?' She took a piece from the dish and put it to the child's lips. Catherine bit into it obediently, her enjoyment evident. 'Yes, it is nice, isn't it, darling?'

Jack had pulled a chair to the table and was eating his chicken with a fork now, though he didn't eat much of the potato. Jessie let him have what he wanted, though she fed Catherine some of the mash, which she ate obediently.

'I like you,' Jack announced with his mouth full. 'You're not cross all the time.'

'I like you, too,' Jessie said and smiled. In fact she had fallen in love with both of the Kendle children. 'Now eat a mouthful more of the mash and I think you will find there is strawberry jelly for afters.' She was pleased to see that the mash went down in double-quick time.

Catherine had a sleep after her lunch and Jessie read to Jack in the playroom while his sister slept next door. Afterwards, she took them both to see Nanny, who was sitting up enjoying a cup of tea and looking much better than she had that morning. It was when she was on her way back to the nursery that Jessie met Alice, who was frowning and clearly annoyed.

'I've been searching for you all over,' she said. 'Madam wants to see you in the study and she's on the warpath.'

'The study – that's where I spoke to her yesterday, isn't it?'

'Yes, and you'd best hurry up. She isn't pleased about something.'

'What about the children? I was just about to give them their tea and put them to bed.'

'I'll sit with them until you come – but don't be long. I want my own tea before I get changed for the evening. I'm going out tonight, remember. I should have been finished half an hour ago!'

Jessie promised she would be as quick as she could and hurried into the main wing of the house. She wondered what had upset her employer, trying to think of something that she had done wrong without realizing it. As she approached the study she heard raised voices.

'Well, you will be a fool if you make a fuss about it, Mary,' Captain Kendle was saying. 'What harm was done?'

'None as it happens, but there might have been. I don't want that child brought into the main wing while we have guests . . .'

84

'You really are a heartless bitch,' he said harshly. 'You don't care a scrap for Catherine, do you?'

'I am not prepared to have my friends pity me because I have an idiot daughter,' Mary Kendle replied. 'I don't mind her being taken to Mother's room when no one is here, but . . .'

Jessie was so sickened by what she had overheard that she knocked on the door, wanting to shut off the sound of that cruel voice.

'Come in!' Mary Kendle turned to look at her as she entered. 'I suppose you heard that? It's just as well if you did. What on earth do you think you've been doing all day, running about with that child all over the place? First the garden, then Mother's room and goodness knows where else!'

'Catherine needs fresh air sometimes,' Jessie said. She spoke out in her usual way, not angrily, but not giving ground either. 'It's not good for her to stay in the nursery all the time. Lady Kendle said it was all right. She said I could take Catherine there whenever I liked. I didn't know you wanted her hidden away.'

'Well, really! I don't know who you think you are, young woman, but—'

'She is Catherine's nurse and a big help to you,' Captain Kendle reminded her with a warning glance. 'Jessie didn't mean to upset you, Mary – and she is quite right, Catherine does need to be taken out sometimes. Good God! Do you want to keep her a prisoner for the rest of her life?'

Mary looked at him, her mouth opening and closing like a fish out of water. It was clear she had suddenly realized what a difficult position she would be in if Jessie left. She turned away, taking a cigarette from a silver box on the table and lighting it with a fancy silver table lighter. It was clear she was angry, but when she faced them again her temper was under control.

'I prefer that you restrict Catherine's fresh air to early in the morning, and any games are to be played well away from the front of the house. There is plenty of room in the kitchen garden or in the fields. I am sure you understand my feelings on this, Jessie.'

Jessie didn't understand them at all. For two pins she would have given her notice in right then, but if she did there would be no one to look after Nanny or the children. Nanny might be sent to the Infirmary, and those children were in need of some love.

'Yes, ma'am. I am sure I can manage to keep Catherine away from your friends while they are here.'

'And I would rather you didn't take her into Mother's room.'

'I think Mother would have something to say about that,' Captain Kendle murmured softly. He hadn't looked at Jessie and she dared not look at him.

'For the next day or so. Just while my friends are here.' Mary puffed nervously at her cigarette. Jessie guessed that Captain Kendle didn't often put his foot down, but when he did she was forced to accept his word as law. 'Do you understand me, Jessie?'

'Yes, ma'am.'

'Very well. You may go now.'

As Jessie was leaving she saw an elderly gentleman with silvery hair coming towards the study from the opposite direction. She thought he must be Sir Joshua. He was remarkably like his son, she thought. It was the first time she had seen him, and felt hesitant, wondering if she should greet him, but he went into the study without speaking or looking at her. She heard Mary greet him in an agitated voice.

'Dearest Father!' she cried. 'You look wonderful. Do tell Harry he is a perfect beast to me . . .'

Jessie heard no more as she started down the back stairs towards the kitchen. If it weren't for Nanny and the children she didn't think she would want to stay in this house another night.

Six

Jessie calmed down as she gave the children their tea. She felt nervous about seeing Captain Kendle after hearing that argument in the study, but when he arrived he seemed to have forgotten about it.

'Have you finished your sums?' he asked his son, his eyes following Jessie as she picked up Catherine and took her to wash the strawberry jam from her face and hands. 'Or have you been too busy?'

'I did them while Jessie was showing Catherine my picture book.'

Jack fetched a small writing pad, displaying his work proudly. His father went over the sums, correcting one and explaining the mistake. He then set some more sums for Jack, but his attention was drawn to Jessie and his daughter once more.

'What is this, Catherine?' Jessie was asking as she pointed to a picture. 'Do you know? It's a cat. Can you say cat for me?'

Catherine was sucking her thumb. Jessie removed it from her mouth and she chuckled. 'Cat for me,' she said and promptly put her thumb back in her mouth.

'That's clever of Catherine,' Jessie said. 'Say cat, darling. Tell me again what's in the picture.'

'Cat,' Catherine said and patted her face. 'Jessie nice. Cat nice. Catherine want cat.' She rubbed the picture with her chubby hand and chuckled again.

'I think that is the most I've heard Catherine say in one go,' Harry said and Jessie looked up, her heart jumping. She hadn't realized that he was so near. 'Will you put her down for a moment, please? I would like to talk to you.'

Jessie obeyed and he glanced at his son, then back at her. 'Could we go into the next room, Jessie?'

She understood. Jack already heard and understood more than was good for him. She followed Captain Kendle into what was meant to be a sitting room for the children's nurse, and he closed the door behind them. The room was a little untidy, littered with Jack and Catherine's things, and Jessie apologized.

'I haven't had time to tidy up yet, sir.'

'It doesn't matter. First I want to apologize for what happened earlier. My wife cannot accept Catherine's disability. She rejected her soon after she was born. When we realized . . . It may seem cruel to you, but she cannot help her feelings.'

'Catherine can't help being as she is, sir.' Jessie dared not look at him for fear of betraying her own feelings. 'Besides, she is just a little slow. With patience she might be taught a lot of things.'

'She will never be normal, Jessie. They told me she had been damaged at birth. She took too long in coming and they used forceps on her. Her twin had been born first and it is possible that she was starved of oxygen in the period between. I don't think the doctors really know why, but the fact remains – she is retarded. My wife was also affected by the birth; she is often depressed, restless. She has never been quite the same since.'

'I am sorry, sir. But Catherine understands more than you might imagine. I think I could teach her a lot of things.'

'A few words, perhaps,' Harry said. 'Believe me, Miss Hale, if I thought there was a chance I would move heaven and earth to give her what she needs.'

Jessie raised her head to look at him. His eyes had that haunted look she had seen once before and she knew that his anguish was genuine.

'With care and attention she could have a better life, that's all I'm saying, sir. It isn't right just to give up on her because she's slow. She may not be as bright as Jack but she deserves to be loved.'

'Then I hope you will give her what she needs,' he replied. 'Are you comfortable here? Have you all you need?'

'I am quite content, sir.' Jessie hesitated, then said, 'I don't know what is required of me in a situation like this. I may do things I shouldn't, but I want to do what's best for the children, Lady Kendle and Nanny.'

'My wife was upset earlier. She has thought better of it now. You are to have a free hand with the children – but she would prefer that you keep Catherine away from her guests.'

'Yes, sir. Of course I shall do as she asks.'

Harry ran a hand through his dark gold hair, his bluish-grey eyes intent on her face. 'Even if it kills you?'

Jessie was shocked for a moment, then she caught a glint of humour in his eyes. 'I'm afraid I was born stubborn, sir. It gets me into trouble and some would say I don't know my place.'

'Ah . . .' A soft chuckle escaped him. 'But what is your place, Miss Hale? I wonder if any of us know these days. We've all been turned topsy-turvy, as Nanny would say. It's partly the war, partly that the world is changing, the old order tossed aside. The new thinking is that we are all the same – that's it, you know, equality for all. I am sure it will come when the Labour Party gets into power, and they will one day. I'm a radical; my father believes it and sometimes I do myself.'

'I think you are teasing me, sir.'

'Yes, perhaps I am, but you've made me laugh. You don't realize what a miracle that is, of course. But I digress. My reason for this talk was not the state of the world but to ask about Nanny. Is she going to be all right?'

'She seems to be getting better but she will need lots of rest. I am not sure that she will be able to return to her duties again.'

'I wasn't so concerned about that, rather what she wants. Will she be happy to stay on here as a dependent or should I find her a cottage on the estate? Would she be able to look after herself?'

'You must ask her, of course,' Jessie said. 'But I will give you my opinion. I think she would be better here. Nanny is part of the family. Even if she can only help a little, she would prefer it. Besides, I don't think she should live alone. If she were to have another stroke and lay all night without help she might die. There is a possibility that she might go and live with her sister in Torquay, but I'm not sure it's what she wants – or that the offer is open to her now.'

'I see. It may be best to do nothing for now. Thank you for putting my mind at rest. I'm afraid we've taken advantage of her, expected too much.'

'Her experience will be a help to me while I learn to look after the children, sir. I can manage everything else myself.'

'What a confident young woman you are, Miss Hale. It was our good fortune that you came to us.'

'I shall do my best, sir.'

'Then I shall not interfere,' he said. 'Good evening, Miss Hale.'

'Good evening, sir.'

Jessie followed as he led the way back into the playroom. Jack was showing Catherine his picture book. He looked up as they entered.

'Catherine can say dog now. I've taught her. Wasn't that clever of me?'

'Well done,' his father said and ruffled his hair affectionately. 'I'll have to see about getting you that pony.'

'Can I really have a pony?' Jack jumped up, suddenly eager. 'When, Father? When can I have a pony?'

'Soon,' Harry promised. 'I'll look round, see what I can find. Say goodnight now, Jack – and be good for Jessie.'

'I'm going to have a pony of my own!'

Jack ran round the room with his arms out, his excitement bubbling over as his father closed the door, but Jessie smiled and let him get on with it. He wasn't doing any harm. She saw that Catherine was absorbed with her dolls and spent the next hour or so tidying the nursery and washing the children's clothes in the little room provided for their laundry.

The children were bathed and in bed by seven. Catherine went to sleep almost at once but Jessie had to read Jack a story from one of his favourite books before he would settle.

He fell asleep at last and, putting all but one small shaded lamp off, she tiptoed out.

She went along the hall to see how Nanny was, finding her dozing and seemingly peaceful. Then she went to visit Lady Kendle and make sure she had taken her medicine, doing a little tidying and plumping up pillows and cushions to make sure that she was comfortable before going downstairs for her evening meal.

'I should think you are ready for this,' Cook said and pushed a cup of tea in front of her. 'Your dinner is in the oven. I thought you were never coming.'

'Jack was a long time going off and then I popped into see Nanny and her ladyship.'

'You should have left the boy to it once you got him to bed,' Cook said. 'You've been on the go the whole day.'

'Yes, but I've enjoyed myself,' Jessie said and sipped her tea. 'It was fun being with the children and Lady Kendle is so easy to look after.'

'It's a long day, and you've not finished yet. You'll be taking drinks up later, I expect.'

'For Nanny and Lady Kendle,' Jessie agreed.

'As long as we know the routine,' Cook said and gave her a straight look. 'You've given this household a good shake-up today, Jessie. Can we expect more of the same?'

'The children enjoyed their food. We'll try giving them the same as they have upstairs, unless it's something spicy or cooked with wine. If you're having something suitable in the kitchen that will be fine – but not eggs or mince all the time.'

'Right you are. It's rabbit pie for us this evening. That all right with you?'

'Lovely. I'm not a fussy eater and everything you cook is delicious.'

Cook was satisfied with her answer and left Jessie to eat her supper in peace while she took her ease by the fire.

It was a similar evening to the first, though Alice wasn't there. Mrs Pearson had taken her place in the upstairs dining room, but in every other way the routine was the same.

91

Maggie was even friendlier than before and Jessie shared her time between the kitchen, Nanny and Lady Kendle. She was made to feel welcome everywhere and when she sat down to write her letter to Archie that night she realized that it was beginning to feel like home.

The weekend was rather more hectic because of the guests, though Jessie kept well away from them. She took the children for a long walk after breakfast and they ended up visiting the farm, which was at the end of a long, rutted track beyond the home park.

There was no sign of Jack's father that morning but the farm workers knew the master's son and welcomed their unexpected guests. They were taken to see new calves in the pens and then the farmer's wife came out to ask them into her kitchen.

'This is a surprise, miss,' she said. 'I'm Bess Goodjohn and you'll be the new girl up at the Hall, I dare say.'

'I'm Jessie Hale. Please call me Jessie. This is very kind of you, Mrs Goodjohn. Jack wanted to show me the animals but we didn't want to be any trouble.'

'We're pleased to see you, Jessie. Master Jack comes with the captain of course, but we haven't seen Miss Catherine. She's a little love, isn't she?'

'Catherine is very good. She's a little tired at the moment I think. We've had a busy morning.'

'Well, sit yourselves down and have a cup of tea. There's milk or my own lemon barley for the children.'

'Lemon barley please, Mrs G,' Jack piped up, clearly at home with the plump, smiling woman. 'It's good, Jessie. You should try it.'

'Thank you, I will,' Jessie said. 'Catherine can share mine, Mrs Goodjohn.'

'Call me Bess, if you like. Most do, except for Master Jack and his father; they've got their own name for me. Captain Kendle started it when he was a young man, before he went off to the army, that is. He was a lovely young man in those days and his boy is just like him, bright as a new button.'

The lemon barley was cool and delicious. Jessie made a note to ask Cook if they could have a jug in the nursery sometimes. She would have to be diplomatic, of course, but it would make a welcome change for the children.

The walk home seemed longer because Jessie had to carry Catherine, who was happy but tired after her exhausting morning. It was obvious that she was not used to much exercise. Nanny was too old to take the children out for long walks, and Captain Kendle took his son sometimes but not his daughter. She did not think the neglect was intentional on his part; it was natural for fathers to take more notice of their sons and in many families of this kind children were ignored completely until after they left the schoolroom. It seemed odd to Jessie that children should be kept apart from their parents, but she knew it happened. She was learning a lot about the gentry from Nanny, who liked to talk about what she thought of as her family.

Jessie's own day was much as the previous one, except that she was not summoned to the study, nor did she see Captain Kendle. He did not visit his son all day. Jack told her his father would come when the guests had gone.

'Father gave me lots of sums to keep me busy. He comes when he's not busy.' Jack frowned. 'He's busy lots of times.'

'Yes, I expect he must be,' Jessie agreed as she got on with ironing the clothes she had washed the previous day, but her opinion of the captain was a little diminished. Surely a few minutes could be found for visiting his children!

It was not until she went down for her dinner that evening that she saw Alice, who had been rushed off her feet all day looking after the guests.

'Did you enjoy the dance?' she asked.

Alice pulled a face. 'It was all right. My feet hurt the whole time and I've got a blister on my little toe.'

'You should've let me stretch your shoes,' Carter said, coming in with a basket of logs for the kitchen fire at that moment. A newspaper lay on top of the logs and he threw it on the table in front of Cook. 'Have you seen that? Nothing but trouble everywhere. We'll have strikes again before we're done. You'd think folk would be glad to buckle down to a good day's work now the war's over, but all they do is grumble.'

'A lot of people haven't got work,' Jessie said as she saw the article that had caused Carter's outburst. 'You would think those that have would be glad of it.'

'There's some will never be satisfied,' Cook said. 'What's behind it all? That's what I'd like to know.'

'Agitators, that's what,' Carter said. 'Travelling up and down the country holding meetings and stirring up trouble.' He opened the paper and jabbed his finger at a photograph. 'He's one of them. The police arrested him but the magistrates gave him a caution and let him go. Afraid of upsetting them new-fangled unions, I shouldn't wonder.'

Jessie looked at the picture that accompanied the article. The nerve endings at the nape of her neck tingled as she picked up the paper and stared at it. The photograph was dark and poor quality so she couldn't be certain, but she thought it was the man from the train. What had he said his name was? Oh yes, Paul Smith. She read the article. It was about a disturbance that had taken place on the evening of the day she'd arrived at Kendlebury Hall. The man referred to was named as Paul Keifer and was said to be working for the unions as an agitator.

'He looks a right troublemaker,' Carter said. 'I met his sort when I was younger. I worked up north in the shipyards before I went into service, in the transport side for the management. Met some rough types there. They would as soon spit in your face as look at you.'

'None of that talk in my kitchen,' Cook said. 'Are you going out on your half day, Jessie?'

'I haven't given it a thought,' she replied, pushing the paper away. She didn't want to think about the man on the train, though if he was an agitator it might explain why he had boarded without a ticket. He certainly wasn't the kind of man she wanted to know! 'I'm not sure – did Mrs Kendle tell me it was on Monday?'

'That's right,' Cook said. 'I'm Tuesday. Mrs Pearson's Wednesday and Maggie's Thursday. Carter takes his when

94

he likes. Alice has Friday, though she wasn't off until gone four this week. She'll go home on Sunday afternoon for a few hours to make up for it. We don't have a cooked meal on Sunday nights. They have it in the middle of the day instead.'

'What will happen with the children if I take my time off?'

'Alice and Mrs Pearson will manage between them,' Cook said. 'You want to take what's due to you, lass. It's only fair.'

'Yes, I shall sometimes,' Jessie replied. 'But I've only just got here and I don't think I need to take it this week. Nanny may be better soon and then she can watch them while I'm out.'

'Don't let Madam know,' Carter warned. 'She'll expect it all the time if you give way to her.'

'I'll take time off when I really want it, but not yet. However, I do have letters to post. Can I do that in the village?'

'I'll take them for you,' Carter said. 'Bring them down in the morning and I'll post them in Torquay. I'm driving Madam in on Monday morning and your letters will go quicker from there.'

'Thank you. I'll bring them down and leave them on the table later this evening.'

Jessie spent half an hour settling Lady Kendle for the night. They talked about the children and Jessie's day, but there were no personal revelations that night. Lady Kendle seemed tired and only sipped her drink.

Nanny was more talkative. She wanted to know about Jessie, about her life in London, and she told Jessie about her own childhood in the north.

'There were ten of us at home,' she said. 'My father worked in the coal mines and Ma took in washing until the laundry started up. Once folk started going there she lost most of her customers. I was nine when I was put to work in the sorting room. You wouldn't believe the stink in there! I hated it and I got out just as soon as I could. It was more than four years though, and I'd moved up to the wet room, got chilblains there.

'Then I heard someone was looking for a nursery maid. The Kendles were visiting with friends up north and their girl had run off and left them in the lurch. I'm talking of Sir Joshua's parents, of course. I never expected to get the job, but I think they were desperate. The nanny they had was a tartar. She soon put me in my place but I learned fast. I helped look after Sir Joshua's brothers and sisters, though he had left the nursery when I joined it.'

'Did he have many brothers and sisters?'

'He had three brothers and a sister. They're all dead now. Two died before they were of school age, one had a riding accident when he was twenty, and the girl died a few years back. Sir Joshua was very fond of his sister and her death broke him up – especially after losing his eldest son.'

'So you've been with three generations of Kendles then?'

'Yes, that's right. I replaced the old nanny when she left to retire and then stayed on with Sir Joshua when he married. They had several children, but they weren't lucky either. It's an unlucky family in some ways.'

'What do you mean, they weren't lucky?'

'They had three children,' Nanny said. 'Master John, Master Harry and Miss Priscilla. Captain Kendle was the youngest. Lady Kendle had a miscarriage with her fourth child. She was never the same after that. She wasn't an invalid then, of course; that came later. She had an accident after Master John was killed . . .'

'I had wondered why she found it so painful to get about. She isn't actually crippled, is she?'

'No, not quite, but the pain can be terrible at times. She fell down the stairs and injured her back, you see. She was in bed for a long time and they thought she might never move again, but she gradually got so that she could get out of bed with help, but she can't walk more than a few steps and the pain is always with her. But I think she still feels the pain of losing Master John as much as that in her back.'

'What happened to him?'

'They didn't say a great deal at the time, but the boys were out with a shooting party and somehow Master John got in the way of the guns. One of them shot him. They brought him home with the blood pouring out of him and his mother saw him. She was ill for weeks, and it was when she was feeling poorly that she had the accident. They had the doctor to Master John but it was useless. He lingered the night but by morning he'd gone.'

'That must have been a terrible time for the family,' Jessie said. She thought it explained the sadness she had witnessed in Lady Kendle on her first night. 'Is Captain Kendle the only one of the children left?'

'Bless you, no,' Nanny said. 'Miss Priscilla was married ten years ago; she was older than either of the boys, you see. She has three children of her own. Lovely girl, as you'll discover when she comes to visit. Pity she can't visit more, but her husband is something in the government. They spend part of their time in Yorkshire, which is his home, and the rest in London. She can only come for a few days once or twice a year.'

'It is a shame she can't see her mother more.'

'Yes. She cheers us all up when she does come.' Nanny looked at Jessie thoughtfully. 'You're a bit like her in a way. She has a very direct manner, too, and she says what's on her mind. Argues with her father a lot, and takes Captain Kendle's side. They are fond of one another, you know.'

'I hope she doesn't get into as much trouble as I do,' Jessie said and laughed. She was still smiling as she left Nanny's room and went along the hall to the nursery. She just wanted to see the children were all right before she went to bed.

As she entered she caught the scent of sandalwood and her heart missed a beat; it was the scent of the cologne Captain Kendle used and she could see him standing by the playroom window, looking out at the night.

'Don't go,' he said without turning round. 'It's a beautiful night, don't you think, Jessie?'

'Yes, it is,' she replied, moving to stand beside him and look out. The sky was a velvety black and sprinkled with stars.

'They are both fast asleep,' he said and turned to look at her. 'I come here sometimes at night if I've been too busy

97

earlier, just to look at them and to think. I like to remember the way it was before . . . After all, it was my room for years. Priscilla was grown up and my brother was killed in an accident when he was twelve. I was ten at the time. Everything changed then . . .'

'It was a terrible thing,' Jessie said. She could see that haunted expression in his eyes and thought she understood. 'To lose your brother that way.'

'Do you think the sins of the father are visited on the children, Jessie?'

'No, of course not. Why should they be?'

'I hope not. I pray it isn't my fault that Catherine is the way she is. I should hate her to suffer for my sins.'

'That's nonsense. Catherine's birth was unfortunate. It had nothing to do with you.'

Harry was silent for a moment, then said, 'My father blamed me for my brother's death, you know. I was bored with the shooting. I didn't like it much. It seemed cruel and senseless to me . . . all those birds getting shot in one day. I made John come with me.'

'How could you do that? He was older than you.'

'I told him about the badger set I'd found. He wanted to see. We left the shooting party and went off for more than an hour. When we came back there was no noise. We thought it was all over and we were laughing, larking about. John was ahead of me. He ran across the line of the guns just as they started shooting again. They had just stopped for a drink . . .'

His story was even more shocking than Nanny's had been, perhaps because she could see that it had affected him deeply, scarring him. Jessie stared at him in silence for a few moments, unsure of what to say.

'That doesn't make your brother's death your fault,' she said at last. 'It was an accident.'

'We were warned not to wander off. We knew it was dangerous. John wouldn't have gone to look at the badgers if I hadn't persuaded him. My father blamed me. I think Mother did, too, though she has never said it to my face.'

'Your father was wrong,' Jessie said. She didn't know why

she was talking like this. It wasn't her place to express her opinion on something of which she knew so little, but she sensed the desperate need in him, the guilt that had lived with him all these years, and she wanted to ease his pain if she could. 'Accidents happen. It wasn't your fault, and it isn't your fault that Catherine is a bit backward.'

'A bit backward – is that how you see her?' A smile flickered in his eyes. 'If only I could see it that way.'

'She's a bright little thing really,' Jessie said. 'Give me a little time and you'll see a change in her.'

'Shall I? You almost make me believe it.' He was silent for a moment and then moved towards her, bending his head. She knew he was going to kiss her and she knew she ought to move away, but somehow she couldn't. His kiss was soft and gentle, a mere brush of his lips against hers.

'Thank you for not making a fuss,' he said when she made no comment. 'It wasn't a prelude to seduction, Jessie. It was just for comfort. I was feeling pretty desperate when I came here. You've made me feel better. Thank you for that, too.'

'I didn't do much, sir,' Jessie said. 'I think I should go now. Goodnight, sir.'

'Goodnight, Jessie. Sleep well.'

'And you, sir.'

Jessie walked along the hall to her own room. She hesitated and then locked her door. She didn't really think he would try to come in, but it was wise to be sensible. That kiss had made her tingle right down to her toes. She would have to be careful or she would find herself becoming too attached to Captain Kendle.

She had sensed his loneliness, and she knew his marriage wasn't all it should be, but that wasn't her affair. Nothing could come of a relationship between them; it would be doomed from the start – if she allowed it to start.

She sat brushing her hair for some minutes before getting into bed to read a few pages of her book. It was a long time since she'd thought about a man's kiss. No one had made any impression on her since Robbie. She'd had plenty of chances. Brothers and friends of the other nurses at St Joseph's had asked her out and one of the doctors had shown some interest until she'd made her own feelings clear. She hadn't wanted anyone to take Robbie's place – and she still didn't – but she had felt something this evening, a stirring of feelings she'd believed long dead.

This was ridiculous! Jessie told herself to stop being foolish. Captain Kendle was married and even if he hadn't been there was a huge divide between them. She would only be hurt if she allowed herself to think of him as anything other than the father of Catherine and Jack.

She turned her thoughts to the children. Jack could be a handful at times. They'd had one or two small battles that weekend, but he wasn't too difficult if you treated him firmly but fairly. She knew he'd played Alice up while she was in with Lady Kendle, but Alice lost her temper too easily. She was too impatient and resented looking after the children, even for a short time.

Catherine was no problem. Jessie was finding the child a delight. She was always happy, playing contentedly until Jessie was ready to look after her, but her eyes were ever watchful. Jessie was sure she knew far more of what was going on around her than everyone thought. She wouldn't talk unless she had to and she preferred to crawl rather than walk, but she could walk if she wanted; it was just that she could crawl faster.

Jessie was sure she was responding to the attention she was getting. Perhaps she would never be like Jack, but she could still have a happy life if her parents could learn to accept her for who and what she was.

Sighing, Jessie pushed the problem from her mind as she settled down to sleep, but another one immediately replaced it. Was the man she'd met on the train really a political agitator? Oh, what did it matter? She wasn't likely to see him again.

Jessie turned out her lamp, closed her eyes and went to sleep. It would soon be morning and she had another long day ahead of her.

Jessie woke and lay staring into the darkness, wondering what had disturbed her. Then she heard the door handle turn and

100

remembered locking her door the previous evening. It had seemed sensible, but supposing she was needed? She jumped out of bed and rushed to the door.

'Who is it?' she asked. 'What do you want? Is someone ill?'

There was no answer but Jessie thought she heard someone walking away. She unlocked her door and looked out but the hall was empty. Had whoever it was gone or had she imagined the whole thing?

Captain Kendle wouldn't have come to her room, would he? Stranger things had happened. Aunt Elizabeth had warned her to be careful.

'Some men can't keep their hands off the maids,' she'd told Jessie. 'I'm not saying your Captain Kendle is like that, but it's best to be careful.'

She would raise her eyebrows if Jessie told her about the kiss, but she wasn't going to tell anyone. Jessie was sure it was just an innocent gesture, for comfort as he'd said. He hadn't meant to seduce her and she hadn't been in danger of being seduced. If she'd been frightened she would have made her displeasure known, but he'd been gentle and sweet and she'd quite liked being kissed by him.

She was suddenly sure it hadn't been him who had tried her door. That only left Sir Joshua and Carter, both seemed equally unlikely. Unless Nanny was wandering. Perhaps she'd felt ill again?

Jessie pulled on a dressing robe. She went down the hall, carefully opening Nanny's door a crack. A gentle snore told her that all was well. A visit to the nursery revealed Jack and Catherine in their beds.

It was a mystery. Jessie returned to her room, locking the door behind her again. She would make sure she did it every night in future, though she would leave the door that led through into the nursery wing unlocked in case the children needed her in the night.

She frowned as she got into bed. There were only three men in the house now that the guests had gone home. It had to have been one of them. She just wished she knew which of them had tried to enter her room unannounced.

What would she have done if it had been Captain Kendle? Jessie wondered. She hoped she would have had the strength of mind to send him away, but she wasn't sure. She wasn't at all sure that she would want him to leave.

Seven

Jessie wondered if her mystery visitor would try again, but several nights passed and nobody tried to come into her room again. She was half inclined to think she might have imagined it in the first place.

She was a bit worried about meeting Captain Kendle again after their kiss, but when it happened it was accidental and passed off without embarrassment. She was returning from one of her long walks with the children and he saw them, waiting for Jack to run up to him, to be swung high in the air until he shrieked with laughter. He smiled at Jessie, gave Jack a peppermint out of his pocket and when Catherine asked to be picked up because she was tired, carried her himself.

Giving her to Jessie as they approached the house, he said, 'She seems to walk better than she did. Perhaps it's because of all the fresh air and exercise she's been getting.'

'Yes, sir. It's not as easy to crawl outside as it is in the house. She wants to keep up with Jack so she has started to run after him. She can't catch him, of course, but she doesn't fall over so much now.'

'So I noticed,' Harry said and smiled. 'You *are* making a difference with her, Jessie.'

'Thank you, sir.'

Jessie was pleased with his praise and walked into the house with a smile on her face. She was heading for the stairs when Carter came into the hall. He gave her an odd look as she passed him, then called out something she didn't quite catch.

Jessie turned to look at him. 'What did you say?'

'Pride goes before a fall, that's what I said,' he muttered and she caught a flash of something that might have been jealousy in his eyes. 'Be careful, Jessie, that's my advice to you.'

'What do you mean? I don't understand you.'

'You understand right enough,' he said and turned away to the kitchen.

Jessie decided to ignore his remarks. She was settling in well now and didn't want any trouble with Carter. It made her think that it might have been him that tried her door, but since it hadn't happened again she wasn't going to make a fuss.

However, it made her uneasy about asking him to take her into Torquay on her afternoon off and she asked Nanny about the train when she decided that she would take some free time. She had been at the house for nearly three weeks now and she hadn't bothered to take more than an hour or so off from her duties.

'Yes, there's a train into Torquay,' Nanny told her. 'But you'll need to catch the five thirty back or you will be stranded until the next morning, and it's a long walk home from the station. It's a lot easier to ask Carter to pick you up in town. He doesn't mind. Besides, he goes in often to bring back provisions for Cook; he can kill two birds with one stone.'

'I'd rather be independent if I can.'

'Has he made a pass at you?' Nanny asked. 'I know he was a bit of a lad when he was younger but he's usually sensible – at least when he's sober.'

'Does he drink a lot?'

'No, not often. I've known him to have one too many at Christmas or New Year, but otherwise he's fairly reliable.'

Seeing her suspicious look, Jessie laughed. 'He hasn't done anything, Nanny. I just like to be independent if I can, that's all.'

'You haven't got anything to hide, have you? No secret lover you want to meet?'

Jessie saw the mischief in her eyes. 'No, no lovers. All right. I suppose I'm being silly. I'll go on the train and ask Carter to meet me from the station when I get back.'

'If he does cause you any trouble, tell me. I'll put him right.'

Jessie was pleased to hear the militant note in her voice. Nanny was making a good recovery and was perfectly able

104

to wash, dress and look after herself. She was still having her meals in her room, but had offered to sit in the nursery with the children while Jessie had her time off.

Jessie felt quite excited to be going to the busy seaside town that afternoon. She'd only visited the sea a few times and never before in this part of the world, which she knew to be especially picturesque. The train journey took only twenty minutes or so and she was thrilled by her first glimpse of the beautiful wooded coastline. The cliffs looked pinkish in the clear light and seemed to climb forever to the sky, and the dark blue sea stretched endlessly into the distance, sparkling and enticing in the winter sunshine. The wind was very cold, of course, but Jessie found it exhilarating.

Jessie spent most of the afternoon exploring. She had come to buy knitting wool, postcards, some toiletries she needed for herself, and also one or two small presents to give at Christmas. Once that was done she wandered along one of the twisting cliff paths, stopping every now and then to gaze out at the sea. Below her the foam was tossed high into the air as the waves boiled and thrashed about spurs of jutting rock. It was all so beautiful, she thought, standing at the edge to gaze down at the beach below.

She could see two people walking along it, intent on each other. As she watched, they stopped and embraced, their kiss deeply passionate and intimate. Jessie felt embarrassed and turned away, but even as she did so the woman laughed and broke away, running ahead of her companion. When she stopped and looked back, Jessie saw her face and her heart stopped. It couldn't be! No, she was wrong. She had to be wrong! That wasn't Mary Kendle down there . . . and it certainly wasn't Captain Kendle with her.

Jessie drew back, hoping that she hadn't been seen. She hadn't meant to spy on something that was so private, and yet it had happened on a public beach. There were few other people about because it was too early yet for the tourists to be here in force, so perhaps the lovers had thought themselves safe to kiss on a beach they had almost to themselves.

Jessie wished she hadn't seen it. She was almost sure that

the woman wasn't Mary Kendle. How could it be? Of course it couldn't! She was mistaken.

She hurried down the cliff path as she realized the time. The afternoon had passed so swiftly that she had to hurry to catch her train. She managed it by mere seconds and found herself wishing that she'd had longer. If she had asked Carter to fetch her from the town she could have spent that much more time exploring.

He was waiting for her at the station in the Daimler. He gave her a sideways glance as she got in beside him.

'Had a good afternoon then, Jessie?'

'Yes, thank you. The time went too quickly though.'

'I could always take you in earlier or fetch you back. You have only to ask. Madam sometimes needs me, but she prefers to drive herself. She went in after lunch.'

'Oh . . .' Jessie's heart thudded. It could have been Mary Kendle she'd seen on the beach – but surely it wasn't. That would mean . . . something she didn't want to know. 'Perhaps I'll ask another time, thank you.'

Carter accepted that then lapsed into silence. She wondered if she had offended him but when he followed her into the kitchen he was his usual cheerful self, teasing Maggie and chatting to Cook about something he'd read in the paper.

'Did you get what you needed, Jessie?' Cook asked as she poured her a cup of tea.

'Yes, thank you. I'll drink this and then go up to the nursery and see how things are,' Jessie said. She was feeling a little anxious in case it had been too tiring for Nanny looking after the children.

'I'll keep your supper warm for you then. I'm just about to get their dinner upstairs. Mary Kendle came in a few minutes before you.'

Jessie finished her tea and snatched a rock bun from the cooling tray to keep her going until she had her meal. She was thoughtful as she walked upstairs. Mary Kendle could have got home before her even if she had been on that beach. It had taken Jessie at least ten minutes to walk to the station and twenty minutes on the train; the drive would probably take half that time if the roads were not busy. But of course

106

it couldn't have been her! She wasn't being unfaithful to her husband, was she?

As Jessie approached the nursery she heard voices and hesitated, surprised. Mary Kendle hardly ever came near the nursery.

'I wanted your opinion, Nanny,' she was saying. 'You have so much more experience. Captain Kendle thinks the new girl has done wonders, but I . . .'

Jessie didn't wait to hear more. She went straight in, surprising her employer into a blush.

'You're back then, Jessie,' Nanny said. 'They've both been good. I put Miss Catherine to bed after her tea because she was tired. Master Jack has been painting that castle you helped him make. It looks very good now he's nearly finished it.'

'It's for his soldiers,' Jessie said and smiled at her. 'Catherine walked such a long way this morning. I expect she was tired, but we should get her up for a while or she might not sleep through the night.' She looked at Mary Kendle. 'Would you like to see Catherine for a few minutes, Mrs Kendle?'

'Not at this moment.' Mary frowned. 'My husband is thinking of getting another expert opinion on her. He thinks the first doctor may have been wrong – that she may be less retarded than we had thought. I wanted to ask Nanny's opinion first.'

'Jessie sees more of her than I do, ma'am,' Nanny said. 'She seems better in herself for the fresh air she's been getting, but I couldn't tell you more than that. I'm not a medical person.'

'She talks more than she did and she tries to run after Jack when we're out,' Jessie said. 'I think she seems very bright in herself, though I can't be sure how much she is capable of learning.'

'And have you had medical experience of children like my daughter?'

Jessie cringed as she said those words, as if Catherine were some sort of a freak. 'No, ma'am, I speak only of what I have observed in Catherine.'

'Then perhaps you should keep your opinions to yourself. My husband believes you know what you are talking about and he is determined to seek further advice. I believe we shall be disappointed, but he will have his way.' Mary glared at Jessie. 'I just hope it will not be a complete waste of time and money.'

She nodded to Nanny and walked from the room, ignoring her son, who was playing with his soldiers and looked up as if in hope of a kind word from his mother.

Jessie went through into the children's bedroom and began to tidy it, though there wasn't much out of place. She was so angry that she thought she would explode. How could any mother be so careless of a child's welfare? Even if the visit to the doctor didn't help, surely it was worth trying.

Nanny followed her into the bedroom after a moment. 'I shouldn't let her bother you,' she said when Jessie thumped a pillow. 'She always did have a sharp tongue. Pretty, of course, and an heiress – but I thought Master Harry could have done better for himself.'

'I could have hit her!' Jessie said between her teeth and, seeing that Catherine had woken, went to pick her up. 'Hello, darling. Want to come and play for a while?'

Catherine was wet. Jessie was teaching her to use the chamber pot and sometimes they were successful, but not always. She changed her nappy, feeling a little anxious as she put the child down and watched her crawl across the floor to find and play with her dolls.

'It isn't for us to say what's right and wrong between them. I suppose they are happy enough in their way.'

'Believe that and you'll believe anything,' Nanny said with a sniff. 'Master Harry is miserable even if he tries not to show it. I'm going to visit Lady Kendle. The children had their tea at three thirty but they didn't want much. You'd given them a good dinner before you went.'

They had walked back into the playroom together. Jack looked up as Nanny went out, the door closing behind her.

'It was boiled egg for tea. I don't like eggs much.'

'Well, perhaps you would like a biscuit,' Jessie said with a smile. 'I bought a packet of chocolate ones. Would you like to have one or two now?'

Jack said that he would. The only time he'd been given chocolate biscuits was on those rare occasions that his mother sent for him to appear when she and her friends were having tea, and he'd had to wear the hated sailor suit, which rather took the shine from the treat. He was eating his second biscuit when the nursery door opened to admit Captain Kendle. Jessie had taken Catherine on her lap and she too was busily chewing on a biscuit, her mouth ringed with chocolate.

'What's this?' Harry asked with a mock scowl that deceived no one. 'I don't remember anyone giving me chocolate biscuits before bed when I was in the nursery.'

'I hope you don't mind,' Jessie said. 'It's a special treat I bought in Torquay for the children.'

'You shouldn't spend your own money on them.'

'I wanted to, sir. I also bought some wool to knit them jumpers, but that came from the nursery fund.'

'You must ask me if you need more money for the children. I came to tell you that I have just telephoned to make an appointment with a doctor in London for Catherine on the tenth of next month. I wanted to wait until after Christmas, because it will throw all my wife's arrangements out otherwise. I shall need you to accompany me to take care of her. My wife has other arrangements – a visit with some friends of hers in Kent, I believe. I understand Nanny is feeling well enough to keep an eye on Jack.'

'Can't I come too?' Jack asked. 'Please, Father. I shan't be any trouble, shall I, Jessie?'

She looked at his pleading face and smiled. 'Your father knows best, Jack. I expect it will mean a lot of sitting about and waiting. It wouldn't be much fun for you.'

'We could take him if you didn't mind looking after both of them,' Harry said, surprising both her and himself. 'It will mean staying overnight at the London house, of course. We can't do both journeys in one day and it might be too much for Nanny to have Jack all that time. She is better, I know, but not completely well again.'

'Will you promise to be good?' Jessie asked and laughed as she saw Jack's eager face. 'Then I think we might take you. I'm not sure if we shall have time to do anything more than visit the doctor, but if we do, where would you like to go?'

'Can we see the guards changing at Buckingham Palace? And the zoo?' Jack asked and his father smiled.

'Perhaps Jessie will take you to the zoo while I take Catherine to the doctor.'

'Catherine want zoo,' a little voice piped up and Harry felt a tug on his trousers. 'See elphant.'

Harry looked at Jessie over her head. 'Did you tell her that?'

'I read a story to them this morning about an elephant at the zoo,' Jessie said. 'Catherine has a good memory, don't you, darling?'

'She has certainly improved enormously these past few weeks,' her father said. He reached down to take the little girl on to his knee. She looked at him solemnly, having seldom found herself in this position before, then made a chuckling sound as she reached up to pat his face. 'So you want to go to the zoo, do you? We had better take you and Jack then.' He looked across at Jessie and smiled, making her heart lurch at the touching picture of father and daughter together. 'It may mean an extra day in London, but what does that matter?'

'It doesn't matter to me, sir.'

'You might visit your aunt one evening,' he said. 'That's settled then – and now I want to see your sums, Jack.' He put Catherine down and she scampered across the floor on her hands and knees to where she had left her dolls earlier.

Jessie turned away. Her heart was racing at the thought of spending three whole days with the children and their father.

Jessie got some odd looks when she told the others what was happening. Carter muttered something she couldn't hear and hid behind his paper when she looked at him. Maggie gave a little scream of envy and asked if she could change places with her. Alice lifted her brows as she left the kitchen and Cook gave her a straight, hard look.

'I hope you know what you're doing, Jessie.'

'I'm not doing anything except my job,' she replied, feeling a bit annoyed but determined not to show it. 'Captain Kendle can't see to the children himself, and Mrs Kendle has arranged to visit some friends in Kent.'

'Will she be travelling with you part of the way then?'

'I've no idea,' Jessie said. 'I wasn't consulted about the travel arrangements. I suppose we shall go on the train. There's nothing very terrible about that, is there?'

'I wish it were me,' Maggie said, looking at her enviously. 'Can't you say you need help and take me too, Jessie?'

'I would if I could,' Jessie said to please her. 'I was thinking we might have an afternoon off together one week, Maggie. We could go to one of those tea dances Carter told us about, if you'd like that – and if Nanny would look after the children on a Thursday instead of a Monday.'

'Would I just!' Maggie said. 'I don't mind if we go to the pictures or a dance. I hardly ever bother going into town on my own, but it would be fun with you.'

'Why don't we do it next week then? I'm sure Nanny wouldn't mind having the children – especially as we'll be away for several days next month.'

'Will you ask her?' Maggie said, her face lighting up. 'Carter will take us and fetch us – won't you?'

'Don't see why not,' he said and grinned at her. 'I want a dance though, Maggie, as my reward.'

Maggie giggled and looked at Jessie. 'Should I let him come with us, Jessie?'

'I don't mind,' Jessie said, though she did and half regretted making the offer. She hadn't expected Carter to invite himself along. 'I'll talk to Nanny. I'm sure she won't mind.'

'As long as Madam doesn't find out and make a fuss because you're both gone at the same time,' Cook said. 'Still, you haven't taken all your days off so she can't say much.'

'I can't see what difference it could possibly make,' Jessie said. 'Maggie doesn't do much for the children except to take their tea up, and it wouldn't matter if Alice did that for once, would it?'

'What are you asking for Alice to do?' the girl asked as she came back into the kitchen and then nodded agreeably as Jessie explained. 'I don't mind for once – and I'd like to have Monday afternoon off next week if that's all right with you, Cook. I've spoken to Mrs Pearson and she says I can if you've no objection.'

'All this changing about,' Cook grumbled. 'I suppose it's all right if Mrs Pearson agrees, though I can't see why you need to change, Alice.'

Alice had gone pink, her eyes looking beyond Cook as she said, 'I have to see someone, that's all.'

Cook muttered something but Jessie could see it was just a case of having her routine changed, nothing more. She helped Maggie with the washing up as she often did, and by the time the kitchen was to rights Cook had recovered her usual goodwill.

'So what will you wear to this dance then, Maggie?' she asked. 'You'll want a pretty dress but nothing too fancy; it's afternoon not evening.'

Maggie pulled a face. 'I'm not sure I've got anything suitable.'

'Are you any good at sewing?' Jessie asked and Maggie nodded. 'Come up to my room and have a look in my wardrobe. I've got a couple of dresses you can choose from, but you'll need to alter the hem on the one you want to borrow.'

'Can I really wear one of your dresses?' Maggie's face lit up. 'I couldn't borrow that green one you wore this afternoon, could I?'

It was one of her favourites, but Jessie smiled and said that of course she could if it was the one she wanted. Cook said Maggie could go up with her now so they went upstairs together, and Maggie took the dress away to try on. Jessie went down the hall to make sure that Lady Kendle was comfortable.

She took the drinks up later as usual and spent some time talking to Nanny, who said that it made no difference to her what afternoon she looked after the children.

'I'm feeling a lot better than I was before you came,' she told Jessie and smiled. 'I shall soon be able to help you more than I have until now. There's no need for Alice to bring the children's tea up. I can quite well carry it up myself.'

'You let Alice do it if she has time,' Jessie said. 'You've been doing too much for too long, and you deserve to take things easy.'

112

It wasn't until she was ready for bed that Jessie had time to read the letters she'd found waiting for her on her return from her trip to Torquay. There was a long, chatty one from her aunt, who seemed to be as busy as ever, and a shorter one from Archie just to say that he hoped she was keeping well and settling in nicely at her job.

Jessie was relieved that he hadn't written anything more intimate, and she tucked the letters away in her writing case before putting off the light and going to sleep.

Maggie was like a little girl waking up to find that Father Christmas had been and left her a sack full of presents. She was wearing Jessie's dress, which she had altered to fit herself, a new pair of shoes that her mother had bought her for an advance birthday gift, and she'd had her hair in papers to curl it all morning.

'Do I look all right?' she asked Cook and Jessie. 'I don't look daft, do I?'

'You look pretty,' Jessie said and it was true. The green dress suited Maggie as well if not better than it ever had Jessie and she decided to make her a gift of it, though she wouldn't say anything yet. It was Maggie's birthday in a few days and it would be a surprise for her to be told she could keep the dress she liked so much.

'Very smart,' Cook said, giving her a straight look. 'Just you behave yourself, my girl. Don't do anything your mother wouldn't approve of. I don't want you getting into trouble and leaving me in the lurch.'

Jessie heard a little gasp and turned round to find that Alice had just come into the kitchen. She had an odd expression on her face, but she smiled as she saw Jessie looking at her.

'You look nice, Maggie,' she said. 'Have a good time.' She reached into her pocket and brought out a small bottle of lavender water. 'Here, I was going to give it to you for your birthday, but you might as well have it now.'

'Oh, Alice, that's ever so good of you,' Maggie said and unscrewed the cap to dab some behind her ears.

'Come on then, time's a-wasting,' Carter said from the

113

door. He was wearing a pale grey suit and smart shoes and looked very different with his hair slicked down with perfumed oil that was so strong Jessie could smell it across the room.'

Maggie was in a hurry to get off. Jessie lingered a moment after them and was told not to let her get into trouble.

'She's a good girl, but daft,' Cook said. 'I don't want anything to happen to our Maggie.'

'It's an afternoon dance,' Jessie said. 'I imagine it will be very staid and ladylike, Cook. Besides, Maggie has Carter and me to look after her.'

'Yes, I know, but keep an eye on her. Make sure she only drinks tea.'

Jessie agreed with a smile. Cook seemed to think they were going to a den of iniquity, but Jessie thought it would probably be a little boring. Still, she wasn't going to spoil Maggie's big treat by saying so.

Maggie was already in the front seat of the car when she arrived. Jessie thankfully slid into the back, pleased that she didn't have to sit beside Carter. She listened to Maggie's excited chatter all the way to the small hotel on the seafront where the tea dances took place.

The room had only three couples dancing when they went in, but it was early yet and Carter assured them that it would fill up later. He had secured a table for them by the time they returned from hanging their coats in the little cloakroom, and he asked Maggie for a dance straight away.

'You don't mind, do you, Jessie?' she asked.

'Of course not. I'm happy to watch,' Jessie replied.

However, she hadn't been sitting by herself long before a man walked up to her and asked her if she would care to dance with him. Jessie said thank you, because he looked respectable, and when they got talking she discovered that he was employed by the management to dance with any lady that came in and sat alone.

Jessie was secretly amused that he had taken pity on her, but she hid her smile. When Carter brought Maggie back to their table, the little room had begun to fill up and Jessie saw that some men and women had entered in a group. They weren't in couples, although they were together, and before she had hardly sat down, Jessie was asked to dance by one of the newcomers. She agreed and then saw that Carter was dancing with Maggie again.

After the second dance, the waitress came to take their order and Maggie was asked to dance by the young man who had just partnered Jessie. Carter asked if she would like to dance and she thought she might as well get it over with so she agreed with a smile.

Carter was quite an accomplished dancer and when she complimented him he told her he had taken part in several competitions when he was younger, and won some of them.

'You might think I'm just a nobody,' he said. 'But I've had my moments.'

'I am sure you have,' she replied. 'I think we should try to be civil to each other, don't you? For the sake of peace in the kitchen.'

'Suits me,' he said and shrugged.

After their dance the tea was brought and Carter excused himself, going off to dance with a lady some years younger than himself who he obviously knew well. Maggie was asked to dance again, and Jessie found herself sitting alone for a few minutes.

'Would you like to dance or would you rather have your tea?'

Jessie looked up and gave a little gasp of surprise. It was the man from the train!

'Mr Smith,' she said. 'If that is your real name.'

'It's Paul,' he replied and gave her an odd smile. 'The rest of it changes from time to time for the sake of convenience – and you're Jessie, aren't you?'

'Yes.' She wasn't sure whether she was pleased to see him or not and her next question was rather demanding. 'Why are you here?'

'I'm travelling on business,' he said, answering her equably. 'I work for the unions and I give talks all over the country. I'm giving one at a hall in Torquay this evening.'

'You told me you sold ideas.' She couldn't help her voice sounding accusing.

'It's true in a way. I sell the idea that the working man has the right to freedom, that he doesn't have to lie down and let the bosses walk all over him. All we need to do is unite. A man can't stand up to his employer alone, but if he is part of a union he has a chance of being listened to. It's slow going but we are gradually getting that idea across to the working man.'

'You're a political agitator,' Jessie said. 'I'm not sure I approve of you, Paul Smith.'

'I'm sorry about that,' he said and frowned. 'Perhaps I'd better go away and stop bothering you.'

'Yes, perhaps you had,' Jessie replied. 'My friends will be back in a moment and one of them might recognize you from the picture in the paper.'

'Excuse me,' he said and gave her a curt nod. 'I made a mistake. I thought you were one of us . . .'

Jessie watched as he walked away. She felt a bit sorry that she had sent him off like that, but he had lied to her and she was almost sure that he had ridden on the train without paying for his ticket. At the time she had condoned it, but if he was working for the unions that changed things. She couldn't see the point of making all this unrest amongst the working men, when there was so much unemployment. Besides, if Carter had recognized him from the newspaper photograph she could just imagine what he might have said.

Carter and Maggie returned to have their tea. When they had finished, Carter asked Maggie to dance with him again and a young man who said his name was Alan Griggs approached Jessie.

'Would you like to dance?' he asked and smiled at her.

'Yes, thank you,' Jessie replied and stood up. Across the room she saw Paul Smith watching her and scowling. She avoided meeting his eyes and smiled up at her partner.

'I didn't expect it to be as busy as this here.'

'Oh yes, these dances are very popular,' he told her. 'I come every Thursday because it's my day off. I go to the Imperial Ballroom on Friday evenings. It's where they hold the big competitions once a year. Have you ever entered a competition?'

'No, I haven't, Jessie said. 'But Carter has – he's the man we came with this afternoon.'

'Oh, yes, I've seen him before,' her companion said. 'But you haven't been here until now, have you?'

'No. I came for Maggie's sake really,' Jessie said. 'She is dancing with Carter now. This is her first dance.'

'You're not courting, are you?'

'My fiancé was killed in the war,' Jessie said. 'I don't go out much.'

'I see. I was just wondering if I might see you here next week.'

'I don't think so,' Jessie replied and smiled because he looked disappointed. 'My afternoon off is usually on a Monday.'

He nodded, looked gloomier than before and returned her to her table as the music ended. He asked Maggie to dance next, and Jessie sat down to finish her tea.

'She wants to watch that one,' Carter said, his eyes following the pair. 'Different girl every chance he gets.'

'He said he'd seen you here before.'

'I come when I can.'

'I think we should be going soon,' Jessie said. 'We ought to be back by six just in case.'

'In case of what?' Carter asked. 'We've only just got here. Not bored already, are you? Or isn't there anyone here posh enough for you, Miss Hale?'

'I thought we were going to call a truce?'

'I'm only warning you for your own good,' he said. 'Never trust the gentry. They don't mix with our sort. It's like oil and water. You'll get your fingers burned if you don't watch out.'

'Thanks for the warning,' Jessie said. 'But it wasn't needed. I'm in no danger of falling into that trap.'

'You can't always help yourself,' he said. 'I've got nothing against you, Jessie. It's just that I've seen it all before.'

'What do you mean?'

He shook his head. 'I'm going to dance with a friend. We'll leave at a quarter to six. We shan't be late back. Besides, you're entitled to be out until seven on your afternoon off.'

There was nothing Jessie could do but accept his decision. She wasn't due back before seven, and she didn't want to spoil Maggie's afternoon. Yet there was a niggling worry at the back of her mind, though she had no idea what was worrying her.

Eight

Cook gave them an odd look as they walked in the kitchen door but it was Alice who dropped the bombshell.

'There's been a right kick-up upstairs,' she said. 'Madam was furious when she was told both you and Maggie were out this afternoon. Lady Kendle was taken bad and we had to have the doctor. Mrs Pearson couldn't leave her ladyship and Madam had friends visiting. It took me two trips to carry in all the tea things, and when she rang for more hot water I was seeing to the doctor. That didn't suit her, I can tell you.'

'How is Lady Kendle now?' Jessie asked, choosing to focus on what she thought was the most important piece of Alice's information. 'Was she very ill?'

'She had a funny turn, that's all I know.'

'I had better go up and see her straight away.'

'Madam said you were to go to the study and wait for her.'

'But won't she be at dinner a while yet?'

'Yes, but she said . . .'

'In that case I've plenty of time to ask how Lady Kendle is and help Nanny get the children into bed before I see Lady Kendle,' Jessie said with a stubborn look on her face.

'Well, I've told you what she said.' Alice pulled a face. 'You're in trouble now, Jessie. Be careful or there's no telling what she will do.'

'She can only dismiss me. In for a penny in for a pound, as my aunt says. You've told me, Alice. It isn't your fault if I choose to think other things are more important than kicking my heels in the study. Besides, I needn't have been back for another half an hour.'

Jessie went out without giving either Alice or Cook a chance to reply. She was feeling apprehensive as she ran quickly up the back stairs. She wouldn't have minded being told to go when she'd first arrived, but it would upset her now because she had grown fond of the children and she believed she was helping Catherine.

Lady Kendle was lying with her eyes closed and looking pale and drawn, but she opened them as Jessie approached. 'I'm sorry to have caused so much fuss,' she said. 'But I'm afraid everyone was very worried about me. So silly.'

'It was hardly your fault.' Jessie looked at her anxiously. 'How are you? I'm so sorry to have been out when you needed me.'

'You are entitled to your free time, Jessie. I'm feeling a little better now. Besides, it was nothing really. Just a little pain in my chest and some difficulty with breathing, but it only lasted a few minutes. Why Sir Joshua insisted on calling the doctor I do not know. I dare say I ate too much at lunch.'

'I very much doubt that, ma'am. What did the doctor say?'

'He thinks it may have been a heart tremor, but he's a fusspot like the rest of them. And I really do feel much better now. It was probably indigestion.'

'Did he leave you any pills to take?'

Lady Kendle pointed to a little bottle on the side and Jessie checked them. They were what she would expect the doctor to prescribe as a mild sedative to ease any stress caused by her upsetting afternoon.

'Did he say he would be calling again?'

'Yes, tomorrow. Totally unnecessary, of course.'

'I am certain he feels it necessary,' Jessie said. 'I can only apologize again for not being here when you needed me.'

'You could not have known.'

It was true that Jessie could not have known she would be needed; it was also true that she was entitled to her free afternoon off, but she knew that her absence at such a time must have made things difficult.

After making sure that Lady Kendle was as comfortable as possible in the circumstances, Jessie went up to the nursery. Nanny had already put Catherine to bed but Jack had insisted on staying up to see her. He clung to her when she tucked him up in his bed and begged her not to go away. It was clear that he sensed trouble. Someone must have said something in front of him and he was afraid that Jessie would leave him.

'I don't want to leave you,' she told him and kissed his cheek. 'If I had to it would be because I was given no choice. I only work here, Jack. I have to do as I'm told.'

'I hate her,' he said fiercely. 'If she sends you away I shall kick her!'

'You must not say such things. You don't hate your mother, Jack. You are cross with her and that is a very different thing.'

'Promise you won't go!' he begged, tears in his eyes.

'I shan't go without saying goodbye, but perhaps I shan't have to leave at all. I'm in a bit of trouble because things went wrong today, but I haven't done anything terrible. Cheer up, darling. I expect everything will be just the same tomorrow.'

Jack looked at her doubtfully but she stroked his hair, kissed him again and left him to snuggle down in his bed. Nanny was waiting for her when she went back into the playroom.

'Madam was very angry,' she said. 'Alice had to manage tea alone and there were six guests, and then the doctor arrived in the middle of it and Madam was left ringing with no one to answer.'

'That's hardly my fault,' Jessie said. 'They need another maid here to help Alice—' She broke off as Alice poked her head round the door.

'You're wanted in the study and you'd better hurry.'

Jessie smoothed the skirt of her dress and tucked a stray hair behind her ear. She hadn't had time to change into her uniform but it didn't seem to matter much as she was probably going to be dismissed anyway.

'Wish me luck, Nanny,' she said and smiled even though she didn't feel much like smiling.

'It's not fair,' Alice said, surprising her. 'You haven't done anything so very wrong. Besides, I don't know how we'll manage without you.'

'You managed before I came, but thanks just the same. I shall miss you all.'

Alice gave her an odd look before she turned away.

Jessie felt apprehensive as she made her way into the main wing and turned towards the study. She paused outside, hearing voices. That must be Sir Joshua with Mary Kendle; it wasn't Captain Kendle.

'Trust Harry not to be here when he's needed. If I dismiss her without his knowledge he'll probably throw a fit.'

'You must do as you please, my dear,' Sir Joshua said. 'The way my son carries on these days is no help to anyone. If it were not for you . . .'

Jessie knocked. She didn't want to overhear a private conversation. After a moment's pause she was invited to enter. Mary Kendle turned cold eyes on her.

'So you've decided to favour us with your presence at last. I hope you have an explanation for your conduct today. You were absent when we needed you most.'

'I changed my afternoon off, ma'am. Mrs Pearson made no objection. It was only my second period of free time since I came some weeks ago.'

'That isn't the point. You should have asked me if you wanted to change your afternoon. It made things very awkward for me. Had you been here Mother might have had attention sooner than she did.'

'I regret that I wasn't here,' Jessie said. 'But it could have happened at any time.'

'It happened on a day when you should have been here!' Mary snapped. She looked at Jessie as if she disliked her intensely. 'And I believe it was your suggestion that you and the other girl should go out together.'

'Yes, I made the suggestion.'

Jessie's head went up. She wasn't going to grovel. It was unfortunate that Lady Kendle had been ill while she was absent but she was entitled to her free time. If the staffing arrangements had been adequate for a house like this it wouldn't have mattered that Maggie had also been out.

'I really cannot have staff rearranging things to suit their convenience. You should have asked my permission.'

'I imagined such things would be left to Mrs Pearson's discretion.'

Mary's eyes glinted because of course such matters were always left to the housekeeper's discretion, and she would not have wanted to be bothered if she'd been asked. It was in her mind to dismiss the impertinent Miss Hale, but to do so would be inconvenient. Finding a replacement for Jessie would not be easy.

'You have seriously displeased me,' she said. 'If something of this nature occurs again I shall not hesitate to dismiss you. Very well, Jessie. You may go.'

'Yes, madam. Good evening, madam, sir.'

Jessie inclined her head. She refused to apologize or to thank her employer. She was angry as she left the room and returned to the servants' part of the house. Had she not cared so much for the children, Jessie would have been glad to leave. Yet mixed with her anger was guilt and regret. If anything had happened to Lady Kendle while she was out she would have felt terrible.

She went first to Nanny's room and told her the news.

'Madam must have thought better of it,' Nanny said. 'She was in such a temper earlier! But she knows it wouldn't be simple to find a replacement willing to work the way you do. It isn't easy to find any servants in a place like this since the war. And she isn't the easiest person in the world to work for either. We're only just managing as it is. I can help with the children now and then but I'm too old to look after them on my own. If you went I should retire and live with my sister. I warned her this afternoon that I couldn't stay on if you went.'

'Than I probably have you to thank for my job,' Jessie said. 'I'll go down and tell the others and then I'll bring the drinks up.'

She bent to pick up some scraps of washing that had been left on a chair.

'I was going to take that down in the morning,' Nanny said.

'I'll drop it into the laundry room on my way.'

'Have you had your supper?'

'No, but I'm not hungry. I'll ask Cook for a cup of tea and a slice of cake.'

'Don't you neglect yourself!'

'I shan't,' Jessie said and smiled at her. 'I'll be back in an hour or so.'

She went down the stairs and into the laundry room, stopping in surprise as she saw Alice was there and in some distress.

123

She was sitting on the edge of a scrubbed pine table, crying. She looked up as Jessie entered and rubbed her face with her hand to wipe away the tears.

'Sorry to intrude. I brought Nanny's washing.'

'Did you get the push?'

'Just a warning.'

'The bitch thought better of it then. Just as well. Maggie said she was leaving if you did.'

'That's not why you're crying. Is something wrong, Alice? Can I help?'

Alice stared at her for a moment in silence, then, her voice harsh with emotion, 'Not unless you know someone who can get rid of a kid for me.'

'Get rid . . .' Jessie was startled and then realized what Alice meant. She was shocked and upset, because she understood the hurt and fear that lay behind Alice's statement. 'It's illegal to have an abortion. You know that, don't you?'

'They do it though,' Alice said defiantly. 'It happens in London. I've heard about places you can go to have it done.'

'They are dreadful little back-street places,' Jessie said, feeling anxious for her at once. 'Don't do it, Alice. It's very dangerous. You could die. Have you told the father?' Alice nodded, her face miserable. 'He won't marry you?'

'He asked if I was sure it was his. He knows it is but he doesn't want to get married – not to me anyway.'

'Rotten devil,' Jessie said and looked angry. She hated men who took what they wanted and then shirked all responsibility. It was terribly unfair and frightening for the girl who found herself in such a situation. 'You've been unlucky, Alice. What do your parents say?'

Alice's face said it all. 'My father would kill me. I daren't tell him. I was thinking of going to London to get rid of it. I can sing a bit and I thought I might go on the stage.'

Jessie felt sad for her. 'If you are sure you can't tell your parents, there are places that would take you in until the baby was born. They have the baby adopted for you – you have to agree to that for a start, I'm afraid.'

'I'd end up in a reformatory!'

'Not if you go to a place I know of. One of the nurses I

was friendly with got into trouble that way. She said the Sally Army was good to her. They are fairly strict while you're in the home, of course, but they don't send you to a reformatory.'

'They just preach at you and sing hymns all the time,' Alice said and blinked her tears away. 'I'd rather get rid of it. I hate it!'

'Hate the father if you like, he deserves it – but the baby didn't ask to be born.'

'Don't you preach at me. You'll be saying I should keep it next.'

'I wasn't and I shan't; you'll do what you want. I might have been in the same situation if Robbie hadn't held back because he didn't want me to be landed while he was away in the war. I would've gone all the way that last night of his leave, but he said we would wait. I sometimes wished that I'd had his baby. At least I would have had a bit of him to love and care for.'

'Did you love him very much?' Alice was staring at her as if seeing her in a new light.

'Yes, very much.' Jessie smiled at her. For some reason it didn't hurt to talk about Robbie as much as it had once. 'He was such a lovely lad, always making plans for the future, generous and thoughtful. I was lucky. Luckier than most, because I had Robbie's love for a while. Do you love the father of your child, Alice?'

'Not any more. I thought I did but not after the way he's behaved.' Alice frowned. 'You won't tell anyone? Only I want to work a bit longer before I leave my job here, save as much as I can.'

'No, of course I shan't tell anyone your secret. And you will need money. My friend was told she would be charged a hundred pounds for an abortion and she couldn't find that kind of money – that's why she chose the Sally Army and adoption instead. If you want their address, just in case you change your mind, I'll write it down for you and I'll give you a few pounds before you leave. Not much, but it all helps.'

'Would you really?' Alice looked at her oddly. 'That's real nice of you, Jessie. I thought you were a bit stuck-up when you came here, laying down the law and changing things, but you're not. I'd be grateful for anything you could let me have and I'll pay you back one day.'

'Don't worry about that,' Jessie said. 'It isn't much – about ten pounds – but you can have it and welcome.'

A tear trickled from the corner of Alice's eye. 'Thanks, Jessie. It's very good of you. I shall work until the end of the month and then I'm off. They say it's dangerous to leave it any longer than that so I shall have to collect my wages and disappear before anyone knows what's going on.'

'I'll give you the money and the address tomorrow,' Jessie said. 'And now I had better go and have a cup of tea and a slice of cake if Cook hasn't given up on me entirely.'

Alice gave her a watery smile. 'You're the best thing that's happened around here for a long time,' she said. 'Maybe we'll see each other again. Will you give me an address for you – your aunt's place? I can send your money there when I've got it.'

'When you're on the stage and rich and famous,' Jessie said and smiled as she went out.

The smile left her face as she closed the door. Poor Alice! She had her dreams but she would find it very different when she got to London and woke up to the reality of her situation.

Jessie was just helping Lady Kendle to settle comfortably the next morning when Alice came into the room. She bobbed a curtsey to the invalid and begged her pardon for interrupting.

'I'm sorry, ma'am, but there's been an accident. Jessie's wanted downstairs at once.'

'Is someone hurt?' Lady Kendle asked and looked anxious as Alice nodded her head vigorously. 'Off you go then, Jessie. I shall be fine now, but someone must come back and tell me what's going on later.'

Jessie promised she would and hurried after Alice.

'What's happened?'

'It's one of the gardener's lads,' Alice said. 'He has cut his arm badly and he's in the kitchen bleeding all over the place. Captain Kendle has phoned for the doctor but he told me to get you because the doctor is out and it will be a while before he can come.'

126

Jessie flew down the stairs, knowing that such an injury could be very serious. When she got to the kitchen the lad was stretched out on a rush mat, his face very white. Cook and Maggie hovered uncertainly over him, too frightened to touch him.

Someone had knotted a tie above the deep wound to try to stop the bleeding but it wasn't tight enough and the blood was still coming out in gushes.

'I shall need a wooden stick – one of your cooking spoons, please, and some linen strips,' Jessie said. She knelt down on the mat beside the lad and smiled at him. 'This is going to hurt a bit, I'm afraid, but I need to stop the bleeding.' His eyelids flickered but it was obvious he was fainting from loss of blood and hardly heard her.

'Here you are, Jessie – a spoon and some clean muslin.'

She took the items held out to her and made an efficient tourniquet, then removed the tie and makeshift bandage that someone had put on earlier. The gash was deep and had cut through the muscle to the bone, making a terrible mess of the lad's arm. Jessie knew that he would be lucky if he ever got the full use of his limb back again after a cut like this. She had wondered if she ought to use the materials she carried in her nursing bag, which was in her room, to try to do a temporary repair, but the extent of the injury would need a competent surgeon and she might do more harm by attempting it. Instead she pressed the torn muscle and flesh back into place and made a pad of gauze, binding it tightly to keep it in place as best she could. She had just finished her work when she was aware of someone standing beside her and she glanced up to see Captain Kendle watching her.

'It's a nasty cut, isn't it?'

'Very deep, I'm afraid,' Jessie said. 'He ought to go straight to hospital. I've stopped the bleeding for the moment but if he doesn't receive immediate attention he could lose the arm or at the least the use of it. He could die if he loses too much blood.'

'I'll take him myself,' Captain Kendle said. 'You had better come with me, Jessie. Is there anything you can give him for pain if he comes to on the way?'

127

'I'd better not give him any medication in case it interferes with the hospital's medication,' Jessie said. 'But we might give him a little brandy – if there is any around.'

Brandy was fetched. Jessie was offered Maggie's coat to save her going back for her own and the three of them trooped out, Captain Kendle carrying the lad while Carter opened doors and got the car ready to receive him. He had laid a blanket on the back seat of the Daimler and Jessie got in first. She sat with the injured lad's head on her lap throughout the drive. He moaned a few times but the loss of blood had been severe and he was mercifully unconscious the whole time. Her heart ached for him. He couldn't be more than fifteen and it was likely that he would be crippled for life.

The drive seemed to take ages, but at last they were at the hospital and the young lad was transferred to a stretcher and rushed inside. Jessie watched as he was taken immediately to an operating theatre that had been alerted to receive him, her throat closing with emotion. That poor, poor boy!

She turned as someone spoke to her and Captain Kendle offered her his handkerchief. Until that moment she hadn't realized there were tears on her cheeks.

'He's so young,' she said. 'You know he could lose that arm, don't you?'

Harry nodded. 'I've seen wounds like that in the trenches – and worse. Some of them recovered, some didn't. We've done our bit, Jessie. I've sent word to his parents, but I'll bring them to the hospital as soon as I've got you back.'

'Oh yes, thank you.' He was thoughtful and kind. Jessie stared at him, her heart swelling with an emotion she had never thought to feel again. How could she ever have imagined he was cold? 'I had better get back in case I'm needed.'

'They can manage for a while,' Harry said and his mouth compressed into a thin line. 'This was an emergency. If he'd woken up and started pulling at the tourniquet we might have lost him before we got him here.'

Jessie nodded but made no comment. She thought by his expression that he must have heard about all the trouble over her absence the previous day. To bring it up now would have seemed to criticize his wife Jessie thought, and maintained her silence.

In fact the drive back to the house was mostly silent, with only a few comments from Harry Kendle to Carter. Jessie could see that the captain's face had assumed that remote, harsh expression it often wore and she wondered what was on his mind.

Harry broke the silence when she was out of the car, going after her to catch her alone before she went into the kitchen.

'I wanted to tell you, my mother's illness makes no difference to my plans for next month,' he told her. 'If Mother is worse I shall arrange for a nurse to come in, but hopefully it was a mild attack. My father will be here, of course. He is able to make any decisions necessary about her health.'

'It is your decision, of course,' Jessie said, though her heart skipped a beat with pleasure. 'If Lady Kendle is unwell again it might be better for her to go into hospital for a couple of days to have tests. I should imagine that could be arranged to coincide with the trip to London.'

'Yes, that is an excellent suggestion if Mother would agree. I shall speak to my father.' Harry smiled at her, causing her heart to do a rapid somersault. 'I don't know what we should do without you now. If Wylie's boy lives it will probably be down to you.'

'I'm sure you would have got him there in time somehow,' Jessie said with a little shake of her head.

'I'm not so sure of that. I must speak to Jethro Wylie. He will be frantic about his son by now.'

Jessie went into the kitchen, where she was met by the tantalizing smell of baking and three pairs of curious eyes. Cook, Maggie and one of the gardeners were sitting at the table having a cup of tea and enjoying a gossip.

'I told young Jed to watch out with that there scythe,' Ned Dobson said, shaking his head sorrowfully over it. 'But he be only a lad and they never listen.'

'Will he be all right?' Maggie looked anxious as she turned to Jessie. It was clear from her tear-stained face that she had been crying. She wasn't much older than the lad they had rushed to hospital and had a tender heart. 'He won't die, will he? I've never seen so much blood in my life.'

'He did lose an awful lot of blood, but he's in hospital now and they will save him and his arm if they can.'

The mat that had taken the brunt of that blood had been scrubbed and taken outside to dry, but looking down at herself Jessie saw that the apron she was wearing over her uniform was stained with blood. She took it off and Maggie held out her hand for it.

'I'll put that in cold water for you, Jessie. I'm not sure it will come out, but we can try.'

'I had better go up to the children.'

'You'll have a cup of tea first,' Cook insisted. 'Nanny knows where you've been and she's given the children their lunch. Would you like a drop of brandy to settle your nerves, lass?'

Jessie refused with a smile. It wasn't the first time she'd seen wounds as deep as Jed Wylie's. In France she had seen men brought in with shattered limbs and half their face gone, but she hadn't mentioned her experiences to Captain Kendle and she wouldn't now. There were some things it was best not to talk about. The memories still haunted her dreams sometimes, though not as often as they had once.

She drank her tea then went upstairs to the nursery.

When Jack saw her he gave a whoop of delight and flung himself at her, hugging her waist as if he would never let go of her again.

'I thought you'd gone,' he said. 'Nanny said you would be back but I thought she was just saying that.'

'I had to go to the hospital with the gardener's boy. He had cut his arm,' Jessie said. 'Didn't I tell you I wouldn't leave without saying goodbye?'

'I know, but I thought you had. Grown-ups tell lies. It's all right now you're back.'

'Shall we go for our walk?' Jessie asked and glanced at Nanny. 'Will you let Lady Kendle know that the lad is in hospital and being cared for, please? I know she was anxious.'

'I was going to visit her when you got back anyway,' Nanny said. 'We enjoy our little chats these days. You get off, Jessie. It's a lovely morning for a walk and it will do you and the children good after all the upset.'

'Yes, it is a lovely day,' Jessie agreed.

She was feeling much better as she got the children ready for their walk. Jed Wylie was being cared for and there was no more she could do for him. The warmth of the sun was exceptional for the time of year and the children's laughter brought a smile to her face, banishing the haunting memories of a period of her life that was best forgotten now.

It was only as she returned from her walk just before lunch and saw Captain Kendle standing in the yard at the back of the house, deep in conversation with the gardener, that the truth hit her.

She was in love with her employer, Mary Kendle's husband. She hadn't meant it to happen, hadn't thought it could because of her love for Robbie, but although Robbie was still there in her heart, Harry Kendle was wedged in there beside him.

He turned and smiled at her and Jessie's heart raced. This was the last thing she needed. She was such a fool! It was bound to cause her nothing but heartbreak.

She loved Harry Kendle and she loved his children. She ought to leave this house as soon as someone could be found to take her place. It was the sensible way, the right thing to do. Jessie knew it but she also knew that she wasn't going to leave.

Not just yet. Not unless it became impossible for her to stay.

Nine

Christmas in the Kendle household meant a lot of extra work for Cook and the others. Mary Kendle had friends to stay, which meant that for four days they hardly had time to take a moment for themselves. However, they had a special supper in the servants' hall on Christmas Day and exchanged small gifts.

Jessie was given a box of scented writing paper as a joint present from all the staff and she gave them the little boxes of sweets she had bought in Torquay.

She had also knitted scarves for Jack and Catherine and she gave them both an orange and packets of sweets in their stockings, which had caused endless delight in the nursery, because their father had contributed small gifts when he'd learned of Jessie's intention.

They were taken to their grandmother's room after breakfast and there they were given their main presents, which in Catherine's case was a doll and clothes. Jack was presented with a very expensive model train set and various soldiers, but it was the stockings that had given them the most pleasure.

Jessie had received a gift in the post from her aunt, and a book of poetry from Archie together with cards from various friends she had known before leaving London. However, when she went into her bedroom that night, she found a small package lying on her bed. Opening it, she discovered a box of exquisite lace handkerchiefs.

The small card just wished her happiness and was unsigned, but she recognized Captain Kendle's handwriting at once because of the sums he wrote out for his son. Jessie was quite sure who had put the gift there, and she felt a little tingle of unease. She had already received an extra three pounds in her wages as a gift from the family, and this was something special from Captain Kendle himself.

He ought not to have given her the handkerchiefs, and she ought not to feel so very happy because he had . . .

Despite her determination not to give way to her feelings for Harry Kendle, Jessie found herself looking forward to the London trip and the three days she would spend in his company. She kept her fingers crossed that nothing would happen to prevent it and was reassured to learn that Lady Kendle had agreed to go into a private hospital for tests on her heart condition.

'It will make things easier while you're away, Jessie,' she told her. 'Sir Joshua is worried about me even though I feel quite well at the moment. But with Mary going away for two months . . .' She smiled as she saw Jessie's expression. 'You didn't know, of course.'

'I thought it was just for a couple of weeks, ma'am.'

'She is staying with friends in Kent for two weeks but after that she goes with them to their villa in the south of France. She went last year even though things were still difficult after the war, but she enjoyed it and that is all that matters. Mary needs something to take her mind off her problems and Harry doesn't object. He could join her if he wished but he is too busy with one thing and another. He runs the estate, of course, but he also has workshops in Torquay. Did you know that?' Jessie shook her head. 'He employs craftsmen who make rather lovely furniture. It's all done by hand, time-consuming and expensive. Mary thinks it's a waste of resources; the money could be put to better use elsewhere, perhaps, but Harry says the business is making some money and will do better when the country's stabilized again. This war has turned us all upside down, Jessie. It seems that Harry has to run all the time just to stand still.'

'Yes, I can see he must,' Jessie said, understanding now why Captain Kendle was so often away from home. She found it interesting to learn about his business venture. She was learning more about him all the time, and she liked what she

133

heard; she liked it that he preferred to use craftsmen rather than resort to the production line to make more money.

Lady Kendle and Sir Joshua departed the day before Jessie was due to leave for London, and Mary Kendle had gone to her friends two days before that.

'We shan't know what to do with ourselves,' Cook said. 'It will be like a holiday.'

'It's always better when Madam is away,' Alice told Jessie. She had come to her room to sit on the bed and watch her pack. 'Will you get a chance to see your aunt while you're in town, Jessie?'

'Yes, I think so. Captain Kendle said I should go one evening. It's easy enough on the bus when the children are in bed.'

'You know your way round London,' Alice said with a sigh. 'It will all be new to me when I get there.'

'You won't leave yet, will you? I shall see you again before that?'

'I shan't go until the end of this month,' Alice said. 'But that's the latest I dare leave it if I'm going to have an abortion.'

'You haven't changed your mind? I do wish you would, Alice. You don't have to keep the baby, but that's up to you, of course.'

'I'm thinking about it,' Alice said. 'I still think I want to be rid of it but I'll see when the time comes. I shall have to leave this place anyway. I could never keep something like this a secret – they wouldn't take me back if I went off for a week or two without saying why. Besides, I fancy my chances on the stage.'

Jessie nodded. She saw no point in pressing the argument further. Alice would make up her own mind when she was ready.

'I shall miss you,' she said. 'Perhaps we can meet one day. You can always write to me at my aunt's house.'

Jessie asked Nanny and the others if there was anything they wanted her to bring from town. Nanny and Cook both said no but Maggie wanted several small items and Jessie promised to get them for her if she could.

134

She had wondered if Carter would be driving them all the way to London but was told that he would take them only as far as Torquay where they could catch the mainline train.

'My father may need his services. Besides, Jack wants to go on the train,' Harry explained when he came to the nursery to make the arrangements for the following day. 'The children get sick in the car on long journeys and I think the train is a better way for them to travel. You can manage them, can't you, Jessie?'

'Yes, of course, sir.'

'I thought you could.'

Jessie was warmed by his smile.

They travelled first class and were served lunch in the dining car. It was comfortable and pleasant and, apart from changing Catherine twice in the toilets, everything went smoothly.

Mrs Carmichael was pleased to see Jessie again. She exclaimed over how well she looked.

'The country air has brought colour to your cheeks, Jessie. Are you settling in well?'

'Yes, very well, thank you.'

Jessie gave the children their tea and tucked them up in bed. For once Jack was sleepy and his eyes closed almost as soon as his head touched the pillow.

Jessie went to her own room to change and freshen up after the long and tiring journey. She put on an attractive green and white striped dress with buttoned sleeves and a white frill around the neck; it made her look younger than she did in uniform and she smiled as she looked at her reflection. There was something in her eyes, a light that had been missing since Robbie was killed, and she thought that that was a big part of the change Mrs Carmichael had seen in her.

She was going downstairs for her meal when she met Captain Kendle. 'Ah, I was just about to come up for you,' he said. 'I've asked Mrs Carmichael to lay supper in my study for us. I thought you would find that more comfortable than the dining room.'

'But . . .' Jessie stared at him uncertainly. 'I eat with the staff at Kendlebury, sir.'

'Yes, I know. It wouldn't suit for you to dine with us there, Jessie. My father and Mary are sticklers for the old order, but here there are just the two of us, so where is the harm? Besides, I want to talk to you about the children.'

Jessie hesitated. It wasn't right and they both knew it, but she found herself giving way.

'Well, perhaps just this once then.'

'Tomorrow I shall be dining out with a business friend and you'll want to visit your aunt. It's only once, Jessie.'

There was a note of pleading in his voice and Jessie was lost. She knew even as she agreed that this could be the beginning of something she would come to regret, but somehow she couldn't find the strength to draw back.

Supper had been laid on a small table put up for the purpose, with a white cloth, good porcelain, silver and sparkling glasses. The meal consisted of fresh salmon, delicious creamed potatoes and slender green beans, followed by a wine syllabub in long fluted glasses. There was a crisp white wine that had been chilled to just the right degree to accompany the meal, with coffee and chocolates to follow.

Jessie enjoyed every morsel. She wasn't in the least shy because Harry talked about the children most of the time, putting her at her ease.

'Jack has another two years before he goes to boarding school,' he told her. 'I went when I was six, but I hated it and ran away. My mother brought me home and hired a tutor. My father was disgusted. He thought me weak, you see. He still feels the same.'

'He can't think that, not after what you did in the war.'

'Yes he can and does,' Harry said with a wry grimace. 'But I'm used to it. I only mention my experience because I value your advice – do you think Jack is ready for a tutor at home?'

'He is very bright, full of energy, but still young. I can only give my own opinion but I would say the autumn would be soon enough.'

'Let him have the summer to run free? I agree with you.

So that's settled. Jack can have a few more months of playing with you and Catherine, then I'll arrange for him to have lessons in the mornings. The vicar said he would send his curate and that will suit us all. He can come to the house at first and then when Jack is accustomed to the idea I'll take him to the vicarage. There are a couple of other boys who have lessons there and it will get him used to the idea of boarding school.'

'He will enjoy his lessons once he settles down. He is a very active boy and it will do him good to stretch his mind.'

Harry nodded. 'That leaves Catherine. Is she still improving in your estimation?'

'Yes, I believe so. She is beginning to ask for the toilet, though we had an accident on the train but I expected that. However, she is talking much more than she used to, as you must have noticed.'

'She certainly makes herself heard.' Harry smiled indulgently. 'You've done wonders with her, Jessie. Whatever the doctor says I know she is much happier than she was before you came.'

'Yes, she is certainly happier.'

There was a pause as they looked at each other, then Jessie bent her head to sip her coffee, her heart racing at the intent expression in his eyes. Surely she could not be mistaken about that look? She had seen it often enough in Robbie's eyes, and in Archie's the night he had asked her to marry him.

'You know that I am happier too, don't you?' he asked softly. 'You've worked a miracle on us. I thought I would never feel like this again.'

Jessie looked up as she heard the note of urgency in his voice. He had risen and was standing next to her, offering her his hand. She hesitated, then gave him her hand and he pulled her gently to her feet. For a moment she gazed into his face and then she was drawn into his arms. At first he held her gently in an embrace that made her heart hammer wildly but did not frighten her. His eyes seemed to be searching deep into her mind, trying to penetrate her thoughts as he looked for a sign, and perhaps he found it, because then he bent his head and kissed her on the lips.

It was not a demanding kiss; instead it seemed to coax, to beg for her response, which she gave willingly. His arms tightened about her, holding her pressed against him so hard that she felt the evidence of his arousal and her breath came more quickly. It was so long since she had felt this way, too long, and she was melting, her resistance weaker than it ought to be.

'Do you know I love you?'

'You can't – you mustn't,' she whispered, her throat tight with emotion. 'It would be wrong for us to love each other . . .'

'For us?' He smiled and kissed her brow. 'That means you feel something for me, too. Why would it be wrong, Jessie?'

'You know the answer to that. You're married. A divorce would tear your family apart and shame us both. I shall have to go away.'

'Only if you take me with you,' he whispered fiercely. 'Do you know how often I have wanted to run away from it all, Jessie? I've never wanted to manage the estate, never expected it would fall to me. It should have been my brother, and my father can't forget that. Everything I try to do is wrong. I don't mind that, but there are times . . .' He sighed. 'Mary isn't my wife in anything but name these days; she hasn't been since Catherine was born. Sometimes I think she despises me as much as my father does – that she believes Catherine's trouble was my fault . . .'

'That's unfair,' Jessie said and gazed up at him. Seeing that haunted expression in his eyes, she kissed him gently on the mouth. 'Let me go now. If I am not to leave you we mustn't do this. I don't want to be just another maidservant who got into trouble with her employer and had to leave under a cloud.'

'It wouldn't be that way for us,' he told her, but he let her go when she pushed against his chest. 'I don't want to hurt you, Jessie. It's the last thing I would do. I love you. I want you to be my wife – and if I can't marry you then I would live with you away from my parents' home somewhere. Abroad if it came to that.'

'And what about your family?'

'We would take the children with us.'

'And break Lady Kendle's heart? Even if you have no feelings for your father, you must have them for her.'

'Yes, of course I care about her,' Harry said, running his fingers through his hair distractedly. 'I suppose I care for my father and the estate in a way or I wouldn't have put up with so much – but I love you. I don't see why we can't be together.'

'We can – but only as master and your children's nurse,' Jessie told him. 'We can be friends, spend a little time together with the children away from the house, but it has to end there. You know it does.'

'So you don't love me enough? Together we could defy the world, break the old taboos – take what we want and be damned to the rest!'

'Please don't look at me that way,' Jessie begged as his passionate words made her tingle down to her toes. 'Don't you know how easy it would be for me to say yes to a home where we could be together? But in time you would want your own class, your friends – and I would seem nothing but a nuisance to you. You might become ashamed, wish that you had never met me. You know I'm not like you. I don't have the same background, the same culture . . .'

'Don't you know all that nonsense counts for nothing these days? It's gone, scattered like fallen leaves before the wind. We're all going to be equal if this labour movement gets off the ground – and maybe that won't be a bad thing. Kendlebury is a dinosaur out of its time and useless.'

'I don't think it's useless,' Jessie disagreed. 'It's beautiful and your children love their home. They love their grandmother and their mother – yes, they do, Harry, even if you don't think so. Jack looks for a word from Mary whenever she comes to the nursery.'

'That is a rare thing! She isn't interested in them. Even at Christmas she wouldn't have them with us in the drawing room. They were confined to my mother's room. She isn't a loving mother. You know she isn't.'

'But that doesn't stop Jack loving her. I don't think Catherine realizes, but Jack certainly does.'

139

'He'll get over it. You're the one he really cares for, Jessie. He would soon forget her.'

'Stop it, Harry. You know all this is just a dream. When it came to it you couldn't just give everything up for someone like me.'

'Couldn't I?' He smiled down at her. 'Are you willing to give me a chance, Jessie?'

She turned away, her heart racing. When he looked at her like that she wanted to believe him. She wanted to believe with all her heart in the world he had described for her, but a part of her – the saner part that had managed to remain aloof from the raging emotions in her heart – knew it couldn't happen. A shiver went down her spine as he put his arms about her, his lips warm against the back of her neck as he lifted her hair and kissed it.

'Don't leave me, Jessie. Give me something to hope for, something to make living worthwhile.'

She turned to face him, lifting her face for a kiss that left her breathless and shaken, wanting more – so much more.

'I'm not sure,' she said at last, the words forced out of her by the need she sensed in him that was echoed inside her. 'Give me time. Let's see how you feel a few months from now. Perhaps when Jack is ready for school and . . .'

'You are asking me to prove my love, is that it?' He touched her face softly. 'Well, I shall prove it, Jessie. When Mary comes home I'll ask her for a divorce.'

'No, Harry! Promise me you won't. It's much too soon. You have to think this through, be certain. *I* must be certain. This affects both of us, not just you – and we have to think of what's right for the children.'

He smiled. 'At least that made you use my name. It's either divorce or you live with me as my wife in everything but name, Jessie – but I'll let you think about it until Mary comes home and until then I'll be good.'

'If only you meant that,' she said and he laughed down at her. 'It's no good promising if you can't keep your promise, sir.'

'So we're back to sir, are we?' His eyes were soft and full of teasing laughter. 'We'll see, Jessie. And now I shall let you go or the servants will start to gossip, and we can't have that just yet, can we?'

Jessie shook her head. As soon as he moved away she wished she was back in his arms, that she had tossed her cap over the windmill and given into the prompting of her heart. Yet when she was alone in her room she knew that she had merely escaped for the moment. Harry wouldn't be content to leave things as they were. He wanted her, claimed to love her and be willing to change his life for her – but even if he was willing, could she let him sacrifice so much for her sake?

Jessie found it difficult to sleep that night. She blamed the strange bed but knew it was more likely Harry Kendle's passionate words and the memory of his kisses, which lingered like a blessing on her lips, that had caused her restlessness. She had a disturbing dream that woke her with a start but it faded quickly and she only remembered afterwards that it had had something to do with Robbie. Had he denounced her for her faithlessness, because she had fallen in love again? Jessie wondered but then dismissed the thought. Robbie wasn't like that. He would want her to be happy.

But it was unlikely that her feelings for Harry Kendle could bring her happiness. Jessie tried to push the forbidden interlude from her mind as she got the children dressed and fed that morning.

They were taking Catherine to see the doctor at eleven o'clock and if there was time they would visit the zoo, which had stayed open for the end of the school holiday. It was bitterly cold but bright, a pale sun threading its way through a break in the clouds. Jack wanted to know why they couldn't go exploring straight away.

'Because Catherine has to go to the doctor.'

'Why? She isn't ill, is she?'

'No, not ill,' Jessie said. 'It's a special doctor, Jack. It's the reason we came to London, remember? We'll go to the zoo this afternoon or tomorrow.'

'Can I come to the doctor too?'

'Your father wants you to stay here with Mrs Carmichael. We shan't be too long.'

141

Jack was a bit grumpy but his father's word was law and he had the promise of an afternoon at the zoo to look forward to. When he was told that Carmichael would take him to feed the ducks and pigeons in a nearby park, he was content.

Jessie was nervous in the taxicab taking them to the appointment with the doctor. Supposing she was wrong to have raised hopes for Catherine's abilities? Yet she knew there had been an improvement in the child in so many ways.

The clinic was a private one, smart with thick carpets and a comfortable waiting area. She did not expect to be taken into the consulting room but Harry insisted.

'You know Catherine better than anyone, Jessie. Doctor Robinson will want to hear what you have to say.'

Jessie held the little girl's hand, letting her walk at her own pace, which was slow and unhurried since Catherine had no reason to exert herself. Doctor Robinson smiled approvingly as he welcomed them. He was a tall, thin man with a serious face, but his smile was genuine and friendly.

'So this is Catherine,' he said. 'And how old is your daughter, Mrs Kendle?'

'She's two years and eight months,' Harry replied before Jessie could. 'Until the last month or so she couldn't walk much, but she's improved recently, hasn't she, Jessie?'

'We've been going for long walks,' Jessie said. 'I'm Catherine's nurse, sir. I've been teaching her new words and she talks more than she did, don't you, darling?' Catherine cooed and smiled but didn't say a word. She was gazing wonderingly at the strange, large man and her eyes looked very bright, as if she wondered who he was and where he belonged in her world.

'I see, Jessie. How have you taught her?'

Jessie explained about the picture books and various other things she'd done to encourage Catherine.

'She can do lots more things now, can't you, Catherine? I think she may be lazy, sir. She'll only do what she wants, though she can move fast enough when she feels like it.'

The doctor nodded, bending down to pick Catherine up. She went without protest into his arms, her eyes wide with wonder.

'Hello young lady,' he said. 'Will you talk to me, Catherine? You're a very pretty young lady, aren't you?'

'Nice,' Catherine gurgled and patted his face as she always did when she approved of someone, deciding to share her secret with him. 'Catherine go zoo see elphant with Jessie.'

'Are you going to the zoo?' Doctor Robinson asked and glanced over her head at Jessie, who smiled and nodded. 'There are tigers and monkeys at the zoo, Catherine.'

'Want see elphant.'

'Would you like to look at a picture book with me?'

Catherine nodded her head. He put her down and led her across the room to what was clearly a play area for his patients. There were numerous picture books, various puzzles and games, and the doctor spent the next half an hour or so playing with Catherine. He made occasional notes as he observed her movements and reactions, his manner gentle and patient as the child stumbled over the unfamiliar tasks.

Jessie longed to be able to help her, knowing that she could improve Catherine's responses just by repeating them over and over until she grasped what was needed, but the doctor had warned her she must not. What seemed like games were actually controlled tests to allow him to assess her movements and learning ability. He brought her back to Jessie at last and smiled.

'Perhaps you and Catherine would wait outside for a few minutes, please, Jessie.'

'Yes, of course.'

Jessie took Catherine to the waiting room. Her heart was racing and she felt nervous, but Catherine seemed sleepy and was quite content to sit on her knee. Jessie's apprehension increased as she saw Harry's expression as he came out of the consulting room after what seemed an eternity. She looked at him anxiously but he said nothing until they were in the taxi being driven home and Catherine had fallen asleep on her lap.

'Doctor Robinson says she needs a lot of care and attention if she is to get on as she should. Her development has been neglected. Our fault, of course, but we didn't realize what she was capable of.'

143

'What is she capable of?'

'He says that she is bright and will make considerable improvement given the right care. She needs the right kinds of toys – the kind of thing he was using today – and I shall see that she gets them, of course, but she will probably never progress beyond the age of a child of eleven or twelve. However, she could live quite happily within her limits and be capable of having a satisfactory life.'

'I see.' Jessie bit her lip as she saw his stern expression. 'Did you hope for more? Are you disappointed?'

'No, that is far more than I was led to believe at the beginning. I'm just a little anxious,' he said. 'With care and love Catherine can be happy and fulfilled in herself, but he said something else that worried me.'

'About Catherine?'

'Yes.' Harry looked at her. 'It seems that we weren't told everything about her the last time, because they thought she might not live long. She has a weakness in the wall of her heart that could make her more susceptible to illness than normal children. Doctor Robinson told me that she may not live beyond her teens – if she reaches that age it will be a small miracle.'

'Oh, I am so sorry,' Jessie said and her hand reached for his to offer comfort. He grasped it tightly and she sensed his grief, though it showed only in the nerve flicking in his cheek, his expression giving nothing away. 'I can hardly believe it. She seems so well.'

'I asked if there was anything we could do – like an operation – but he said it wasn't something they knew how to treat yet, that it might get progressively worse as she gets older. On the other hand she could grow out of the condition. In the meantime we have to be patient and realize that it takes her longer to do things.'

Jessie's eyes widened. 'Is that why she only does what she has to? Have I made things worse by taking her for long walks?'

'No. No, you mustn't think that. He praised what you've achieved with her in such a short time and told me it was important that the bond continued. It is better for her to get

144

lots of fresh air, but it's the reason she needs to sleep such a lot. Until you came I thought it was a sign of her mental disability, but he says it's because she gets tired quickly. She has bursts of energy and then she needs to sleep.'

'Poor darling,' Jessie said and blinked back the tears as she looked at the child sleeping in her arms. 'She is so beautiful. We must make sure she is happy, Harry.'

'Trust you to think of that.'

Harry's voice was choked with emotion. Glancing at him she saw that his face was working with grief.

'Sometimes doctors are wrong, Harry. Besides, he said she could get stronger.'

'You won't leave her? She needs you, Jessie. Promise me you won't go away.'

'I shan't leave her. I love her.'

'Yes, I know you do. I shudder to think what her life would have been if you hadn't come to us. I had accepted that she would never do anything much. I didn't try to help her and Nanny was too old to see what you saw, Jessie.'

'Don't blame yourself for that, Harry. Catherine is what matters now. We have to do what we can to make her life good for as long as she survives, and she mustn't suspect anything, ever. We have to be strong for her.'

Harry looked at her in silence. He knew what she was saying, what she had not said in so many words. Jessie could stay with them only on certain terms. If he pressed his own claims, his own needs, she would have to leave. He thought of insisting on divorce, even more wildly of Mary's death, which would set him free without scandal or a breach with his whole family. For a moment he longed for it so fiercely that he was shocked by the hatred he felt towards his wife. Mary didn't love him. He sometimes suspected that she had a lover, but he was trapped. Divorce would destroy his mother – and there was Catherine. She needed stability, the peace of her home. She was more vulnerable than he had thought. Yet he did not want to give up his dreams.

'Perhaps one day . . .'

'Please don't,' Jessie said. 'We can be friends, Harry. We can be happy sometimes, away from the house, together with the children. We can share them. We can have that much.'

They could have that or nothing. Harry turned away, closing his eyes for a moment as the pain washed over him. He wanted so much more, but it was too difficult to attain; he couldn't fight them all unless Jessie was willing, and she was too caring, too generous to cause pain to the others. It was perhaps the reason he loved her and there was nothing he could do. Catherine needed Jessie. She needed the love that only Jessie could give her to make her short life as happy as possible.

'Yes, we can have that,' he said at last.

Catherine stirred in Jessie's arms as the taxi drew to a halt. She looked up at her, her innocent eyes wide and enquiring, so beautiful that she almost wrenched the heart out of Jessie.

'Go zoo now?' she asked.

'Yes, we're going to the zoo after we've had our lunch,' Jessie said and kissed her. Catherine had suddenly become infinitely more precious.

'Well, there you are, Jess.' Aunt Elizabeth wrapped her in an embracing hug as she went into the warm and well-remembered kitchen that evening. 'I was beginning to think you weren't coming after all.'

'I'm sorry to be late,' Jessie said and gave her the box of chocolates she had bought for her at an exclusive shop. 'We took the children to the zoo this afternoon and then we had tea at a posh restaurant and bought a couple of toys at a marvellous shop before we went home. You should have seen them, Auntie. Catherine adored all the animals, but especially the elephant. The keeper let her stroke the one they have walking about. It took a bun from her and she laughed and laughed. Jack liked the tigers best, but they both had a wonderful time. They were so tired when they got home that they went off to sleep at once but I had to see to them before I could leave.'

'Of course you did, love. I don't mind. I've put an apple pie in the oven for you but that won't hurt for a few minutes. Come and sit down and tell me how you got on this morning. What did the doctor say about the little girl?'

Jessie explained and her aunt listened, looking distressed and shaking her head. 'Well, that is a sad thing. You must stop there and take care of her now, Jess. You couldn't think of leaving the family in the lurch after that.'

'No, I couldn't,' Jessie agreed. 'She's such a little darling, Auntie, and Jack is so bright and clever. I love them both. It's almost like having my own children.'

'Don't forget they aren't,' Elizabeth said, looking at her anxiously. 'Remember that the family could ask you to leave whenever they like.'

'That won't happen,' Jessie said and smiled as she remembered Harry's last words to her before they parted, thanking her for a wonderful afternoon at the zoo.

'I don't think I ever knew what it was like to be this happy before,' he'd told her. 'Thank you for giving me this, Jessie.'

'Well, just remember it could happen,' her aunt said. She had hoped that Jessie might decide to come home in a few months, but she could see that wasn't likely. 'You look well, Jess. Living in the country must suit you. You don't miss the shops and the theatres then?'

'Sometimes,' Jessie replied. 'I miss you, Auntie, and I miss our talks over supper. It would be nice to go out together again, but I'm not sure when that will be. I couldn't think of asking for time off, not at the moment – and it will be worse when Alice leaves.'

'Alice – she's the parlourmaid, isn't she? Didn't you say she wasn't as friendly as some of the others?'

'She wasn't at first,' Jessie agreed. 'But we get on well now. I'm sorry she's thinking of leaving, but she wants to come to London. She might write to me here.'

'I'll send her letter on if she does,' Elizabeth said, pausing for a moment before continuing. 'I'm thinking of opening a shop to sell the bread and cakes soon, Jess. The bakery is doing reasonably well, though not as well as I'd like. Eddie thinks we could do better if we had a shop. He's got a good business head on him, I'll say that for him.'

'Are you sure you want the extra work? He can't run the bakery and the shop, can he?'

'No, I'll be doing that myself,' her aunt said. 'To tell you the

147

truth, I haven't enough to do these days. If you'd been unhappy where you are I was going to suggest we run it together – the place I'm thinking of is big enough for a teashop as well. You quite liked working in a teashop before the war, didn't you?'

'Yes, it was a pleasant job,' Jessie agreed. She'd heard the sigh in her aunt's voice and felt sorry. 'I'm sorry, Auntie dearest. I would have liked that if it hadn't been for Catherine.'

If she had never gone to Kendlebury, never fallen under the spell of the family, never fallen in love with Harry Kendle and his children.

'Well, it can't be helped,' her aunt said. 'I shall find a girl to help out when I want her, and you're doing something worthwhile, Jess. I wouldn't want you to give that up, not while you're happy.' She smiled as she got up to take the apple pie from the oven and bring it to the scrubbed pine table. 'There's cream to go with this. You said not to make supper, but I'm sure you can eat some of this, can't you?'

'It smells gorgeous,' Jessie said and smiled at her. She was very fond of her Aunt Elizabeth. 'Cook makes delicious food but she can't make apple pie like yours.' It wasn't quite true but it pleased her aunt, and she wanted to make up for letting her down over the teashop.

'Did you get a chance to pop in and say hello to Archie?'

'He was closed when I came past and I didn't want to stop because I was already late.'

'He's got a young man working there part time now,' her aunt said, looking thoughtful. I'm sure I don't know why he took him on. I shouldn't have thought there was enough work for two of them.'

'Archie likes to go to house sales to buy his books. Perhaps it gives him more freedom.'

'Perhaps it does,' her aunt agreed. 'He was asking if I thought you might come up to town for a little holiday sometime. I told him I would ask you but I didn't think that was possible.'

'It isn't easy for me to come up to town unless it's with Captain Kendle and the children, but it would be nice if you could get down to see us one day, Auntie. You could stay in a small family hotel in Torquay and I could bring the children to see you.'

'That would be nice,' her aunt agreed. 'Yes, I might take a little holiday before I open the shop. I haven't been away in years. That was a good idea, Jess. I'll think about it and let you know.'

Ten

It was like going home when they returned to Kendlebury. Jessie looked at the golden glory of the old house as it nestled into the sunshine, letting the sense of peace sink in to her soul. She realized how much she had come to love the place and wondered how Harry could even think of giving it up for her sake. She would never want to leave if it belonged to her.

Just for a little while she could pretend it did. The house was a different place without Mary Kendle. There was a much more relaxed atmosphere. Cook was happy as she worked, no longer seeming so rushed or worried when she was serving up meals, and Maggie went around whistling tunelessly. Even Alice seemed less miserable than she had been when Jessie left for London.

'I've told my mother,' she confided to Jessie when they had a moment to talk in private. 'She says that I should go to the Sally Army like you said. Ma would let me stay at home and keep the baby, but Da would go mad. Besides, she thinks I should try my luck on the stage afterwards. She's always thought my voice too good to waste.'

'You could stay on here a bit longer if you decide to have the baby,' Jessie said. 'I'm glad you told your mother, Alice. At least she won't be anxious when you go away.'

'I feel better now I've told her,' Alice admitted. 'I'll probably stay on here until Mrs Kendle comes back and then I'll go. You're sure the Sally Army will arrange it all for me?'

'Quite sure, if you go to the address I gave you. They take in a lot of girls like you. Some of the girls stay there for weeks beforehand, others just go in for the birth, but you have to agree to give the child up – unless you can prove that you're going to be able to provide a good home, of course.' She smiled at Alice. 'I'm sure you won't regret your decision.'

'Well, I'm not definite yet but Ma wants me to have the baby. She doesn't hold with abortion.'

'You'll make up your own mind.' Jessie was thoughtful. 'I wonder what will happen here when you leave.'

'Mrs Pearson's sister has a daughter in service. She was saying the other day that Lily isn't happy where she is. I expect she will get her to come here if she can.'

Jessie wondered how that would work out but kept her thoughts to herself. She was too busy and happy to worry much about anything.

Lady Kendle seemed refreshed after her brief stay in hospital.

'They gave me some pills to take,' she told Jessie. 'They appear to be doing me good. Besides, it was just a little warning, nothing to worry about. The specialist told me I would probably go on for years.'

'I am very pleased to hear that, ma'am.'

'My husband was relieved,' Lady Kendle said. 'Now, what about you, Jessie? My son tells me the doctor was most insistent that the bond between you and Catherine should not be broken. Are you prepared to stay on with us for some years to come?'

Jessie felt herself blushing under the other woman's scrutiny. There was something odd in that look, as if she suspected a secret – but perhaps that was Jessie's imagination. She couldn't know anything, because there was nothing to know.

'I shall stay for as long as Catherine needs me, if I am permitted, ma'am.'

'You are thinking of Mary's behaviour when I was ill?' Lady Kendle frowned. 'I believe she was harsh with you. I can't promise that it won't happen again, but I can promise that you won't be turned out without good reason. Sir Joshua is still master here and I've told him that I need you. He will make sure that Mary understands that in his own way. My husband is a just man, Jessie, though some have cause to doubt it. But I know him better than most, and I know that he would never go against my wishes in this matter.'

'Thank you, ma'am.'

'All I ask is that you do nothing to make me change my mind.'

The look that accompanied her words convinced Jessie that she was aware of her son's feelings towards her. He might not have spoken of them, but his mother had sensed the change in him. Jessie's cheeks were warm as she met the older woman's gaze.

'I understand there are some things that cannot be forgiven, ma'am. I hope that I shall never disappoint you.'

'I believe that you will try not to,' Lady Kendle said and smiled. 'Now, tell me, did you have a chance to see your aunt?'

'Yes, just for a short time. She is thinking of opening a teashop.'

'That sounds interesting. Didn't you tell me she already owns a bakery?'

'Her husband left it to her. She still owns it but she doesn't run it these days, and she has time on her hands since I left.'

'Yes, I am sure she must miss you, but the shop will be an exciting venture for her.' Lady Kendle nodded her approval and Jessie left her to sit comfortably in her chair by the window while she went to the nursery. Nanny had given the children their tea and Jessie washed them before putting them to bed.

It was always a special time of the day. They smelled so sweet and looked like little angels as she tucked them up in their beds. Catherine was clutching the elephant her father had bought for her, her arms curled protectively about it as she settled down to sleep. Jack had been given a stuffed tiger as his souvenir of the trip, but it had been put on the shelf with his other toys and clearly meant less to him than his soldiers. Jessie wondered if Catherine had ever been given a gift she really wanted before, and realized that she probably hadn't. No one had ever considered what she might like, giving her dolls as a matter of course when it was her birthday or Christmas.

'So,' Nanny said to her after they left the children to sleep. 'You're not regretting coming back then? Mrs Pearson

152

wondered if you might feel homesick after you'd been back for a few days.'

'No, though I did feel a bit sorry that I couldn't help my aunt set up her teashop.'

'You would be more independent working for her.'

'Yes, perhaps,' Jessie agreed. 'We get on so well together, you see – but the children are more important for the moment. My aunt wouldn't want me to leave when I'm needed. Has Captain Kendle told you what the doctor said?'

'About Catherine having a weakness in her heart?' Nanny nodded and looked sad. 'I'm sorry for the poor little lass. She hasn't had much luck in her life, has she?'

'No.' Jessie was sombre. 'All we can do is love her. She needs all the care and kindness we can give her, Nanny.'

'Yes, I can see that and she gets none at all from her mother. Her father has started to take more interest in them both of late, and that's a good thing. I was worried about him; he seemed so sunk into himself, no time for anything but work, but he's more like he used to be before the war now and I'm glad of it.' She looked at Jessie thoughtfully but there was no criticism in her expression. 'I thought I might go and live with my sister once you were used to things here. She came to see me while you were away. We had tea in Mrs Pearson's parlour and talked it over – but I can stay on for a bit longer, until Jack goes to school, perhaps, to make it easier for you. If I'm still of use to you . . .'

'You know you are. I value your advice. Besides, Jack loves you and he respects you. If I have trouble I only have to tell him that Nanny wouldn't be pleased and he subsides.'

'I've always been firm but fair and he knows it. He can be a little monster at times, but he's a good lad – very like Master Harry was as a boy.'

'So you won't think of leaving yet – unless you've been feeling unwell again. I wouldn't want you to do too much.'

Nanny assured her that she was feeling quite like her old self and Jessie went downstairs to have her supper.

Cook put a plate in front of her and poured a cup of tea. 'Captain Kendle tells me he wants a picnic tomorrow. He's taking the children out for a few hours.'

153

'Oh . . .' Jessie was surprised. They had been home for two days now and she'd seen nothing of him. He hadn't been near the nursery, but he'd warned her that he would be busy for a while. 'I wonder where he's taking them.'

'You'll find out soon enough,' Cook said. 'He told me to pack enough for four. You'll be needed to look after the children, of course.'

'Yes. He couldn't manage them alone. I wish I knew where we were going so I knew what they ought to wear.'

'Well, a picnic isn't very formal, is it? Not when it's for children anyway. Different if it was for a shooting party. We used to send the second-best silver and glass then.'

'Do they still have them?' Jessie asked, remembering the accident that had killed Sir Joshua's eldest son.

'Not since the war. Sir Joshua says he isn't up to it these days and the captain says he had enough of guns in the war. Alf Goodjohn from the farm keeps us supplied with game in season. I think he sells any surplus to a hotel in Torquay, but the captain knows about it.'

'Knows about what?' Carter asked as he came into the kitchen. 'He didn't know about this until I showed him.' He threw a small pile of leaflets on to the table. 'Distributing these all over town they were.'

'What are they?' Cook asked, because he was clearly annoyed about something.

'The work of political agitators!'

Jessie picked up one of the leaflets and read it. Written in dramatic style it was inciting the workers of factories, shops and public services to stand up for their rights.

'This is rather strong language,' she said with a frown. 'It implies that all employers are the same, exploiting their workers and treating them with contempt.'

'It's true enough in a lot of cases,' Cook said. 'You wouldn't credit how hard it is for some, Jessie. We've got it easy here compared to most.

'Don't forget I was born in the East End,' Jessie said. 'My mother died of diphtheria because she was the only one willing to nurse her neighbours.'

'It's hard for some, I'll not deny that,' Carter said. 'But

they aren't all like that. Captain Kendle looks after his people, and they appreciate it. The foreman gave me these leaflets. He said he's had someone round trying to make trouble but he sent the fellow away with a flea in his ear.'

'Well, there's no harm done there then,' Cook said.

'But there might have been. We'll have strikes all over before they're through. You mark my words. I don't know what this country is coming to!'

Jessie was silent as she listened to their discussion. She wondered if the man distributing the leaflets was Paul Smith. He had certainly been in Torquay a few weeks earlier, but perhaps he had merely been the instigator of the unrest.

She put the worrying thought from her mind. It was really none of her business, though she was glad it hadn't caused trouble for Harry Kendle. She didn't imagine he could afford to have the work disrupted at his factory.

She spent a little time with Maggie and then went upstairs to write some letters. Archie had written to say that he'd been disappointed not to see her when she was in town. Jessie wrote back to say she was sorry that she hadn't had time, but she knew that wasn't quite the truth. She might have been able to pop in for a few minutes if she'd really tried, but it had seemed best to stay away.

There was no point in letting Archie think that she might marry him one day. She had never considered it, but now the idea was even more impossible. She might have no hope of a relationship with Harry Kendle, but she was in love with him and she couldn't think of marrying anyone else.

When Jessie woke the next morning she found an envelope had been pushed beneath her door. Its message was simple. Harry was taking them to see a pony he was buying for his son and planned to have a picnic somewhere on the way back.

Jack will need his riding things, he had written. *Something that washes easily for Catherine would be advisable. And make sure you all wrap up warmly. Please be ready as soon after nine as you can.*

Jessie wondered why he hadn't come to the nursery to tell her in person, and yet in her heart she understood. Harry was

155

being careful. If he came to her there late at night as he had once or twice in the past, he might not be able to resist kissing her again, and someone might walk in and see them.

The knowledge that she was going to be alone with him and the children had given her sweet dreams. Yet they were also disturbing. Despite her determination that they could never be more to each other than they were, Jessie knew the temptation was there for both of them.

She wore a simple green striped dress. The skirt ended just above her ankles, which was slightly old-fashioned these days but suitable for her position as nursemaid. It had short, tight sleeves and a little collar of white lace, but she wore sensible flat shoes because she thought they might be walking over fields. She only owned one coat, which was a dark blue and had served her well for several years, but she added a thick pink scarf and wool hat and decided she didn't look too bad.

Jack made no objection when she suggested he might like to wear his riding breeches and boots.

'Is Father taking me to the farm?' he asked.

'He is taking us all somewhere, but it is a surprise. Cook is making us a picnic.'

'I've never had a picnic. What is that?'

Jessie explained and the child's face lit up. He was excited, unable to wait for his father to appear. It was just as well that he hadn't been told exactly where they were going, Jessie thought.

Catherine was clutching her elephant. She had refused to be parted with it and Jessie let her do as she pleased. She had shown little interest in the other toys her father had bought for her, though Jessie had shown her how to build the bricks into different shapes. Her main interest so far was in knocking them down again, but she was becoming much better at asking for her chamberpot and Jessie was encouraged. Catherine seemed bright, healthy and happy. What more could they ask?

Jessie's heart raced when Harry came to collect them. He was also wearing riding breeches with a casual jacket that had leather patches at the elbows. He looked relaxed and very attractive, and when his eyes met hers Jessie's heart did a rapid somersault.

156

'Where are we going, Father?' Jack asked at once. 'Why are you dressed for riding? Are we going to the farm?'

'Questions! Always questions,' Harry said but his eyes held a secret laughter. 'You will just have to wait and see, young man.'

Jessie hid her smile. Harry looked younger, his manner so changed that he might almost have been a different man from the one she had first met.

'You are happy today,' she said softly as he stood aside for her to pass with Catherine.

'I've stolen a holiday with my family,' he said. 'Why shouldn't I be happy?'

'No reason.' Jessie was warmed by his look and his words. He thought of her as his family. Perhaps he really did love her as much as he said. Perhaps they would be together one day. She allowed herself to dream for a few minutes. 'Is it far?'

'Not too far,' he replied. 'You are as bad as Jack. Wait and see!'

Jessie laughed. His mood was infectious. It was going to be a good day.

The reality was every bit as good as she imagined. The farm that had bred Jack's pony was twenty miles away, on the other side of Torquay, but that was a pleasant drive in the Daimler. Jack sat in the front with his father, Jessie in the back with Catherine. The little girl was excited and looked out of the car window, pointing at animals she saw as they passed. Cows, sheep and horses, cats and dogs all caught her attention and she chattered away until she suddenly fell asleep.

Jack was oddly silent and Jessie knew he was very excited. He suspected they might be going to buy his pony but did not dare to hope in case it wasn't true. It was only when his father drove into a stable yard and stopped that his silence was finally broken.

'Are we?' he asked in a scared, breathy voice. 'Are we going to buy my pony?'

'Only if you like him, Jack,' Harry replied with a smile. 'We've come to see if he suits you and you must say if you don't like him.'

157

'What's his name?'

'That's for you to decide.'

Jack could hardly wait to see the pony his father had picked for him. He looked as if he would burst with excitement. It was a sturdy little thing, chestnut in colour with a silky cream mane.

'He's beautiful,' Jack breathed, his eyes glowing. 'Can I ride him, Father? Can I ride him now?'

'Are you sure you're ready? You're not scared of him?'

'He's only little,' Jack declared boldly. 'I've ridden on your horse. He's much bigger than Wellington.'

'Wellington?' Harry looked at him, much amused. 'Why do you call him that?'

'Because he has a red coat like my soldiers – and I like the Duke of Wellington best, because he won all the battles.'

'Well, it's an odd name for a pony, but it's your choice.'

Jessie was holding Catherine up so that she could stroke the pony's nose. She gurgled with laughter but made no protest when her brother mounted the pony, nor did she clamour to be given a ride. It was as if she understood and accepted that the pony belonged to Jack.

Harry led his son around the yard for a while. Wellington seemed docile and obedient, very suitable for a young boy's first mount. After some twenty minutes or so, they went into the paddock and Harry mounted a horse to ride round with his son.

'Would the little girl like a ride around the yard, miss?'

Jessie turned as the groom spoke to her. He had brought a tiny Shetland pony out and was offering to give Catherine a turn.

'That's kind of you. We'll see what she thinks.' She lifted Catherine so that she could pat the pony as she had Wellington, but it rolled its eyes and shrilled at her, its lip curling back over its teeth.

Catherine screamed and clung to Jessie, burying her face in her shoulder and sobbing.

'Thank you, but I think we had better not,' Jessie said. 'She usually loves animals, but not this time.'

She walked away, patting Catherine's back and soothing

her, but the sobbing went on. It was several minutes before she quietened. Jessie was anxious. The pony had startled her but Catherine never cried, not once in the weeks she had known her had she shed a tear, even when she fell and scraped her knee on a stone in the grass.

It was cold standing about waiting so Jessie got back into the car, nursing the child and talking to her softly. Catherine hugged her elephant. Her face was quite red but she seemed easier now, and after a while she put her thumb in her mouth and went to sleep.

It was nearly half an hour later when Harry brought Jack back to the car. He was looking pleased with himself, and Jack seemed to be in a happy daze.

'Well, that's settled,' Harry said. 'Wellington will be arriving at his new home the day after tomorrow.' He glanced at the sleeping Catherine. 'Was she crying earlier?'

'Yes. The groom offered her a ride on a Shetland pony but it startled her and she was frightened. I've never known her to get so upset.'

'Odd,' Harry said. 'She wasn't frightened of Harry's pony.'

'Nor the elephant,' Jessie said. 'It isn't like her. I think the pony was nervous and that frightened her.'

'Those Shetlands can be vicious,' Harry said. 'It's a good thing she didn't get on its back. Right then, shall we have our picnic now? It isn't a bad day so I thought we would go to the seafront, make a day of it. We can eat in the car, then go for a brisk walk on the front. We might even go on the beach for a little while.'

'The beach! Can we really?'

Jack was clearly delighted. He had been to the beach only rarely with his father and couldn't believe he was to have two treats on the same day.

'We might even buy an ice cream.' Harry glanced anxiously at his daughter. 'Do you think she is all right?'

'She's just sleeping. She'll wake up soon and want her lunch.'

Catherine was hungry when she woke and delighted to find herself being taken somewhere new. It was her very first time on a beach and she kept pointing at the sea and laughing in her excitement. Neither of the children seemed to care that it was winter or that the wind was quite cool as it blew in from the sea. Jessie told Catherine where she was and that the water was the sea and she clamoured to be allowed nearer.

'Catherine want sea . . . Want sea . . .'

'I don't think the children should be allowed to paddle,' she told their father. 'It is far too cold for them.'

'It won't hurt if they just dip their toes in,' Harry said, overruling her. 'John and I used to swim at Christmas when we could. We shan't let them get their clothes wet. It's better for them to be hardy, they'll need to be when they grow up.'

Jessie was doubtful but both Jack and Catherine wanted to go nearer the sea. So she took Catherine by the hand and led her down to the water's edge and Jack ran ahead of them, plopping down in the sand to strip off his boots and socks and roll up the bottoms of his breeches.

Jessie dangled Catherine above the water, letting her dip her feet a few times, which made her gurgle with delight, but she wouldn't let her run free in case she fell and got herself wet all over. Jack, however, paddled contentedly with his father, who had also taken off his boots and seemed to be enjoying the experience as much as his son. Even the sun had come out as if to bless them, taking the bite from the wind; it was so mild now that it could almost have been spring.

Afterwards, Jessie dried the children's feet well on a blanket from the car and they sat in the sand and built castles, Harry as enthusiastic as the two young ones.

Jessie watched, feeling happy to see them all so relaxed and enjoying themselves. It was just a normal family scene, except it hadn't been normal for any of them until recently. Her eyes were misty and her throat felt tight with emotion. She thought that she would never forget this wonderful day.

It was past the children's bedtime when they returned to the house, but they had eaten scones with jam and cream at a little restaurant near the beach and were not hungry. Jessie had only to wash them and tuck them up in bed and they fell asleep immediately.

She went to visit Lady Kendle next, just to make sure she was comfortable and had taken all her medicine, but there were voices coming from inside. However, her tentative knock received an invitation to enter and she did so, feeling slightly awkward as she saw Sir Joshua was with his wife. She seldom saw him since he never visited the nursery and they met only occasionally.

'I am sorry to intrude,' she said. 'I came to see if you needed anything, ma'am.'

'I think that perhaps I should have one of my pills. This shocking news has upset me.'

'News?' Jessie's heart raced as she filled a glass with water and gave Lady Kendle her pill. She knew the children were safe in their beds but something unpleasant must have happened. 'I haven't heard anything, ma'am.'

'You've been with the children, of course. The phone call came only half an hour or so ago. My son's workshops are on fire. They told Sir Joshua that it was serious and my son has gone to investigate. I don't know how bad it is, but I fear the worst.'

'The place is full of wood and materials used for making furniture. I should imagine it went up like a torch – particularly if it was started deliberately, as the police seem to think,' her husband said.

Sir Joshua looked grey and Jessie could see he was very shocked and distressed, as anyone would be at such news. She herself was stunned and hardly knew what to say or think.

'That's terrible,' she said. 'Terrible! Captain Kendle must be very upset.'

'He was angry,' Sir Joshua said. 'Very angry. I cannot recall seeing him that way before. He left at once, though there is nothing much he can do, of course.'

'He had to see it for himself,' Lady Kendle said. 'And he was very concerned that someone might have been hurt.'

'Oh, I do hope not,' Jessie cried and blushed as Lady Kendle looked at her. 'That would be even more tragic.'

She struggled to keep a tight rein on her emotions. It would not do to let Harry's parents guess how very distressed she was by this news, which must have been devastating to him.

This would be a heavy blow to Harry, for he had told her something of his plans for the future. The workshops were his own investment, his independence. Without it he was reliant on the estate, which had been kept going on his wife's money since the war. Jessie had sensed that he hated being dependent on Mary's money for the estate, and had hoped to manage without it once the workshops were making more money.

Sir Joshua was shaking his head over the affair. 'I warned him not to sink everything into that place. This will ruin him.'

'Surely he is insured,' Lady Kendle said with a frown.

'For the building and perhaps some of the contents – but it will be months before the business is up and running again. He may never be able to restart it. I believe he is heavily committed at the bank.'

Sir Joshua seemed to have forgotten Jessie was there.

'Thank you, Jessie,' Lady Kendle said, giving him a subtle reminder. 'Will you come in later as usual?'

'Yes, of course, ma'am.'

Jessie blushed as Sir Joshua frowned at her, as if suddenly remembering that she was in the room. It was a measure of his concern that he had been so outspoken in her presence. She hadn't known that Harry owed money to the bank, but she had been aware how important the business was to him. Closing the door behind her, she heard their voices begin again and was aware of their anxiety. It was a worrying time for the whole family.

She was anxious for more news, but no one knew any more than the bare facts, though Cook and the others could talk of nothing else.

'It will be them political agitators what done it,' Carter said.

'But why?' Cook asked. 'Surely they wouldn't be so mean.'

'Them sort are up to all kinds of tricks.'

'I wonder what's happening,' Jessie said, unable to bear the tension. 'Do you think the firemen can save the building?'

'There'll be spirits and paint on the premises,' Carter said. 'Various oils and paraffin that they use for cleaning and such stuff. It's bound to be a tinderbox.'

'It's dreadful,' Maggie chimed in. 'Dreadful for the men who work there as well as the captain. Most of them were old

162

soldiers, so my father told me. The captain gave them jobs when there was no work going. What will they do now?'

'They'll be like a lot more,' Cook said. 'On the streets looking for work while their families go short.'

Jessie was sorry for the men who had lost their jobs, but what really hurt was the way Harry must be feeling. Why did it have to happen? And today of all days, when they had been so happy. This tragedy had spoiled everything, souring the memory.

Jessie kept her thoughts to herself. She had to be careful not to let anyone guess that the relationship between her and Captain Kendle had gone beyond that of master and servant.

Lady Kendle told her that Harry was still out when she took up her hot drink. 'I dare say he'll stay in Torquay all night,' she said. 'It is a terrible shock for him, Jessie – for all of us, of course, but so much worse for Harry. He has been in such a black mood since the war and he was just coming out of it, beginning to be more like his old self – and now this. I really do not know how he will cope.'

'You must try not to worry,' Jessie said. 'Captain Kendle will do what he has to and he won't want you to be ill over it.'

'That's what my husband told me.' She smiled and held Jessie's hand for a moment. 'It is a great comfort to me that you are here, my dear.'

'Thank you, ma'am. I am glad to be of use.'

Alone in her room later, Jessie read for a while but couldn't sleep. All she could think about was how happy they had been that day, and how worried Harry must be now. If all his money had been tied up in the workshops he might never recover from a blow like this. He had spoken of leaving his wife, of setting up home with Jessie. She had known even then that it was just a dream, but this made it even more impossible. Without Mary's money to support the estate it might have to be sold – and Harry couldn't do that to his family, however much he might want to be free of his marriage.

It was nearly midnight when Jessie heard something in the room next to hers. It was an odd moaning sound, rather like a whimper. She was out of bed instantly, thinking that it must

163

be Jack having a nightmare. He'd only had one since she began taking care of him, but perhaps all the excitement of the day had been too much for him.

As she went into the little sitting room that was part of the nursery wing she saw someone slumped in the chair, head in hands, and knew at once that it was Harry. The sound she'd heard had come from him, not his son.

'Was it very bad?' she asked and knelt by his side as he lifted his head and looked at her, his face grey with shock. 'Was anyone hurt?'

'My foreman,' Harry said. 'He tried to save some of the finished orders and a burning beam fell on him. Poor devil! He's badly burned. If he lives he may never work again.'

'I'm so sorry,' Jessie said, her heart wrenched with pity for the man who had been hurt and for this man she loved, who had lost so much. His cheeks were wet with tears, which she knew were for his foreman more than his own tragedy. 'I wish I could do something to help.'

'It's too late for Bates,' Harry said. 'And it's probably too late for me. I'm finished, Jessie. It's all gone – building, stock, finished orders, worth ten thousand or more. It was a big order and the customer wanted it all delivered at once. Now there's nothing left. The insurance may pay what I owe the bank if I'm lucky, but I shan't be able to start up again. I just don't have the money. Another two days and the orders would have gone out. With that money I could have hung on, but now it's impossible.'

'Your father wouldn't help you to get on your feet again?'

'Throw good money after bad? Why should he? He thought it was a stupid idea at the start, and Mary agreed with him. Besides, he hasn't got much in reserve even if he wanted to help. Without Mary the estate would have gone under before this.'

Jessie wasn't so sure that his father wouldn't help if he could, but she wasn't in a position to know if the money was available.

'You'll find a way.'

'Shall I?' He looked down at her and she sensed his despair, sensed the black well inside him, the hopelessness. 'What's

164

the point? I've lost all chance of getting free. I can't have you and . . .'

Jessie touched her fingers to his lips. She had no idea what made her say what she did, except that her heart ached for him. He was in such need, such pain, and she loved him so very much.

'I love you,' she said. 'Come to bed with me, Harry. Lie with me, be my love, love me as if I were your own true wife. Just for tonight. In the morning things will seem better.'

She stood up and in the faint light penetrating the window he saw that she was wearing a thin nightgown, the rosy peaks of her breasts clearly visible through the material. It clung to her lovingly, caressing the curves of her breasts and hips, and the slenderness of her waist. For a moment he sat staring at her like a man who thinks he has seen an oasis in the desert but can't be sure it isn't a mirage.

'You don't mean that.'

'Yes, I do,' Jessie said. 'I know nothing has changed for us, but sometimes we have to take our chances, we have to seize what is offered lest it never comes again. We may never have more than this night, but we deserve some happiness.'

'Jessie . . .' He was on his feet, drawing her into his arms, holding her, kissing her with an urgency and a desperation that swept them both away on a reckless tide. 'You don't know how much this means to me.'

Jessie kissed him lingeringly on the mouth, the depth of her love reaching out to him, wanting to heal his grief and hurt, her hands stroking the back of his neck. She felt the force of his need in the shudder that went through him, and she took him by the hand, leading him into her own room. Then she let go of his hand for a moment as she reached up to pull her nightgown over her head, standing naked before him. Harry's eyes feasted on the soft swell of her breasts and the creamy silk of her skin.

'You're so beautiful, Jessie. So very lovely . . .'

Jessie smiled invitingly as she lay down on the bed. Harry was stripping off his clothes, revealing the lean, muscled contours of his own body, his skin a darker tone than hers and sprinkled here and there with blond hair. Then he was beside her on the bed, holding her close, stroking her back as she turned instinctively to him, moulding her buttocks, his lips against the arch of her throat. She could feel the burn of his flesh, the strength of his arousal as he kissed and caressed her, making her tremble with desire. She had never suspected that she could feel this way, never realized what loving actually meant before.

Their first coupling was intense because of their heightened emotions, the stress of the past few hours; a fierce, strange, sweet loving that was over quickly and left them both wanting more.

Afterwards, Jessie lay in his arms as he whispered words of love against her throat, telling her that she was his now and for always.

'I'll find a way,' he vowed. 'It won't be easy but I'll find a way to build up the workshops again. We'll be together, my darling, with the children. I promise you won't be hurt. I shall never forget what you've given me, your sweetness, your love.'

Jessie hushed him with a kiss. He began to make love to her again, slowly this time, letting the desire build between them. Jessie's nails raked his shoulders as he brought her to a wonderful, shuddering climax, his body jerking as he delivered his seed inside her.

'I love you,' he whispered as he laid his face against her breast. 'I always shall.'

Jessie realized after a few minutes that he had fallen asleep. She kissed the top of his head, knowing that sleep was what he needed, what his body craved after the agony of the previous hours. Her own mind was too busy for sleep. She knew that she was happy, happier than she had ever been in her life, but she also knew that what she had done could lose her everything she most loved and valued.

If she were to have a child . . . But she wouldn't. It didn't happen the first time for most women. As for the rest, she was willing to take the risk. Harry might think she was fast for offering herself to him, but she had given him the most precious gift she had to give because he was so close to despair and if he loved her he would know that.

166

But they couldn't do this again. Not if she wanted to stay here as his children's nurse. She would make him see that. Once he was over the first terrible shock of the fire, she would tell him that it couldn't happen again.

Eleven

Jessie hardly saw Harry for the next few days, merely catching sight of him in his car as she was out with the children a couple of times, but he had told her he would be busy. She knew from Carter that he had been at the workshops trying to see if anything could be saved, though very little had survived. The fire had been too fierce, too swift. The police were now certain that it had been deliberately set and there was some worry that the insurance might not pay out.

'But that's wicked!' Cook exclaimed when Carter told her what he'd heard. 'Captain Kendle has a right to be paid for what he's lost.'

'They say it was arson and until they're satisfied that he didn't get someone to do it, they won't pay out.'

'But that's ridiculous,' Jessie said, feeling angry. 'Of course he didn't. He wouldn't do a thing like that. Why should he? He was expecting to make a lot of money from finished orders and now that has all gone.'

Carter gave her a long hard look and Jessie realized that her indignation had led her to betray herself. She blushed and looked away, knowing that he already suspected her of carrying on with Harry Kendle and her outburst would convince him he was right.

'It's a wicked shame, that's what I call it,' Cook said. 'And that poor man – what was his name, him what got burned?'

'Bates.' Carter transferred his attention to Cook. 'He died last night, poor soul. It was hopeless from the start. Captain Kendle went to see the widow. He's offered the family a cottage on the estate. Pamela, that's her name. She's to have a small pension and a job in the house, so I'm told.'

'Who told you that?' Cook stared at him.

'Mrs Pearson. She says Lady Kendle informed her this morning. Mrs Bates is to start in the kitchen and Maggie's to be made up to second parlourmaid.'

'Well, I never!' Cook said. 'And without a word to me. After I've got Maggie trained to my ways.'

'Apparently Mrs Bates was in service before she was married.'

'As well she may have been, but I've got my own way of doing things.'

It was obvious that Cook was put out and a little annoyed at losing Maggie, though it would be a step up for her, of course. Jessie listened to their conversation with half an ear. She was naturally distressed to hear that Mrs Bates had lost her husband because of the fire, but her thoughts were elsewhere.

Harry hadn't come to the nursery since that night. Jessie had half expected, half hoped he would. Yet she knew he was being careful, trying to protect her. She had to be careful, too. She mustn't let things he told her privately slip or everyone would guess their secret. Carter had been watching her speculatively for some while now but she ignored him. He could think what he liked as long as he didn't know anything for sure.

Jessie was thoughtful as she took the children out later that morning. She knew she had been lucky the first time. Her monthly flow had come as usual. They had got away with it this time, but it mustn't happen again.

Jack wanted to go to the farm that morning to see his pony. He was wearing his riding breeches – he hardly left them off these days, though he had been told that he wasn't allowed to ride unless his father or Mr Goodjohn had time to be with him.

'I can stroke Wellington, can't I?' he asked Jessie. 'And give him the carrot Cook saved for me?'

'Yes, of course you can.'

Jessie knew how much he longed to ride Wellington and how frustrating it must be that his father was too busy to give him the necessary lessons. Jack could actually ride quite well, but the pony was new to him and his father was cautious about letting him ride alone just yet.

Neither of the children had taken any harm from paddling in the sea. Jack had had a few snuffles for a day or so but they had cleared up and Catherine seemed very well. She was still clinging to her elephant, but Jessie had taught her how to use some of her puzzles and she was making good progress. Nanny was sure she had grown.

'There was a time when I thought she never would,' she told Jessie. 'I feel bad now about not giving her more attention before, but she never seemed to want to do more than sleep.'

'It's not your fault. Everyone thought she would never learn anything.'

In fact it was shameful that no one had cared enough to try. Nanny had had enough to do with keeping the children clean and fed, but she'd been unwell and too old to realize the neglect Catherine had suffered. Harry Kendle was a very busy man and his mother was an invalid. The blame lay squarely at Mary Kendle's door.

She had been told about the fire at her husband's workshops and must know what a devastating blow it was to him, but she'd made no attempt to come home. Jessie was glad she'd chosen to stay away, because the house was happier without her, but she couldn't help thinking how selfish she was, caring only for her own pleasure. She was an unnatural mother and an uncaring wife, and she deserved to lose her husband's love.

Jessie had felt a little guilty over what she'd done at first. It couldn't be right to lie with another woman's husband and yet it seemed Mary didn't care. If she had she would have come home to comfort Harry instead of going off to the south of France with her friends.

Jessie decided she wouldn't let herself feel guilty. She would treasure her memories and keep them sacred in her heart, though of course she mustn't give way to her desires like that again. Once, for Harry's sake, was forgivable, but she ought not to let it happen again.

It was when they were returning from their trip to the farm

170

that a man approached Jessie. For a moment she didn't realize who he was, but then he took off his cap, seeming awkward as he shuffled his feet.

'Beg your pardon, miss, but I'm Jethro Wylie.'

'You're Jed's father,' Jessie said and smiled at him as she held on to Catherine's hand. Harry Kendle had just driven into the back courtyard and Jack had darted off to meet his father, but she wouldn't let Catherine go after him. 'How is he? Carter said something about him coming home soon.'

'He came home yesterday. I've been wanting to see you, miss – to thank you for what you done for him. I didn't properly understand until he told me what the captain said to him, how it were you what saved him.'

'I did very little,' Jessie said. 'How does he feel now?'

'Very low, miss. His arm be useless now. They had to take it off just above the elbow but it were that or him dyin' of blood poisoning, so they told us. He says he might as well be dead but he'll get over it.'

'I'm very sorry. I was afraid the nerves were too badly damaged. If they hadn't had to take his arm off it's unlikely he could have used it much.'

'His ma's glad to have him back, arm or no arm, and so am I. We'll pull him round, miss. Don't know what he'll do for a living, but we'll find him something.'

'Yes, I am sure you will. He might be a night watchman at a factory or something. As time goes on he'll find it easier to accept what has happened to him, but a lot of men feel the way he does at first. There were hundreds of men who lost their limbs in the war. I nursed some of them and those who survived were the lucky ones. You tell Jed that I knew a lot of men who found a way to go on living without both their legs and often with dreadful scars.'

'I'll tell him that, miss. I doubt he'll listen yet, but it might make him think. He was always a bright lad. Could have done well at school if he'd tried.'

'I wish him well,' Jessie said.

He nodded, put his cap on and walked off, tipping it to Harry as he passed.

Jack was bringing his father towards her. Jessie's heart missed a beat as she saw his smile of welcome.

'You've been talking to Jed's father.'

'Yes. Jed is very upset at the moment. His father says he feels useless.'

'We must find a way to make him feel needed. I could have given him a job at the workshops. He's a bright lad, good with figures I understand. He should have stayed on at school but he wanted to work, and of course his family encouraged him to leave. They saw him working on the estate for his lifetime as his father does.'

'Perhaps he could study with the vicar. He might learn to be a clerk.'

'I'll talk to Jethro again. I'm sure we can come up with something.' Harry's eyes lingered on her face. She felt the heat of his gaze enfold her and knew what he was thinking, because she was thinking it too. 'I've been busy, but things are easing now. I've told Jack I'll take him riding tomorrow.' He glanced down at his son. 'Go and ask Cook for a bun, Jack. Jessie will be in soon.'

Jack ran off obediently. Catherine was sucking her thumb and holding tight to her elephant, her eyes wide with wonder.

'I've missed you,' Harry said in a low, urgent whisper. 'Can I see you, Jessie – tonight?'

Jessie's heart went wild. She knew she ought to refuse. They were playing with fire but she had missed him too, so much. A surge of rebellion went through her. Why shouldn't they snatch happiness where they could? Life was so short, so precarious. It could have been Harry in that fire. If he had been visiting the workshops that evening instead of having tea with her and the children he might have been the one to die. Their love was so sweet and true. Surely it couldn't be so very wrong.

'Yes,' she answered, smiling into his eyes. 'You know I've missed you, Harry.'

'I love you.'

'I had better go in now before someone notices us talking.'

'Yes, I suppose so. I've got something to tell you tonight.'

Jessie nodded and left him. She sensed that he remained

where he was, staring after her until she went inside the house.

Jack was sitting at the kitchen table eating one of Cook's rock buns, and the whole kitchen smelled deliciously of baking. Cook was pouring a glass of lemon barley for him and she offered one to Jessie and Catherine too.

'Would Miss Catherine like a drink and a cake?'

'Yes, I am sure she would.' Jessie gave the child a little push and she went forward uncertainly, wriggling her bottom on to a stool as she took the cake with both hands. She ate it with evident enjoyment.

'There's a little love,' Cook said and beamed at her. 'That Pam Bates came to see me while you were out, Jessie. She's a pleasant enough woman, though still in a bit of a state over losing her husband. That's natural, of course. She's got a boy of eight but she had a miscarriage last year. I suppose you could say that's a blessing in disguise now. She says her son is mad about horses and is looking forward to living near the farm. He'll be going to school for a few years yet, of course, but she thinks he'll be suited to the farm when he's older. And she's worked in a kitchen before, so that's all right. We'll get used to each other, and it's only right Maggie should have a chance to move up.'

'I suppose a job was the best way of helping her.'

'She's luckier than most from what I hear. Captain Kendle can't find jobs for all the men, can he?'

'Not unless he can set up the business again.'

Jessie took the children upstairs when they had finished their cakes. Neither of them were very hungry when their lunch arrived an hour or so later, but it didn't matter for once. They could make up for it at tea.

They played happily together for a while, Jack showing his sister how to play various games. Then Catherine had a sleep while Jack did sums from a book his father had bought him. Jessie ironed their clean clothes and watched over them with a feeling of contentment.

Sometimes when she was alone with them like this she could almost believe they were hers. She knew it was a foolish dream, but it might come true one day. Harry had promised

173

her he would find a way for them to be together and perhaps he would.

In her heart Jessie knew that it would cause too much trouble, that the heartbreak and scandal would be too heavy a price to pay. Yet she could not quite dismiss her dreams.

Later that same evening Mrs Pearson told them that Lady Kendle's daughter was coming on a visit to her mother quite soon.

'That's nice,' Cook said. 'It's a long time since Miss Priscilla came to visit – Mrs Barrington, that is, of course.'

'She's too busy to get down often,' Mrs Pearson said. 'But she worries about her mother. She was telling me on the telephone earlier – and she's upset over this latest bother with the fire.'

Jessie listened as they talked, saying nothing. She didn't know Priscilla Barrington and so she could not add to the general conversation. Alice came after her as she went upstairs.

'I shall have to be careful with Miss Priscilla around,' Alice said. 'She's a rare one for secrets. Seems to know exactly what's going on five minutes after she arrives.'

'She won't know yours if you don't tell her, Alice. You don't show yet.'

'No, but I've been sick several times. Mrs Pearson told me I was looking peaky this morning, and Lady Kendle gave me an odd look when I was doing her room later. I shall have to leave soon, whether I want to or not. I'd rather leave than be asked to go.'

'Yes, I think I would, too.'

'Oh, you won't be asked to leave. Lady Kendle thinks you're wonderful and so does the captain.'

Jessie looked at her sharply but there was no malice in the other girl's remark. She obviously had no idea that Jessie had a relationship with Harry Kendle.

'I shall miss you when you go, Alice.'

'I'll write to you,' Alice promised.

The subject was changed and Alice went off to her own room while Jessie visited Nanny. She had been knitting a pair of socks for Jack but she put her work aside, eager to talk

174

about Mrs Barrington's visit. She was clearly pleased that they were to have a visitor.

'Miss Priscilla always cheers things up,' she told Jessie. 'Like a breath of fresh air she is. She'll put Master Harry back on his feet, you'll see.'

'But what can she do? Is she rich?'

'She has a rich husband,' Nanny said. 'But she'll know what to do. If there's a way of getting the money he needs, Miss Priscilla will find it.'

Jessie wasn't sure how Harry would take interference from his well-meaning sister. He was already trying as hard as he possibly could to find a solution. However, she mustn't prejudge. She hadn't even met Mrs Barrington and she was a little nervous. Everyone said she was a past master at discovering secrets. Jessie just hoped she wouldn't discover hers.

Jessie confessed her secret worry as she lay in Harry's arms that night. Their loving had been passionate, even more fulfilling than the first time.

'You need not worry about Priscilla,' he said and touched her face lovingly with his fingertips. 'She has always been on my side. If she knew she would say good luck and be happy.'

Jessie didn't argue. How could she when she didn't know his sister? She couldn't help worrying about it during the week before the visit. Harry was coming to her bed every night now and though she welcomed him with love in her heart she was nervous.

Harry had told her that he believed he'd partly solved his problem.

'There's a barn I could use to set up the workshop until the old one is rebuilt,' he told her, looking excited. 'Some of the tools were saved. Quite a few are the personal property of the men themselves and they take them home; others were dragged out into the yard and escaped the worst. I would need to buy larger things, benches and vices, and cramps, that kind of thing. It's the wood and other materials that cost, of course – and the wages until we are up and running.'

'Would the bank lend you some more money?'

'They aren't keen until the insurance comes through, and

they are being difficult at the moment. They'll pay up in the end, of course, but until then it's awkward. However, my father has offered me a small loan. It's hardly enough but it's all he can afford and very good of him. He has actually been very decent over this, better than I expected.'

'I'm glad,' Jessie said. It meant that he could put some of his craftsmen back to work, but it also meant that he would be even more tied to the estate. She knew that he was pleased with the offer and also that she mustn't question, mustn't ask about the future.

Henry sensed her reserve. He raised himself on one elbow, gazing down into her face. 'You're thinking it means I can never leave Mary?' He smiled as she remained silent and traced the line of her mouth with the tip of his forefinger. 'You don't need to say. Of course I know how you feel. You've given me so much, Jessie. Until you came into my life I thought I would be better off if I'd died in the trenches with the others. Now I have something to live for and I don't intend to let it go. I said I would find a way and I shall. I'm going to France to see Mary. I'm going to ask her to divorce me.'

'You mustn't,' Jessie said. 'Supposing she refuses? What will you tell her if she asks why?'

'Nothing about you. Mary is no happier than I am. She has her . . . friends. She may welcome the suggestion. I don't know for sure, but I believe she has a lover.'

Jessie remembered seeing the couple on the beach in Torquay. She had thought the woman was Mary but couldn't be sure. She wouldn't tell Harry, could never tell him, but she thought Mary had been with her lover that day.

'Are you sure you ought to do this?'

'Yes, of course. It's the best way.'

'But your mother . . .'

'She will be shocked when I marry you, but she'll get used to it.'

'And your father?'

Harry smiled grimly. 'He was always after the maids in the old days, when I was just a boy. I imagine my mother knew but she turned a blind eye – they did in those days, stiff upper

176

lip and all that. I dare say I've got half-brothers and sisters somewhere. One or two of the girls left in a hurry.'

'Poor girls,' Jessie said. 'I wonder what happened to them.'

'Father paid them off, I expect. He was fair enough in that way and it used to happen all the time,' Harry said and kissed her softly on the mouth. 'It won't happen to you, Jessie. I promise you. If you have a child it will be mine, acknowledged and loved. We'll be together one day. I swear it on my brother's grave.'

She heard the intense note in his voice and surrendered to his loving. Harry truly cared for her. There would be problems, gossip, harsh words and knowing looks to be faced, but somehow they would get through it together.

Jack had riding lessons with his father every day for the next week. He was growing in confidence and Harry said it wouldn't be long before he could ride with just a lad from the farm to watch over him.

'We'll finish our lessons when I come home,' he told Jack. 'Your aunt is coming this evening and she'll keep an eye on you. Priscilla was always a brilliant rider so you'll be fine with her.'

Jessie was nervous about meeting Mrs Barrington, but when she did she liked the other woman immediately. Priscilla was an attractive, open, active person with a bright manner. She wasn't like her brother in appearance – her hair was darker in colour, her eyes more grey than blue – but sometimes when she smiled the resemblance was there.

'So you're Jessie,' she said and shook hands firmly. 'I'm Priscilla. I'm so pleased to meet you at last. Mother and Harry have both told me how wonderful you are, and how lucky they are to have you.'

'Oh no,' Jessie said and blushed. 'I just do what I can, that's all.'

'Not from what I hear.' Priscilla laughed. 'I think Harry has fallen for you, Jessie, but you mustn't tell him I said so.'

'No, of course not. I'm sure it isn't true.' Jessie's cheeks were burning and she couldn't look at the other woman.

177

'I know my brother and something is making him look younger these days.' Priscilla's eyes narrowed as she looked at Jessie. 'You would be the very thing for him if he weren't married. It's a pity Mary won't run off and leave him; it would make things so much easier.'

'Priscilla!' Lady Kendle was shocked. 'Please do not embarrass Jessie. She doesn't know what a tease you are.'

'I'm sure Jessie has too much sense,' Priscilla replied, but her gaze was intent, thoughtful. 'They tell me Catherine is much better since you came. I am looking forward to seeing her – and that monster Jack. Harry tells me he is teaching him to ride. I've been asked to oversee him while my brother nips over to France. I can't imagine why he wants to go. The country is bound to have bad memories for him.'

'He wants to see Mary, of course,' Lady Kendle said, rebuking her daughter. 'It is only natural.'

'Pull the other one, Ma! Their marriage was a complete mistake. Her money has helped the estate, of course, but as I keep telling Father, it would be far better to sell this place. It's far too large for you these days. You need lots of money to run a house like this, more than Harry is ever going to make.'

'Priscilla! Your tongue always did run away with you.'

'Well, why not tell the truth? Everyone knows, of course they do. The servants usually know before we do – and I'm sure Jessie won't gossip. She doesn't look the type, too intelligent.'

Lady Kendle sighed. 'Do you imagine we could sell? Harry says it would make a decent hotel if it were nearer Torquay.'

'Father should look for a rich American,' Priscilla said and laughed. 'Advertise in the *Times* and tell them about the ghosts.'

'What ghosts?' Jessie asked, intrigued. She hadn't heard anything about ghosts.

'The one that walks the corridors moaning and trying the bedroom doors,' Priscilla said and Lady Kendle frowned at her.

'That isn't funny, Priscilla. Please stop this nonsense at once. You know that your father would never sell, and for the moment we manage well enough.'

178

'On Mary's money,' Priscilla said. 'I feel sorry for Harry. He only married her because Father pushed him into it.'

'Now that is more than enough,' Lady Kendle said. 'Would you leave us please, Jessie? I wish to talk to my daughter alone.'

Jessie could see that Lady Kendle was very angry. She did not care to have such private family business discussed so openly in front of the nursemaid, and in her heart Jessie couldn't blame her. Priscilla's statement had not come as a surprise to her, because Harry had already told her, but she understood that his mother would not want it to be gossiped about downstairs.

It was a sad tangle, she thought as she went to bed that evening. Harry was tied to a wife he didn't love because of his loyalty to his family, and though he had promised to make changes, Jessie was afraid of the trouble it would undoubtedly cause.

Harry had told her he wouldn't come to her room while Priscilla was in the house. 'She would be bound to walk in or something,' he said. And while Priscilla wouldn't criticize, he didn't want anyone to know about their affair until he had settled things with Mary.

In fact Priscilla did not come to Jessie's room that evening, but the next morning she came to the nursery to collect Jack.

'Want to come riding with me then, brat?' she asked as he flung himself on her with enthusiasm. 'What about you, Jessie? Are you going to bring Catherine to watch?'

'Perhaps another time,' Jessie said. 'She's a little sleepy this morning. We had a good walk yesterday. I might let her play with her toys today and bring her tomorrow, if that's all right?'

'You know what's best for her,' Priscilla said and bent to lift the child in her arms. 'She's grown since I was here, haven't you, my sweet? What a lovely little thing you are.'

Catherine patted her face and cooed but didn't say anything.

'Come along then, Jack,' Priscilla said, putting her down again. 'We'd better have a look at how you're getting along with your pony, young man.'

After they had gone, Catherine seemed disinclined to do

much other than hug her elephant. Jessie was a little concerned about her, but Nanny said she had often been like that in the past and it was nothing to worry about.

Jessie nursed her for quite a long time that morning, reading to her from a picture book and telling her stories. After a while Catherine fell asleep and Jessie laid her on some cushions on the floor so that she could play with her toys if she woke up.

She took some washing downstairs and spent an hour or so rinsing the clothes through and chatting to Maggie's mother, who had come in to do a main wash for the household.

'Maggie was that excited when she went dancing with you and Carter,' she told Jessie. 'But you got into trouble for it, I understand.'

'It was just a misunderstanding,' Jessie told her. 'We must do it again one day if it can be arranged. There's been so much to do that I haven't bothered to take an afternoon off for ages.'

When she went back to the nursery Nanny was sitting watching Catherine, who had woken up full of energy and was playing with her bricks.

'She's been building some interesting shapes,' Nanny said. 'But she always knocks them down again.'

'As long as she is happy,' Jessie said. 'I'm relieved she's more herself again. I was beginning to worry about her, and with Captain Kendle away . . .'

She was interrupted as the nursery door burst open and Jack came flying in, well pleased with himself. He couldn't wait to tell his news. His aunt thought he was a wonderful rider and had told him he would soon be able to start jumping over hurdles.

'Oh, not yet, surely,' Jessie said. 'You mustn't try that until your father comes back, Jack. I don't think he would permit you to jump your pony for a few weeks yet.'

'Nonsense!' Priscilla said, coming in at that moment. 'I've never seen a lad with more promise. Harry is an old woman sometimes.'

Jessie frowned but held her tongue. She knew nothing about riding, but she did know that Jack was impetuous and his father had meant to go slowly with him.

'Hello, Nanny,' Priscilla said and kissed her wrinkled cheek. 'Be a darling and go and tell Mummy I'll be along soon, will you?'

'What are you up to, Miss Priscilla? Something, I'll be bound.' Nanny said with a mock frown, but she went off obediently, leaving Jessie alone with Harry's sister.

'Perhaps we could go in the sitting room,' Priscilla suggested. 'I'm dying for a cigarette and the children are all right for the moment, aren't they?'

Since Jack was showing his sister how to play a game, Jessie agreed and they went into the next room, where Priscilla immediately lit up. She offered her cigarette case to Jessie, who shook her head.

'You don't, of course. Sensible woman,' Priscilla said and sighed. 'I should never have started. I'm hooked on them now I'm afraid, but at least it's better than drinking to excess – or those awful drugs some idiots take these days.' She shuddered. 'I had a friend who became an opium addict; it completely ruined her of course.'

'I haven't come across anyone like that,' Jessie admitted. 'It must be a terrible affliction.'

'Oh, absolutely,' Priscilla said. 'But awfully smart in some circles. Not mine, thank goodness.' She gave Jessie a long, hard look. 'Are you in love with my maddening brother?'

Jessie flushed and looked away. 'Why do you ask? Has your mother said something?'

'Mummy? Good lord, no. She wouldn't approve, of course. Divorce would be the last straw for either of the parents, but I think it is exactly what Harry needs. Mary doesn't love him. She never did.'

'Why did she marry him?' Jessie asked, relieved to turn the subject. 'It wasn't for money.'

'Lord no, she has all the cash,' Priscilla said and laughed. 'She bought herself a title, Jessie. Harry will be Sir Harry one day, you see. Her family is rich but not quite the thing – commerce. The Kendles have been here in this house since the dodo, or almost. Mary was quite impressed with that when she married Harry, but I think it means less to her now.'

'That isn't very nice,' Jessie said slowly. 'If she isn't happy, would she divorce him?'

'I've no idea. There's no reason why she shouldn't. She isn't a Catholic or anything, but it depends on whether it's what she wants or not. You must have noticed that my sister-in-law is incredibly selfish.'

'I imagine she is accustomed to having her own way.'

Priscilla raised her eyebrows. 'That is a very tactful way of putting it, Jessie. Yes, Mary gets her own way in most things, because of the money, of course. Money isn't everything. I should like to see my brother happy and he won't be if he stays married to that cold fish. She wouldn't let him near her after the birth of the twins.'

'She was upset,' Jessie said.

'So was Harry. It almost broke his heart when they told him Catherine wasn't normal. I think he wanted to be killed when he went back to France, but all he got was a flesh wound and a commendation for bravery.'

Jessie nodded, knowing that for a while Harry had felt he would be better off dead, but things were better now.

'Is Catherine improving?' Priscilla said. 'Harry said she was, but I couldn't see much sign of it earlier.'

'She was tired this morning. It's her heart condition, I expect. Some days I can't stop her talking.'

'Bring her down to the paddock tomorrow,' Priscilla said. 'We might give her a little ride on Wellington.'

'I'm not sure that's a good idea. She got upset the last time she was offered a ride on a pony. It was a Shetland and it rolled its eyes and shrilled at her. She cried for ages.'

'Bad-tempered things. I wouldn't let my children ride those when they were small,' Priscilla said and blew a smoke ring. 'I didn't bring my brood down this time because it was only a short visit, but it's their Easter holiday next month and I'll bring them down for a couple of weeks then.'

'They will be company for Jack,' Jessie said. 'We want him to enjoy this summer because he will be starting lessons at the vicarage in the autumn. Captain Kendle doesn't want him to go to boarding school too soon, because he was miserable there himself.'

182

'Harry told you that, did he?' Priscilla's eyes were bright with amusement. 'And you pretend there's nothing between you. Shame on you, Jessie! If you aren't in love with him now I predict it isn't far off. I just hope he does something about it.' She stubbed her cigarette out in an ashtray and jumped up from her chair.

'I must visit Ma or she will think I've deserted her. Don't look so worried, Jessie. I shall keep your secret – and Alice's, the foolish girl. Tell her to come to me if the parents throw her out. I'll find her a job when she's had the baby.'

'Did Alice tell you she's having a child?'

'No, but I guessed as soon as I saw her. She looked scared to death and pale. I bet she's having a horrid time, just as I did. Don't forget to tell her what I said, will you?'

Priscilla smiled and went out, leaving Jessie to stare after her. She wasn't quite sure what to make out of Harry's sister, but at least it seemed that she would have one member of the family on her side if it came to a divorce.

Twelve

Maggie was in the laundry room, folding some towels ready for the airing cupboard when Jessie went in a little later. She swung round, looking alarmed, but smiled when she saw it was Jessie.

'I thought for a moment it was someone else,' she said. She looked odd – half apprehensive, half angry – Jessie thought and asked if something was wrong. Maggie hesitated, then said, 'It's just Carter. He keeps patting my bum and making faces at me. I don't mind that so much but I'm worried about what he's going to try next.'

'He's old enough to be your father!' Jessie was shocked. 'When did this start?'

'A few days after we went to that dance. He'd always been friendly, but nothing like this. I don't think he means anything by it, it's just a lark, but I'd rather he didn't.'

'You should tell him he's making a nuisance of himself. Do you want me to speak to him, Maggie? I could tell him to leave you alone.'

'No!' Maggie looked nervous. 'He wouldn't like that. He thinks you're a bit above the rest of us. If you said anything he'd be angry. If he goes too far I'll speak to Cook. I think he only does it when he's had a couple of drinks. He's sober as a judge most of the time, but every now and then he has a few.'

'Well, you tell him to keep his hands to himself.'

'I'm probably making too much of it.'

Jessie wasn't so sure about that. She'd thought Carter was a decent enough bloke when she first arrived, but someone had tried her door one night and she had seen Carter giving her an odd look a few times. She knew he thought there might

184

be something going on between her and Harry Kendle, and she wouldn't have been surprised if he'd made a pass at her, but he had no right to upset Maggie. However, Cook would put him right if Maggie spoke to her about it.

Jessie forgot about Carter as she took hot drinks to Lady Kendle and Nanny. She didn't stay talking long with Nanny that evening, because she had some letters to write.

She owed Archie a letter. It was becoming more difficult to write to him these days, because she wasn't sure what to say. She tried to write about what she'd done with the children, what was happening in the garden as the seasons changed, and sometimes about what she'd seen in the newspapers. She was sure her letters must seem dull and that he would be disappointed, but she didn't know what else to tell him.

It was much easier to write to her aunt. She told her about Harry's sister, saying how pleasant she was, very modern and smartly dressed, but was careful not to mention the way she had been teased about her feelings for him.

Jessie hadn't given her aunt the slightest hint about how she felt. Aunt Elizabeth had old-fashioned values. She wouldn't approve of divorce. Jessie didn't dare to think what she would say if she knew the truth of what had happened between her and Harry. She wouldn't be angry and she wouldn't condemn, but she would certainly be shocked.

Sometimes Jessie was shocked at herself. Especially when she lay in bed thinking about Harry, wishing he were with her, wanting him to make love to her, longing for the fulfilment he gave her. She was a wanton woman and she wasn't ashamed of it! In fact she knew that making love had brought her exquisite pleasure, far more than she had ever expected to find.

Jessie smiled as she stroked the pillow where his head had lain, thinking of him there beside her. 'Please let Mary divorce him,' she whispered into the darkness. 'Please let us be together for always.'

She couldn't wait for him to come home, and yet she was afraid – afraid that it would mean the end of her dream.

*   *   *

185

Jessie told Jack that she would bring Catherine to watch him a little later that morning. He went off quite happily with his aunt and Jessie spent some time reading to Catherine. It was nearly an hour later when she reached the paddocks and it was warmer than it had been earlier that day.

At first she didn't realize what Priscilla was doing, but then she noticed the little jumps that had been set round the field. They were very low and probably quite safe but Jessie's heart skipped a beat. She was certain Harry wouldn't approve. He had intended to go much more slowly with his son's lessons.

Jack had seen her. He waved to her from across the field. 'Watch me, Jessie!'

'You be careful,' she called, her heart in her mouth as he urged the pony to a canter and began to clear the hurdles one by one. Supposing he fell and hurt himself? In fact the pony cleared all the hurdles with ease and Jack halted in front of her, flushed with triumph.

'Did you see me, Jessie?'

'Yes, I saw you. You did very well.'

'I'm going to do it again but I want the jumps higher. Will you set them higher for me, Aunt Priscilla?'

'No!' Jessie felt coldness at the base of her neck. 'No, I don't think you should, Jack. Not today, please. Take your pony back to the stable. It will soon be time for lunch. I want you to come home with Catherine and me. You can play with her while I do the ironing. Will you do that for me, please?'

'Can't I jump one more round?' Jack looked obstinate.

'Don't be a spoilsport, Jessie,' Priscilla said. 'One more round, Jack. I'll put the jumps up another notch.'

Jessie watched as she adjusted the hurdles. They were still not very high but the pony found it more difficult to clear them. However, it was managed without incident and Jack was very pleased with himself by the end of the round.

'I'll be able to jump over the top notch by the time Father gets back,' he said to his aunt. 'He'll be very proud of me then, won't he?'

'Very proud, I should think,' Priscilla said. 'You're doing

awfully well, Jack. You throw your heart over and that's a brave rider. I'm extremely pleased with you.'

Jessie said nothing. She was certain Harry hadn't intended anything like this when he put his sister in charge of his son's riding lessons, but what could she say? She was merely the nursery maid when it came down to it. Jack was bound to take more notice of his aunt, especially when he was getting exactly what he wanted.

'Shall we go home?' she asked. 'Cook was making her special lemon barley today and baking something nice.'

'Oh good,' Priscilla said. 'I hope there's seedcake. I love her seedcake. No one else makes it quite the same way.'

Priscilla returned the pony to the stables and then they all walked back to the house together. Catherine walked for a while and then asked to be carried. Jessie picked her up; she was no hardship to carry.

Priscilla was smoking. She talked about various musical shows she had been to see in London, asking Jessie if she liked the theatre. She herself had been to see a Dixieland jazz band at the London Palladium, and was a great enthusiast. When they reached the house they all had drinks and cake in the kitchen before Jessie took the children upstairs.

Catherine fell asleep almost at once.

'I'm worried about her,' Jessie told Nanny that evening. 'She's sleeping more than she was a week or two ago. She seemed a lot brighter then than she does now.'

'I don't think there's anything wrong. She has always been like this,' Nanny said. 'She'll be fine again in a day or so.'

Jessie accepted what she said. She didn't want to have the doctor out for nothing, but she wished that Harry was at home so she could ask for his opinion. Perhaps she was worrying over nothing. She'd been so sure Jack's pony would tumble when the jumps were raised and he'd managed the round quite easily in the end.

However, when Priscilla asked if she was coming to the farm to watch him the next morning she said that she wouldn't this time.

'I'll stay here with Catherine. Jack has you to take care of him.'

'Poor little love,' Priscilla said, looking sadly at Catherine who seemed sleepy and kept falling over on her knees. 'It's such a shame.'

'She was so much better,' Jessie said, her throat caught with emotion. 'I can't understand it.'

'Oh, she's always up and down,' Priscilla replied with a shrug. 'You worry too much about them, Jessie. You can't wrap children in cotton wool. Mine had their share of troubles when they were younger; they picked themselves up again. I don't believe in making too much fuss.'

Perhaps Priscilla was right, Jessie thought after she had gone. She hadn't really had that much experience with children, and all she'd done for them was instinctive, partly from her nursing training, and partly from a natural desire to love and protect.

Catherine was waking up at last, playing happily with her toys. She suddenly seemed bright and full of energy and Jessie laughed at herself. She was seeing demons behind every bush!

When Nanny came in she left her to watch over Catherine and went downstairs to fetch them all a nice drink of lemonade. It was a cool, bright day and she thought it would have been pleasant to walk to the farm after all. It was rather late for that now; Jack would be coming home soon, full of himself as usual.

As she passed the laundry room, Jessie heard a little cry. She stopped, hesitated, and then went in. Carter had Maggie up against the wall and was trying to kiss her. Maggie was struggling, fending him off as best she could.

'I don't think Maggie wants to be kissed. Would you mind leaving her alone, please?'

Carter turned as he heard her voice, a sneer on his face. 'It's just a little bit of fun. Maggie doesn't mind. She knows I wouldn't hurt her. She isn't a sourpuss like you.'

'Yes, I do mind,' Maggie said and thrust him out of her way. 'I've had enough of this and I'm telling Cook. She'll put you right.'

Carter glared at Jessie as the girl went out. 'Happy now? I wouldn't have raped her. I like the girl, that's all. It was just a kiss.'

'Why don't you ask her what she wants instead of just assuming she doesn't mind? Maggie liked you and I thought you cared about her – in the right way, not just as a bit of fun.'

'You're so high-minded, of course,' Carter said. 'Butter wouldn't melt in your mouth, would it? Except that I know what you're up to on the sly. You wait until Mary Kendle gets back. Once she gets a sniff of what has been going on behind her back you'll be out on your ear.'

'I don't have to listen to this,' Jessie said, turning away. 'You don't know what you're talking about.'

'Oh, don't I?' Carter grabbed her as she tried to leave, jerking her round and slamming her against the door. He leaned towards her and she caught the smell of beer on his breath. 'Well, let me tell you, Miss Holier Than Thou, I know exactly what's been going on in your room. I could tell your nasty little secret if I wanted.'

'Say what you like,' Jessie said, giving him a push. 'I really don't care what you do.'

She walked away, her heart beating madly. Had Carter been spying on her? If he had stood outside her room listening in the dark he could have heard her with Harry. But she thought he was just bluffing, just being unpleasant to punish her for spoiling his game with Maggie.

Carter was a nuisance but she was inclined to believe him when he said he wouldn't have raped Maggie. He was just one of those men who thought it was funny to catch girls and touch or kiss them. But Maggie didn't like it and it was time he was stopped. Cook would give him the rough side of her tongue, but it wasn't likely that he would be turned off. Lady Kendle relied on him to carry her downstairs and to take both her and Sir Joshua for little rides in the Daimler when the weather was pleasant. He had been with them for a long time and wouldn't be easy to replace. They would probably dismiss Maggie if she made too much fuss. Kitchen maids were easier to find.

Jessie went into the kitchen. Pam Bates had started work that morning and she was busy preparing vegetables at the kitchen sink. She smiled at Jessie but didn't say much, and Jessie realized she must be feeling very strange. She thought Pam was brave to start a new job so soon after her husband's terrible death, but she probably had no choice. The small pension she'd been given wouldn't keep her for long if she didn't work.

'I've just come for a tray of drinks for the nursery,' Jessie said. 'Shall I help myself?'

'You know where everything is,' Cook said. 'Sir Joshua has a few of his friends coming this evening so I'm busy today.'

'I thought you looked busy,' Jessie said. 'That sauce smells good – has it got wine in it?'

'Yes, champagne,' Cook said and beamed at her. 'It's a kind of custard I make for their pudding and serve cold. I'm afraid it will be something simple for the children this lunchtime. Will cold chicken and baked potatoes be all right?'

'I should think that would be fine,' Jessie said. 'I'll take the tray up then.'

She carried the jug of lemonade up to the nursery. Catherine came running to be taken up on her lap. She was thirsty and drank most of her lemonade down in one go.

'Well, I think I'll go and visit Lady Kendle,' Nanny said after she'd had her own drink. 'She was saying she might like to be pushed round the garden this afternoon, and she asked if I would like to walk with her and keep her company.'

'It would be lovely as long as you keep out of the shade,' Jessie said, going to the back window to look out at the court-yard. 'But the wind may be cold . . .' Something caught her eye. Someone was running towards the house, and Jessie could feel that odd prickling sensation at the base of her neck again. 'I wonder why Priscilla is in such a hurry – and where is Jack?'

'What do you mean?' Nanny came to the window. Priscilla was almost at the house now. Her hair was flying wildly and it was clear that she was distressed. Carter was in the yard cleaning the car and she grabbed hold of him, pointing frantically behind her and saying something that neither Jessie nor Nanny could hear. 'Something's happened. It's Master Jack . . .'

Carter threw his sponge in the bucket and jumped into the car. Priscilla got into the passenger seat immediately and he drove off as though the Devil was after him.

'Something has happened to Jack,' Jessie said, her face white. She was cold all over, shivering, and instinctively she knew that Jack must have fallen from his pony.

'Yes, I think you must be right.'

'I'm going to the farm,' Jessie said to Nanny. 'Look after Catherine. I can't take her with me this time.'

'But you can't do anything,' Nanny said, then, as she saw her face, she said, 'Go on then. You can't rest here and nor can any of us until we know for sure.'

Jessie hurried down the back stairs and out of the kitchen door. She knew from the shocked looks on the faces of Cook and Pam Bates that they had heard something but she couldn't wait to hear what they had to say. She ran across the cobbled yard and through the kitchen gardens, taking the short cut through the narrow lane at the back. When she was taking the children for walks they went through the meadow because it was prettier, but today she had no time to look at the view. All she could think was that something had happened to Harry's son. Jack must have put his pony at the jumps too fast or something. She didn't know how it had happened, but she was sure it was bad. Priscilla had been frantic with worry, and she'd needed the car – to take Jack to hospital?

She prayed to God that he was still alive. Jessie panted as she ran, her chest beginning to hurt as she pushed herself to the limit. She had to get there before they took Jack away. Neither Priscilla nor Carter knew how to treat an injured child. They could damage him just by moving him without proper care. Why hadn't they come for her? Harry would have, just as he had when Jed Wylie cut himself with the scythe. She had to get there before they moved Jack into the car.

Jessie had a stitch in her side but she ran on despite the

pain. As she reached the paddocks, she saw that she was too late. A small group of farm workers were still there, staring after the Daimler as it drew away. Jessie bent double as she tried to catch her breath.

One of them turned and saw her, coming towards her immediately.

'Master Jack put the jumps up while Mrs Bates was at the farm for a few minutes, miss. She came over to ask for a drink because Master Jack said he was thirsty. He must have done it while her back was turned. She's in a terrible state, blaming herself for leaving him.'

'What about Jack?' Jessie asked when she was able to speak again. Her chest still hurt and she was fighting for breath. 'What happened to him?'

'The pony refused at the second from last hurdle. It wasn't bought as a jumper. Captain Kendle never intended that, not for a year or two yet, that's what he said. He wanted a nice steady pony for the boy to ride.'

'But Jack – has he broken a leg or something?'

'I'm not sure, miss. He was unconscious when they rushed him off to the hospital. I think he might have hurt his wrist, because it looked awkward, but . . .' He faltered and glanced down as if he couldn't bear to look at her. 'I think he hurt his head the worst, miss.'

'Oh no!' Jessie stared at him. Head and neck injuries were the worst, and they could have done harm by moving his head without support. It was an easy mistake to make for anyone who didn't have any medical experience. 'Is there anyone with a car at the farm? Anyone who can drive?'

'No, miss, that's why Mrs Barrington had to run to the house and fetch Carter. Mr Goodjohn can drive but he's at the market today. Sorry, miss. If you were wantin' to get into town the next train is at two o'clock this afternoon.'

'I see, thank you,' Jessie said. 'In that case there is nothing I can do but go back to the house.'

'He'll be all right,' Nanny told her when they talked about it later. Jessie was giving Catherine her lunch. She couldn't touch anything herself; her stomach was churning. 'Jack is as tough as old boots, you'll see. They'll keep the lad for a while to check him over, but in a few days he'll be home and into trouble as usual.'

'I do hope so,' Jessie said. Her throat was tight and she felt close to tears, but there was nothing she could do. Lady Kendle had been told the situation and Sir Joshua had telephoned the hospital immediately. 'They said he was still unconscious when his grandfather rang. If only I'd been there when he fell. If only I had been there . . .'

'You couldn't have stopped him,' Nanny said. 'Miss Priscilla should never have left him alone. She knows what a monster he is.'

'Jack isn't a monster,' Jessie said, tears in her eyes. 'He's just a naturally high-spirited little boy, and it's my job to look after him.'

'You were worried about Catherine.'

'Yes, and she's fine,' Jessie said. 'I knew it was dangerous to let him jump those hurdles. The pony wasn't up to it. Harry didn't intend him to jump at this stage.'

Nanny gave her a hard look and Jessie blushed.

'You're Jack's nursemaid,' she said. 'You can only do so much. Miss Priscilla is his aunt and Captain Kendle had told her to go slowly with the child. If anyone is to blame, she is, not you.'

Jessie nodded. She had tried to warn against the jumping, but she ought to have said more. She ought to have told Jack's aunt that his father wouldn't want him to go so fast, but she hadn't considered it was her place – but she wished now that she had. She wished it so much that it hurt. She should have spoken out even if she'd been reprimanded for it. She couldn't bear the thought of that little boy lying unconscious in hospital – and she didn't know what she would do if he were seriously hurt.

'If it had been a broken leg it wouldn't have been so bad,' she said on a sob of grief. 'But it was a head injury and they moved him without a doctor being there. Why didn't they ask me to go with them?'

'I don't suppose Miss Priscilla gave it a thought,' Nanny said. 'She was frantic, you said so yourself. Imagine what she's going through at this moment. She adores Harry and Jack. She'll never be able to face her brother again if something . . . if the boy should be brain damaged.'

'He could die,' Jessie said. 'What will happen then? I don't think Harry can take it, Nanny. It was bad enough losing the workshops, but this – this is too much for anyone.'

'You're looking on the black side,' Nanny said. 'Miss Priscilla and Harry took a lot of tumbles between them. Apart from a broken arm once, neither of them suffered much harm. Jack will be as right as rain soon enough.'

Jessie couldn't comfort herself so easily. She knew how serious a fall like this could be and she was torn apart by her regret and grief. Why hadn't she been there? Why hadn't they taken her with them?

But Carter wouldn't have suggested it after the argument over Maggie, and Priscilla had been too upset to think clearly. Jessie prayed that Nanny was right, and that she was making too much fuss, but the premonition that had haunted her since she'd first seen Jack jumping over those hurdles was stronger than ever.

Jessie went to ask Lady Kendle if there had been any news. She shook her head and looked at her sadly.

'Priscilla telephoned an hour ago. She says there is no change as yet. She was trying to get through to France, but it's difficult to place a call. She says that if she can't get through she'll ring her husband and ask him to send a telegram or fly over if need be. It's the quickest way to reach Harry, though I think it's so dangerous – but George is very good at emergencies. I am sure he will find a way to reach Harry, through diplomatic channels if nothing else.'

'Would it be all right if I went to the hospital, ma'am? I've had a message to say that Mr Goodjohn is home from the market and will take me into the hospital if I want to go.'

'Yes, if you wish to,' Lady Kendle said, seeing the signs of strain in Jessie's face. 'I am certain Nanny can manage Catherine for a while. She is no trouble. Yes, get off now. I am sure Priscilla will be glad to see you. She must be out of her mind with worry over this.'

194

'Yes, ma'am. I am quite sure she is,' Jessie replied. 'I'll get changed and walk down to the farm.'

'I think there is a bicycle somewhere in the yard. You could probably borrow that if you like.'

Jessie thanked her and left to change into a clean dress. She decided against taking the bike and walked down to the farm, where the obliging farmer was only too pleased to give her a ride to the hospital.

'I just wish I'd been here to take you in sooner, Jessie,' he said. 'It's a terrible thing and no mistake. I can't imagine what got into Mrs Barrington's head, letting him raise the jumps like that.'

'I'm sure she didn't realize he had put them up even higher while she was gone,' Jessie said, but in her heart she agreed. Priscilla should never have started to teach Jack to jump without his father's permission.

The farmer's lorry was uncomfortable, bouncing over all the bumps in the road, but Jessie was grateful for the ride. She knew that there was very little she could do when she got to the hospital, but she wanted to be with Jack. It was breaking her heart to think of him lying there unconscious, and she didn't know how she could bear it. She had come to love Jack as if he were her own, and it was like being wrenched apart.

She asked for news at the reception desk and at first they said she couldn't see Jack, because only family were allowed to visit. She explained that she was Jack's nurse and had responsibility for him. She also told the girl that she had been a nurse in the war.

'I'll make some enquiries, miss.'

'Thank you.' Jessie waited anxiously while the girl went off. It seemed ages before she returned but at last she came back with welcome news.

'You can go up for a while, Nurse Hale,' she told Jessie at last. 'The boy's aunt is with him, but she has agreed to go out and leave him while you sit with him. The doctors have said there should only be one person with him at a time, because of the disruption to the ward.'

'I'll be very quiet,' Jessie said. 'I shan't disturb anyone, I promise.'

195

She walked up to the ward where Jack was being treated. It was a small one for patients in a critical condition and had only four beds.

Priscilla was waiting outside in the corridor for her to arrive. Her face was white and tense and she was clearly in a terrible state.

'Harry will never forgive me,' she said. 'I shouldn't have left Jack even for a minute, but he seemed so capable. The pony was jumping well and I thought it was safe . . .' She gave a little sob. 'Jack was so confident, so full of himself, and then he said he wanted a drink but he didn't want to leave Wellington so I went to fetch it. I had mine in the kitchen and I suppose I was chatting for five minutes . . .'

'You couldn't know what Jack would do while you were gone.'

'I should have guessed,' Priscilla said. 'He had been asking me to put the hurdle right up to the top. It wasn't just one notch higher, it was three, and the sudden change surprised Wellington. He refused and Jack went over his head. I saw it about to happen and I tried to stop him, but it was too late. Perhaps if I hadn't shouted . . .'

'You can't blame yourself,' Jessie said, though in her heart she knew Priscilla must blame herself, just as she was blaming herself for not being there. If she had taken Catherine to watch him she could have stopped Jack being so impetuous. She ought to have been there with him, even if she had carried Catherine all the way there and back. 'May I go in now?'

'Of course. I should have taken you with us, but I was in such a panic. I didn't think to fetch you. The doctor told me Jack could have suffered more damage because he wasn't moved correctly, but they aren't sure yet.'

'Yes, I know,' Jessie said. 'I ran all the way to the farm but it was too late. You had just gone.'

'I'll never forgive myself if . . .' Priscilla gave a sob and then blew her nose. 'Take no notice of me, Jessie. Go and see him.'

Jessie went into the ward. Jack was in the bed nearest the door so that the sister could keep an eye on him. She shook her head when Jessie asked if there had been any change.

Jessie sat on the chair beside the bed. The lights were shaded because all the patients in this ward were seriously ill. As yet there wasn't much they could do for Jack. Until he came to they wouldn't know whether or not he had suffered serious damage. He would already have had an X-ray, of course, but Jessie had only so much faith in things like that. She knew that they were still at a comparatively early stage in the development of the technique, and the results were not always as decisive as they might be. Broken bones were easy to detect but brain damage wasn't as clear. They would need to monitor the child and see what his reactions were when he woke up. *If* he woke up . . . But he had to, he had to! He mustn't die.

Jessie took his hand in hers, holding it to her face and then kissing it. 'Please don't die, my little darling,' she said. 'Please don't leave us all. We love you so much.'

There was no reaction, even when she stroked his forehead, not even the flicker of an eyelid. Her heart felt as if it were being torn in two and she didn't know how she could bear the pain. He looked so young, so vulnerable, and so beautiful. He was such a lovely child, a little angel.

Tears coursed down her cheeks, and she bent over him to kiss his forehead, stroking it again as she whispered to him of her love, his father's love and need of him.

'You can't die,' she whispered. 'You can't . . .'

Jack's eyelids flickered. Jessie felt her heart stop and then beat faster. She kissed him again, praying that he would open his eyes and look at her. His eyelids fluttered once more and he made a little moaning sound, but he didn't open his eyes.

Jessie left him and went to tell the sister that she had seen signs that he might return to consciousness within a short time.

'He didn't look at me,' she said. 'But he was aware of me stroking his forehead. I am almost sure of it.'

'Well, as a nurse you know that is a good sign,' Sister said. 'We mustn't hope for too much too soon, but he is strong and we can only pray and watch.'

'Yes, I know. I was so afraid that his spine might have been damaged when he was moved.'

'I think you can be reassured on that,' Sister said. 'He has a fractured wrist and head injuries. We don't know how bad they are at the moment, or what the consequences will be – we must just hope for the best.'

Jessie returned to the bed, sitting by Jack's side for another half an hour before she kissed him and left. There had been no further signs of a recovery and she could not pass on any encouraging news to Jack's worried aunt.

'Do you want to go home?' Jessie asked. 'I can stay for a few hours if you want to change and have a meal.'

'I couldn't eat a thing,' Priscilla said. 'They've given me several cups of tea. No, I think I'll stay here for a few hours longer. My husband managed to get through to Harry. He sent a telegram and had a reply. Harry is flying home this evening as soon as he can get a flight. My husband has arranged special emergency transport through the diplomatic service. With any luck he will be here in the morning.'

'I hope there will be better news by then,' Jessie said. It was only when she got to the foyer of the hospital that she wondered how she was going to get back to Kendlebury. The last train had gone and she had not brought any money for a taxi, though someone might take her if she promised to pay at the other end.

'Jessie, how is he?'

She was surprised as Carter came towards her.

'I think he's holding his own – that's all I can say at the moment. I didn't think you would still be here. Mrs Barrington is staying for a few hours yet and Captain Kendle may be home in the morning.'

'I came back when they told me you were here,' Carter said and looked at her oddly. 'I shouldn't have done what I did this morning – to Maggie or you. It was out of order.'

'It doesn't matter now. I just wished you'd sent for me earlier, before you brought Jack here.'

'We neither of us thought of it,' Carter said. 'Afterwards I remembered how you looked after Wylie's boy and I knew I should have waited for you. I'm sorry, Jessie.'

'As it happens it seems that no further harm was done,' Jessie said. 'Look, I don't want to be bad friends with you – can we just forget all the bother? There are more important things to worry about now.'

198

'Thanks for being decent about it,' Carter said. 'I'll take you home and then see if I'm needed. I may have to come back for Mrs Barrington later, but it all depends . . .'

Jessie nodded. Jack wasn't out of the woods yet by any means. It could still go either way.

Thirteen

Jessie found it almost impossible to sleep. She tossed and turned for ages, then got up and went down to the kitchen to make a cup of tea. She was just pouring it when Priscilla came in, followed by Carter. Harry's sister looked tired and drawn as she sat down.

'Do you think you could spare a cup for me?'

'Of course,' Jessie said. 'You should eat something. Shall I make you a sandwich? I think there's some cold salmon left over from your father's supper party.'

'I couldn't force it down. I wanted to stay at the hospital but they threw me out. Said I couldn't do anything and would be ill myself. I think I was getting in their way. They told me to go back tomorrow afternoon.'

'I suppose that's fair enough,' Jessie said. 'You would be in the way if they wanted to treat him.'

'A doctor came to look at him about an hour before we left. He said they might have to operate if there's no change by tomorrow – something about swelling on the brain.'

'Please God they don't have to do that,' Jessie said. She set the teapot down, closing her eyes against the sting of tears. 'Sometimes a blood clot is formed and puts pressure on the brain. It can be very dangerous. I hope it won't come to an operation.'

'I feel so guilty.' Priscilla leaned her elbows on the table, burying her face in her hands. 'Harry will hate me for this.'

Jessie felt her distress as a physical thing. She reached across the table and touched Priscilla's bowed head. 'It's as much my fault as yours. I should have been there. If I had been Jack couldn't have altered those jumps. I wouldn't have let him.'

Priscilla looked up, her face grey with grief. 'Thank you for offering to share the blame, Jessie, but we both know it was my fault. You were uneasy from the start. I should have watched him like a hawk. I'd forgotten how impetuous he was.'

They sat talking for a while longer but there was nothing to say. Jack's life was in the balance and they could hardly bear the pain. Neither of them dared to think what Harry would do if the boy died.

Jessie was up at her usual time despite her lack of sleep. She could feel the tension in the house. Everyone was affected. Cook, Maggie, Mrs Pearson, Alice, even Pam Bates felt the sense of fear that hung over the family.

As yet there was no news from the hospital. Carter told them that Sir Joshua had phoned at eight that morning but was told Jack was still unconscious.

'They are considering an operation,' Carter said. 'Apparently they think a blood clot may be pressing on the brain. I think they're waiting for his father to get there to give his permission.'

'What does that mean, Jessie?'

All eyes turned on her as she tried to explain that sometimes the cavity around the brain could be affected by swelling caused by a blood clot.

'Is an operation dangerous?' Maggie asked. Her eyes and nose were red. She had been crying for hours and looked awful.

'Yes, I'm afraid it is. All surgery carries risks, and anything affecting the brain requires very delicate work – but it could be the only way.'

'But won't that . . . affect him?' Cook asked, looking distressed. 'You know, the way Miss Cathy . . .'

'It might,' Jessie said. 'There is a very high risk of some impairment.'

Silence fell as they all contemplated such an outcome.

'It would kill his father,' Cook said. 'It might be better if he died.'

Jessie got up abruptly and left the kitchen. She couldn't

201

bear to hear them talk about Jack that way. She kept praying that a miracle would happen and he would wake up with little more than bruises and a fractured wrist.

When Jessie went in to dress Lady Kendle, she told her that Jack's father was now at the hospital.

'I believe he arrived in England during the night. George arranged a private flight to Torquay and he was driven to the hospital in the early hours of the morning. He managed a quick call to his father a few minutes ago. Harry said . . .' Her voice was muffled with emotion as she choked back a sob. 'He thought they might be about to operate.'

'Oh no,' Jessie said and tears began to slide down her cheeks. 'That's terrible news. Even if he lives . . .'

'You think he'll be damaged?' Lady Kendle nodded, her expression grim. 'We were afraid of that. I just don't know how Harry will cope if that happens. First Catherine and now . . .' She broke off, driven to close her eyes for a moment by the force of her anguish. 'We must be cursed as a family, wouldn't you say?'

'Surely not.' Jessie wiped her tears away. Crying wouldn't help. 'It was an accident.'

'Priscilla is desperate. She believes Harry will hate her. They were always so close.' Lady Kendle wiped her eyes with a lace handkerchief. 'I can't think how it will all end.'

'Perhaps Jack will come through this and be fine,' Jessie said, though she didn't sound convincing even to herself.

'You don't really believe that?'

Jessie hesitated, then shook her head. 'I'm not a doctor, but I've seen the results of similar operations and they have often been disappointing. The doctors do their best and one day they will do better, but they're still learning about the way the brain works. Not every surgeon could or would perform such an operation, because it is so difficult. I hoped Jack wouldn't need it – that he would wake up himself.'

'Then we must not hope for too much.' Lady Kendle blew her nose and lifted her chin, clearly determined to control her emotions. 'I shall be perfectly all right now, Jessie. Please go to Catherine. Priscilla said you were anxious about her yesterday.'

'She was very sleepy first thing but she seemed better later. This morning she asked for Jack twice. I am not sure what to tell her.'

'As little as possible, I imagine. She wouldn't understand. She will get used to his not being around in time – as will the rest of us.'

Jessie said nothing. Lady Kendle seemed to think the little girl had no feelings. Jessie knew that was wrong. Catherine might be backward and have a heart problem but she was already missing her brother.

The morning dragged on and on and still no one came to give them any news. Jessie kept busy but her mind was with Jack and his father, and her heart was aching for them both. The nursery clock seemed to tick menacingly as if measuring their heartbeats and outside the brilliance of a magical spring landscape was a mockery, reminding them of all they were in danger of losing.

Nanny sat knitting the socks she was making for Jack, as if she were determined that he would come home and need them. Jessie read to Catherine, cuddling her because she sensed the child's anxiety. Catherine kept looking round, searching for something and every now and then she said Jack's name.

'Soon, darling,' Jessie said, but a cold fear had settled about her heart and somehow she knew that Jack wouldn't be coming home.

It was nearly two o'clock that afternoon when Priscilla came to the nursery with the news they had dreaded. One look at her face told Jessie all she needed to know. She gave a sob of grief and covered her face with her hands as the tears trickled down her cheeks.

'They operated, but he died on the table,' Priscilla said. She was shocked, numbed, her eyes dark-shadowed through lack of sleep. 'There was nothing they could do, apparently.'

'Poor darling Jack,' Jessie choked on a sob. 'It's so cruel, so cruel.'

She felt overwhelmed by her grief, but also angry at the wicked waste of life. Why did it have to be this way? Jack was only a child. He shouldn't have died in a silly accident.

Sometimes Jessie felt there was no God. For how could He let this happen?

'Poor little lad,' Nanny said and put her knitting aside. She looked very old suddenly, her eyes sunken and dull. 'I don't know what Master Harry will do. This will kill him. He was so much better lately and now . . .' She broke off, her voice harsh with emotion.

'Yes, I know what he must be feeling,' Priscilla said. 'I feel awful. I don't know what to say to him.'

'Where is he?' Jessie asked, conquering her anger and grief as she thought of Harry's suffering. 'Have you seen him?'

'No. Mary said he wouldn't speak to anyone. When the doctor told him, he just walked out of the hospital without looking at her and without saying a word to anyone.'

'Mary – she was there?' Jessie was startled. Somehow she hadn't expected that.

'Yes, of course. She's Jack's mother. It's natural she would be there.'

Jessie made no reply. Only a few days earlier Priscilla had been saying that a divorce would be the best thing that could happen, now she was feeling sympathy for Harry's wife. Jessie wanted to scream that it was a waste of her pity. Mary hadn't loved her son. She had hardly bothered to see him.

'He hasn't come home?' she asked at last. 'Captain Kendle . . .'

'No, not yet,' Priscilla said and took out a cigarette. She lit it and inhaled deeply, her hands trembling. 'Knowing Harry he will go off on his own somewhere for hours – or days. It wouldn't be the first time, would it, Nanny?'

'No,' Nanny agreed. 'He disappeared when Master John died – and after his mother's fall. He was just a lad then. He'll come back this time, for the funeral.'

That awful word! Jessie hated the sound of it. She wanted to shut it out, to scream that it couldn't happen, they couldn't put her child in the cold ground. She couldn't believe that Jack was dead. She was numb, still in shock, still not really taking in what Priscilla had told them. Only a few hours ago she'd touched Jack, stroked his forehead, had hope that he might pull through. Now he had gone and she felt as though a part of her had died. Jack had become so dear to her, like her own child. He was the son she might have had if Robbie had lived.

Catherine was pulling at her knee. Jessie picked her up and took her into the bedroom, finding comfort in the routine of changing her. Catherine was soaking wet and anxious. She might not understand what had happened, but she was aware of changes, of something not quite as it should be.

Jessie put a dry nappy on her and then kissed her. She had been so worried that something might happen to Catherine, but it was Jack who had died. The pain she was feeling inside was hard to bear, but she could not imagine what Harry must be feeling.

Mary's presence in the house made itself felt almost at once. At first everyone felt sorry for her, but that lasted no more than a few hours. She did nothing but complain. No one could please her.

'She shouted at me,' Maggie said and blew her nose noisily. She had been crying constantly since the news of Jack's accident and her face was red and blotchy. 'She said if I couldn't stop sniffling I could go back to the kitchen and stay there because she didn't want to see my miserable face.'

'She's grieving,' Cook said. 'It was a terrible shock to her.'

'If she's grieving it's because she had to come home,' Alice muttered. 'I heard her on the telephone. She was complaining that her holiday had been cut short.'

'Well, I never!' Cook said staring in disbelief. 'Can she really be so unnatural? Surely you got that wrong, Alice. It's just nerves, I expect.'

'Nerves or not, she's a bitch,' Alice said. 'I shan't stop here now she's home. I'm leaving at the end of the week and I've told Mrs Pearson.'

'Leaving?' Cook was bewildered. 'You can't do that, Alice.'

'Yes, I can,' Alice said and went out without another word.

'So it's true, then,' Cook said and sighed heavily. 'The lass has got herself into bother. Carter suspected as much but I didn't believe him.'

205

Jessie didn't answer. She went after Alice, catching her at the top of the back stairs. 'Are you really going, Alice?'

'I've got to, Jessie. She lost her temper with me,' Alice said. 'Can you imagine what she would be like if she knew? I never did like her and now I can't stand the selfish bitch. Cook feels sorry for her, but she doesn't know; she doesn't see her as much as I do. I've heard the rows between her and Captain Kendle. I've heard the way she speaks to him, belittles him. Mary Kendle doesn't care that her son died or that her husband is out of his mind with grief – all she thinks about is herself.'

Jessie didn't reprimand her. In her heart she agreed with every word though she wouldn't say it.

'You haven't heard about Captain Kendle – where he is or when he's coming home?'

'Madam was telling someone that he'd gone off and left her to arrange everything. She said it was typical of him, that he was weak and she was sick of doing it all herself. Then she blamed him for buying the pony in the first place.' Alice shook her head. 'If I were him I would never come back. They all treat him as if he were nothing but a workhorse and she is the worst. What has the poor sod got to come home to now?'

Jessie didn't answer. She was praying that he would come to her so that they could comfort each other. Surely he must know that she had loved Jack, that she was grieving too. If Harry loved her he would come to her, wouldn't he?

He'd said he loved her, wanted to marry her – but that was before his son's death. Was he blaming her for not being there to look after Jack? Was she just a servant he had tumbled to amuse himself? No, she wouldn't believe that.

Jessie tried to keep the doubts at bay over the next couple of days. Harry hadn't come home, but his family didn't seem concerned. He would come when he was ready, they all thought. He would be home for his son's funeral.

Jessie found his absence hard to bear, but she knew she mustn't expect too much. Harry was wild with pain, out of his mind. Anyone who lost a child would feel the way he did, especially after what he'd been through. It must have brought

206

back memories of his brother's tragic accident. He couldn't cope, couldn't face his pain, and so he'd gone off like a wounded beast to lick his wounds in private.

All Jessie could do was wait for him to come back.

'And where were you when my son was falling off his horse?' Mary Kendle asked, an angry, bitter note in her voice as she looked at Jessie. It was the day before Jack's funeral and she had summoned Jessie to the study to accuse her of neglect. 'Priscilla told me she went to fetch him a cool drink because he was thirsty. If you'd been there as you are paid to be you could have fetched the stupid glass of lemonade and none of this would have happened.'

Jessie had blamed herself time and again, but to have the accusation flung at her in such a cruel way knocked the breath out of her. For a moment she stared at her employer, unable to answer.

'I had stayed at home because Catherine seemed unwell.'

'Catherine was perfectly well,' Mary snapped. 'Nanny told me she was sleepy. My daughter is always sleepy. You could have left her at home with Nanny. She is quite capable of looking after her. It was your fault that Priscilla had to leave my son to fetch that drink – and I am considering your position here. It depends on Mother. As far as I am concerned you are no longer needed in this house.'

'No longer needed . . .' Jessie stared at her in disbelief. How could Mary Kendle be so cruel? Jessie loved both the children and this was like being torn apart, piece by piece. She had lost Jack and now she was to lose Catherine too. 'But Catherine needs me. She is making progress. The doctor said—'

'I am well aware what he said, thank you,' Mary cut her off abruptly. 'I also know that she is never going to be more than a useless imbecile. I see no point in employing you for her benefit.'

'Lady Kendle . . .'

'Mother says you are useful to her,' Mary said. 'But she might change her mind when I tell her that you have been sleeping with her son.' Mary's eyes flashed with spite as she saw Jessie's flush. 'Did you imagine I wouldn't know? I knew as soon as he told me he wanted a divorce – which I shall not give him, of course. I have no intention of being replaced by a nursery maid.'

'Captain Kendle didn't tell you that,' Jessie said, her head raised proudly.

'He didn't need to,' Mary replied coldly. 'I saw the change in him at once and I knew why. Don't imagine I am jealous. If he hadn't asked for a divorce you could have carried on with your nasty little affair as long as you pleased. But I intend to be the next Lady Kendle and no little slut is going to take that away from me.'

'You're not exactly innocent, are you?' Jessie said, anger making her careless. 'Supposing I tell Harry that I saw you with a man on the beach? You were kissing him—'

'You impertinent slut!' Mary said, took a step towards her and slapped her hard across the face. 'You give me no choice. You will leave my house today. Mrs Pearson will give you six weeks' wages and Carter will drive you to the station.'

Jessie stared at her. Her hands clenched at her sides. She was tempted to strike her back, but held her temper in check.

'I am not leaving here before Harry comes home.'

'You will do as you are told,' Mary said. 'If you do not leave now I shall summon the police and tell them that you have stolen items belonging to me. I think you would experience difficulty in finding work after that. Besides, Harry will choose me when it comes to it. He cannot afford to divorce me. It's only my money keeping this wretched estate afloat.'

'I shall speak to Lady Kendle,' Jessie said, her head high, but even as she left the room she knew it was useless. Mary's word was law in this house and though Lady Kendle had found her useful, she would not support her once she knew that Harry had asked his wife for a divorce so that he could marry Jessie.

'She dismissed you?' Nanny stared at Jessie in disbelief. 'But she wouldn't. Not now, not today. Even Mary couldn't be that cruel – could she?'

'She blames me for Jack's accident. I was paid to look after

208

him and I wasn't there. In a way she's right. I should have been with him. I could have left Catherine with you.'

'You were worried about her,' Nanny said, distressed. She had become fond of Jessie in the past months. Always so helpful and kind, taking on more than her share of the work; it wouldn't be the same without her. 'Have you spoken to Lady Kendle about this?'

'I can't,' Jessie said. 'Mrs Kendle threatened me. She said that she would accuse me of theft if I didn't leave now. I refused to leave before I had spoken to Captain Kendle, but she could make it difficult for me to find work – and she would. Besides . . .' Jessie left the rest unspoken. It was impossible to tell Nanny about Mary's threats to expose her as Harry's lover – or of her own doubts.

Three days had passed without a word from Harry. Jessie was afraid that he had turned against her, blaming her for the accident as Mary did. Or perhaps he had never really loved her. He might be glad to find her gone when he got back.

'I shall give my notice in,' Nanny said, recalling her thoughts to the present. 'I shall go and live with my sister. I can't stay here if you're leaving, Jessie.'

'You must do what is best for you,' Jessie said, knowing full well that Nanny couldn't manage Catherine alone. 'But please stay with Catherine until they find a new girl for her. She needs loving and she's missing her brother.'

'It's you she'll miss,' Nanny said. 'You've been a mother to that child.'

'I love her as much as if she had been my own. I can't bear to think what may happen to her when we're both gone.'

'I'll stay for a while. But only until they replace me. I'm too old, Jessie. I should have gone years ago.'

Jessie had to agree. It wasn't fair to expect Nanny to stay on for ever, but it made her feel sad for Catherine. Who would love the little girl when Nanny had gone? Her mother certainly didn't, and Harry . . . He had seemed to care but Jessie couldn't be sure how he would react. Jack had been his wonderful, clever, lively son. Catherine could never take Jack's place. If Harry was bitter he might turn against her, neglect her.

It broke Jessie's heart to think of Catherine's distress after she'd gone. She hesitated, wondering if she should put her case to Lady Kendle after all, but when Mrs Pearson brought her money to her and told her Carter was waiting, Jessie knew there was no hope.

She cuddled Catherine one last time, her heart breaking. What would Catherine do when all the familiar faces were no longer there? It hurt too much to think of her silent suffering and bewilderment, and Jessie was close to tears when she handed the child back to Nanny.

'Look after her, please.'

'I'll take care of her for as long as I can, but it's you she needs.' Nanny was upset and angry. Life was unfair, especially for girls in Jessie's situation, and there was nothing she could do about it.

'You won't forget my letter?'

'Of course not. You'd better go now. Catherine is beginning to wonder.' Jessie nodded. She could see that the child was anxious, sensing something she did not understand.

'I'm sorry you've had to leave,' Mrs Pearson said as Jessie came down the stairs. 'But I suppose your family comes first.'

'What do you mean?' Jessie was bewildered.

'You're going home because your aunt's ill. Mrs Kendle told me.'

Jessie realized that Mary had given a false reason for her departure. She almost denied it but then decided to keep silent. She couldn't tell Mrs Pearson the real reason for her dismissal. Nanny knew the truth and she would give Harry the letter Jessie had left for him. Perhaps it was best if the others believed she had left of her own accord. Maggie had threatened to walk out once before and the family would find it difficult enough to manage as it was.

Jessie said goodbye to Cook and the others. They all said they would miss her and Alice promised to come and visit her in London one day.

'I should like that,' Jessie told her. 'And I'm sorry if my leaving like this means extra work for you all.'

'You did your share while you were here,' Cook said. 'I don't blame you for not wanting to stay now.'

Jessie shook her head. She was too upset to say very much.

If she had she might have blurted out something she ought not to reveal.

'I shall miss everyone,' was all she permitted herself to say.

Carter was waiting for her outside. He took her case and put it in the boot of the car.

'I'll take you into Torquay,' he said. 'It will save you the extra fare.'

Jessie thanked him as he opened the back door for her to get in. She did so without a word and was grateful that he said nothing more throughout the drive. It was taking her all her time to keep back the tears. He carried her case to the ticket office at the station, set it down and then looked at her oddly.

'I'm sorry you're going. It's unfair. Good luck, Jessie.'

Had he heard something? Jessie sensed he knew the truth but she didn't comment; Carter always seemed to know everything.

'Thank you for bringing me here. Look after them, Carter.'

'I always have,' he said and went off without another word.

Jessie checked the times of the trains. It seemed that she had missed the fast one and the next available stopped at all the country stations. It would take forever to get back to London.

'You would do better to stay overnight and take the morning train, miss,' the friendly desk clerk told her.

'Stay overnight?' Jessie considered this for a moment. Why not? She was free to do exactly as she pleased. She could take a room at a small guesthouse and then she could go to the funeral. As a servant of the house she might not have been permitted to attend, but no one could stop her now. She no longer worked for the Kendles. They couldn't tell her what to do any more.

She would have to be careful, of course, to make sure the family didn't see her. She would sit right at the back of the church, choose a pew behind a stone pillar where she couldn't be seen. And she would pay her respects at Jack's grave when the family had gone. It didn't take Jessie long to find a pleasant guesthouse that had a room to let for two nights.

'Are you on holiday, miss?' the woman who ran it asked.

211

'No. I was working near here but I left my job. I thought I would take a little holiday before I went home.'

'Well, why not?' the woman said and smiled at her. 'I'm Bess Thompson. I don't need anyone myself, but there are several opportunities at the moment, if you don't mind housework. It's the Easter holiday season, you see. Everyone needs extra help for a few weeks of the year. Easter, Whitsun and the summer most of all.'

Jessie looked at her in surprise. 'I hadn't considered looking for a job here. Is it really that easy to find one?'

'Just for a few weeks of the year. It's like a madhouse, see, with so many guests and so much to do. My sister needs help in her kitchen at the moment, just for the washing up. She has a guesthouse just round the corner from me. I should think she'd be glad to take you on. It's just temporary, for a few weeks, mind.'

Jessie thanked her and said she would think about it.

She left her suitcase in the neat room upstairs, with its matching blue-flowered bedspread and curtains, shining woodwork and plain brown carpet. Then she went out for a walk without bothering to unpack; that could wait for later. She needed to get some air, be by herself for a while.

The town was much busier than the last time she'd come, because she hadn't bothered to take her afternoon off since the argument over that silly tea dance, preferring to snatch an hour for herself now and then when she could.

She wandered around the shops, lingering the longest in a craft shop selling beautifully made baskets and finally choosing one intended for needlework as a gift for her aunt.

'That was made locally,' the woman told her. 'Unfortunately, we might not be able to get any more. The man who made them is having to give up because he can't afford the rent of his premises.'

'That would be a dreadful shame,' Jessie said. 'Something individual like this is really nice to have.'

After buying her basket she left the shop, deserting the crowded streets and walking up the hill that led to one of the main hotels; beyond that lay the winding cliff path with its spectacular views out over the sea. It was from there that she had seen Mary Kendle with her lover that day. If he had been her lover, of course. Jessie had never been sure, but the accusation had brought an angry reaction from Mary, so it might well have been true.

Tears were stinging Jessie's eyes as she walked. She blinked and rubbed her hand over her face, trying to keep back the storm of grief that overcame her. But it was too powerful for her and she sat down on a bench halfway down the cliff path, letting her grief flow out as she wept.

'Is something wrong, miss? Can I help?'

Jessie looked up into the face of a stranger. She took out her handkerchief and wiped her face, forcing a smile.

'No, thank you,' she said. 'There's nothing anyone can do.'

'I'm from the Salvation Army,' the woman said. She took a card from her pocket and offered it to Jessie. 'If you're in trouble we may be able to help. You won't do anything silly, will you? Nothing is ever quite as bad as it seems.'

'Isn't it?'

'We're always there to help.'

'Thank you,' Jessie said and took the card because she didn't want to cause offence. 'But I'm really not in any trouble, just unhappy.'

'Remember that God is always there to help.'

'Is He?' Jessie stood up. She was suddenly angry. 'If He's the same God who lets a little boy die from a stupid accident, then I don't care to know about him,' she said and strode off without waiting for the woman to reply.

Jessie returned to the guesthouse and ordered tea. She ate tiny cucumber sandwiches and sponge cakes, then went to her room to unpack her case and write a letter to her aunt. She would tell her that she had left Kendlebury Hall and that she was going to stay in Torquay for a little while, but she wouldn't tell her the rest of her news until she saw her.

Jessie waited until the church was almost full before slipping in at the back. No one seemed to notice her and she was able to hide behind a large carved stone pillar. When the funeral music was played, she hid behind the massive column until

213

the family had passed. Harry and Carter were carrying the small coffin on their shoulders; Sir Joshua and Mary walked behind. It seemed that Mary Kendle had not invited any of her friends to her son's funeral. She couldn't see Lady Kendle with them, but perhaps she hadn't managed to come; it would be difficult with her chair.

Harry's face was deathly pale. He looked as if he hadn't slept since he heard the news and his eyes were red-rimmed with weeping. Jessie's heart went out to him and she wished that she could go to him as he sat down, sit by him and slip her hand into his. She couldn't see Mary once they were sitting down, but she kept her eyes on the back of Harry's head and she sensed his deep misery. It made her heart ache so much she wanted to cry out.

Throughout the service she could hear a drizzle of rain against the brightly coloured windowpanes of the old church. Even the weather was in mourning, Jessie thought, suffused with grief. Tears ran down her cheeks as Harry got up to say a few words about his son.

'He was a ray of sunshine in all our lives,' Harry said, his voice almost breaking. 'God saw fit to take the sunshine away . . .'

Jessie didn't know if he said any more after that. She closed her eyes, unable to bear the waves of pain and hurt that washed over her as she absorbed Harry's grief into herself. She hardly knew what was going on around her, but then the congregation was standing and the coffin was being taken outside.

Jessie sat on in church as everyone filed out, some to join the family as the child was laid in the ground, some to go home to their own families. Jessie sat on until the last, then she slipped out and found a spot where she could see the grave but not be seen by the man who was still standing there alone, his head bowed. He looked absolutely defeated and Jessie's heart bled for him. She longed to go to him, almost did, and then Sir Joshua came back and took him by the arm, leading him away.

Jessie waited until she was sure the cars had gone, then she walked towards the open grave. The diggers were just beginning to fill it in but stopped respectfully as she walked forward, allowing her a moment to throw her rose on to the coffin.

'Goodbye, my darling,' she said. 'Sleep in peace, Jack.'

Tears were sliding down her cheeks as she turned and walked away towards the railway station.

Fifteen

Jessie stayed in Torquay for three weeks, then, when she was sick for the third consecutive morning, she wrote to her aunt and told her she would be coming home at the end of that week.

She was going to have Harry's child! The realization was like a douche of cold water, bringing her to her senses in a flash. She had lost herself in drudgery these past weeks, scarcely leaving the kitchen of Mrs Cuthbert's guesthouse as she fought to control her grief. For a while she had wanted only to numb the pain that had threatened to overwhelm her since Jack's funeral. The sight of Harry's lonely grief had been more than she could bear, but now she knew that she had to face the future.

Jessie believed that Aunt Elizabeth wouldn't turn her away. She was luckier than most girls in her situation. Her aunt would be upset for her sake, but she wouldn't condemn and she would do all she could to help her.

'I shall be sorry to see you go,' her employer said when she told her she was leaving, but accepted her decision with resignation. Girls came and went in this job and it was part of running a boarding house. 'If you're down here next year I'll be glad to have you again.'

Jessie smiled and told her she didn't think she would be back the following year. It was a hard, thankless job and the wages were shamefully low, but she had been glad of aching feet and legs when she went to bed, glad that she was too tired to do anything other than fall asleep. There would be plenty of time to think when she got home.

'I knew there had to be something,' Elizabeth Pottersby said as she looked across the kitchen table at Jessie. 'When you told me you'd left Kendlebury Hall and were staying in Torquay for a while, I wondered why you didn't come home.'

'I needed some time to think,' Jessie told her. 'I didn't even know I was pregnant when I left the family. That wasn't the reason I didn't come home straight away, Auntie. I just couldn't bear the pain of losing the children.' She hadn't told her aunt about going to the funeral or the way seeing Harry standing there alone by the grave had torn her apart.

'You say Captain Kendle made no attempt to contact you?' Her aunt frowned. 'You don't think that he took the coward's way out – letting his wife dismiss you?'

'Harry isn't a coward,' Jessie said. 'He's angry with me. He blames me for not being with Jack that day. If I had been it wouldn't have happened and Harry's son would still be alive.'

'You can't know that, Jess,' her aunt said and looked at her sadly. Jessie wasn't a fool, but she may have given her heart too easily this time. It was understandable. Her position with the children had made her vulnerable and some men took advantage of that. 'If you'd prevented Jack from putting the jumps higher that time he would have found some way to do what he wanted. When someone is determined they usually do what they want in the end.'

'Perhaps,' Jessie said. 'I'm sure that Harry went off as he did because he was in such turmoil. I don't know how he felt when he came home and discovered I'd gone. He may have been relieved. Mary wouldn't divorce him. I warned him of that in the first place, but he wouldn't listen.'

'So now you've come back and there's a child on the way. It's a pickle you've landed yourself in, Jess, and no mistake.'

'I know.' Jessie looked rueful. 'I know I've been a fool and that I should have known better – but I loved him and . . .'

'You thought it might be your last chance for a bit of happiness, your last chance to know what love was all about?' Elizabeth nodded her understanding. 'You regretted that you never had that with Robbie, didn't you?' Jessie agreed and her aunt smiled. 'I can't blame you for wanting some happiness, love. You've had a rough deal. There are hundreds of women like you. The war took their men and there's little chance of them finding another. A whole generation was more or less wiped out. In your place a lot of others would have done the same.'

'Harry loved me, I know he did,' Jessie said. 'I never believed that we could actually make a life together, even when he promised it to me. I knew that it was just a dream, but for a while I allowed myself to dream. He didn't try to deceive me, Auntie. He really meant to do it – but he's lost everything. I don't know how he feels now.'

'I'm more interested in how you feel,' her aunt said. 'What do you want to do, Jess?'

'I want to keep the child,' Jessie said. 'I don't want to have it adopted. I know the Sally Army would help, but I want to keep my child. If you don't feel you can have us here I'll find somewhere to live before then.'

'That's a daft thing to say. If I didn't know that you had to make the offer I'd be insulted. Where should your child be born if not in your home?'

'Oh, Auntie,' Jessie said and went round the table to hug her. 'What have I done to deserve you?'

'I've no idea,' Elizabeth said and gave her a little push. 'Don't smother me, Jess. That's settled then, and the teashop will be open in a week's time so you'll be working there until it becomes too difficult. We might have to get you a wedding ring when the baby is born, to satisfy the old tabbies, but otherwise I see no problem.'

'Thank you,' Jessie said. 'And thank you for not telling me all the things you were entitled to say.'

'It's all water under the bridge now,' Elizabeth said and smiled. 'It will be nice having a child in the house again.'

'So you're back then?' Eddie Robinson leered at her as she went into the suffocating heat of the bakery to fetch a tray of bread. It was opening day at the teashop and her aunt had ordered a special lot of baking that morning. 'Thought you were settled for life down there. What happened?'

'I changed my mind, that's all,' Jessie said giving him a cool stare. Eddie hadn't changed and she knew she would

218

have to put up with impertinent looks and comments from him once her condition started to show, but it was a part of the price she had to pay for taking her brief time of happiness with Harry.

She carried the tray back to the house, the freshly baked bread covered by a thin muslin cloth. Aunt Elizabeth had done a lot of baking herself that morning and trays of her special cakes were cooling on the pine table in the kitchen. It was all being collected together so that the man who worked for Archie at the bookshop could deliver it for them in his van.

'Archie said it would be no trouble,' Elizabeth told her when she asked how they were going to transport all the food daily. 'I was going to hire someone to deliver for me, but Archie said his assistant would do it for a few shillings. Apparently, he does some deliveries for Archie too and it will all fit in together nicely.'

'Have you met his assistant?'

'Yes, once or twice when I've popped into the shop. I always take Archie a few cakes once a week, as you know, Jess. His assistant seems a nice enough young man – though I hope he gets that ink off his fingers before he carries my trays.'

'Ink?' Jessie was puzzled. 'Why should he have ink on his fingers?'

'Archie says he does a bit of printing for him in the room at the back,' Elizabeth said. 'Leaflets telling customers what they can find in the shop, I expect. He seems a lot busier these days, Jess, people in and out most days.'

'The leaflets must be working,' Jessie said and dismissed it from her thoughts.

However, when the small black van arrived a few minutes after her return from the bakery and the driver came to the door to collect the bread and cakes, Jessie began to think again. It was the man she had seen in Archie's shop before she went down to Kendlebury, the man she had shared her lunch with on the train and met again in Torquay at that tea dance.

'Oh, hello,' Paul Smith said and smiled awkwardly at her as she answered the door. 'It is you. I wondered when Archie

Thistle told me you were living with Mrs Pottersby again. I work for Archie now.'

'Yes, so I understand. My aunt was saying she hoped you had washed the ink off your fingers. We were wondering about those leaflets you print for Archie, but I don't suppose we have to wonder any more – do we? I've read some of the leaflets you distributed in Torquay.'

Paul frowned, his eyes narrowing as she spoke angrily. 'Archie isn't involved in any of that,' he said. 'Listen, Jessie. I heard about what happened down there and I'm sorry about that fire. That wasn't my idea. I give you my word. It was some local hothead who went too far, that's all.'

'That's all?' Jessie was furious. 'Do you know that a man lost his life – and Captain Kendle lost all the money he had invested in that workshop? And don't say he could afford it, because he couldn't. It may well have ruined him.'

'Believe me, I was angry when I heard what had happened. We can do without that sort of thing. I didn't want that to happen, you have to believe me, Jessie. We need people to listen and learn, to make peaceful protests – that kind of behaviour sets the cause back years.'

'Has Paul come?' Elizabeth was at the door. 'Well, don't keep him standing there, Jessie. We haven't any time to waste.'

Jessie turned away, her face flushed. She still felt very angry with Paul Smith, knowing that the leaflets he had printed and distributed had been a major cause of the fire at Harry's work-shops. He was indirectly responsible for the death of Pam Bates's husband and Harry's loss, however much he denied it. But there was very little she could do about it for the moment. Archie had given him work so he must know what he did for the unions, perhaps he even supported it.

Jessie pushed her angry thoughts to the back of her mind. For the moment there was the teashop to think about. Her aunt had put a lot of money into setting it up and she needed it to be a success.

'Well, I think we can say that that went very well,' Elizabeth Pottersby said as she locked the door behind the last customer. 'We're all but out of bread and there isn't a cake left in sight.'

'Except this slice of apple pie, which I'm having,' Jessie said and popped it into her mouth, biting into it with a sigh of satisfaction. 'Of course it was always going to be a success, Auntie. How could it not be, with your baking? We shall have them queuing up to order before long.'

'I was a bit worried,' her aunt confessed. 'The profits from the bakery have been dropping a little recently, but this will soon put me on my feet again.'

Jessie was thoughtful. She knew her aunt trusted Eddie Robinson implicitly, said he was the best baker she'd ever had work for her, but Jessie wasn't so sure. She had never liked or trusted the man and she wouldn't put it past him to cheat her aunt – but perhaps that was just because she hated the way he looked at her. She mustn't make hasty judgements, as she had earlier that day.

Having had time to think it over, Jessie's temper had cooled. Paul Smith's leaflets were intended to make the workers of the country unite, and that was surely both necessary and worthwhile. Things had been unfairly balanced on the side of the employer for too many years, and that was wrong. What had happened at Harry's workshops was also wrong, but that didn't make Paul responsible – or Archie for giving him a job.

Jessie and her aunt were pleasantly tired as they took the tram home, walking the last few yards to their house. Unlocking the door, Elizabeth bent to pick up a letter from the mat as she went inside. She glanced at the name written on it and passed it to Jessie.

'It's for you, love, and delivered by hand.'

'I don't know the writing,' Jessie said and wrinkled her nose as she smelled perfume. 'I've smelt that before . . . it's the kind of scent Priscilla usually wears. Do you think it can be from her?'

'I don't know. Why don't you open it?'

'Why would she write to me?' Jessie asked. She sat down at the table and slit the envelope with a knife as her aunt moved the kettle on to the hotplate over the fire. 'Yes, it is from her . . .' She read swiftly. 'Priscilla is asking if I have seen Harry. She says he had a terrible row with Mary the night of the

funeral and then walked out. They haven't seen him since . . .'
Jessie turned the page. 'She says that she thinks he would have
strangled his wife if she hadn't stopped him, and that Mary
has gone to France. She told Priscilla that Harry had run mad
and . . . she wasn't coming back to that house ever again. She
didn't take Catherine with her. She doesn't want her.'

'Well, I never,' Elizabeth said and sat down. She shivered
as a chill went down her spine. 'I never heard of such goings
on. A mother abandoning her child like that! What a wicked
woman she must be. They must be a strange family, Jess. It
may be just as well that you left when you did.'

'I didn't leave, Mary dismissed me,' Jessie reminded her.
'They must be in terrible trouble down there, Auntie. Mary's
money was keeping them afloat. I don't know what they will
do without her.'

'That's hardly your affair, is it? Why did Captain Kendle's
sister think you might know where he is?'

'I think Priscilla knew there was something between us,'
Jessie said. 'I'm fairly sure she did. She's asked if we can
meet. She is in London for another three days and then she
goes back to Yorkshire.'

'Do you want to see her?' Elizabeth was doubtful. 'You're
putting all that behind you, Jess. Wouldn't it be better to just
say no – tell her that you don't want to know?'

'I couldn't do that,' Jessie said. 'I care about them; Catherine
and Lady Kendle and Nanny and the others – and I love Harry.
I always shall, no matter what.'

'But he knows where you are, Jessie. If he wanted to see
you . . .'

'I know.' Jessie folded the letter and put it in her pocket.
She had thought the same thing many times as she lay sleep-
less in her bed. 'I've told myself that a thousand times since
I came home, but it doesn't change the way I feel. I love him
and I want to help his family if I can – besides, I'm worried
about him. Where could he have gone all this time? And why
did he go?'

'Now don't start thinking like that! I can see what's going
on in your mind, Jessie. Even if the quarrel with his wife was
over you, he hasn't come to look for you, has he?'

222

'No, he hasn't,' Jessie said. 'Look, I'm going to think about this, Auntie. Priscilla has given me her telephone number. I'll ring her tomorrow and hear what she has to say.'

'Are you sure you don't mind me using your telephone, Archie?' Jessie asked the next morning when she went into the shop. 'I could use the one at the bakery, but it's so hot in there.'

'Of course you are welcome to use mine. Surely you know that, Jessie.'

'Yes.' She blushed slightly as she saw the look in his eyes. Archie had asked her out a couple of times since she'd been home but so far she had said no. It wasn't fair to string him along in the circumstances. 'It's very kind of you.'

'Anything you want, anytime.'

Jessie went into the little box-like room just off the shop to make her telephone call. She was conscious of the man in the back room setting his printing press, but she pushed the door to so that he wouldn't be able to hear her conversation.

Her heart caught as she heard Priscilla's voice at the other end of the line. 'Yes, Priscilla Barrington speaking.'

'It's Jessie – Jessie Hale.'

'You got my letter? I'm so angry with you, Jessie. Why on earth did you go off like that without a word to Mother or me? She was terribly upset, and Harry . . . He nearly went off the deep end!'

'Harry was upset because I left?'

'Well, what would you think? Leaving Catherine like that at such a time. It was very bad of you, Jessie.'

'You don't imagine I wanted to do it?'

'I know your aunt was ill, but surely Catherine and Harry came first in the circumstances.'

'My aunt wasn't ill. Mary threw me out. She said that if I refused to leave at once she would tell the police that I had stolen from her – and she would have told your mother that I had been sleeping with Harry.'

For a moment there was stunned silence at the other end.

'If that's the truth, it's no wonder Harry nearly killed her. He must have got it out of her somehow. I had no idea. We

223

told him you'd had to leave for your aunt's sake and he was angry and upset, but then something happened. I think Nanny gave him a letter . . . from you, I suppose.'

'Yes, of course. Nanny knew the truth and I wanted Harry to know. It broke my heart to leave – and when I saw Harry at the funeral I felt terrible. I wanted to go to him, to comfort him – but how could I?'

'You were there? Mother thought she saw you at the back of the church but I said she must be wrong.'

'Lady Kendle was there? I didn't see her.'

'She was brought in at a side door because of the chair. You probably couldn't see from the back of the church.'

'No. I was behind a stone column. I couldn't see much but then I didn't want to be seen.' Jessie paused. 'Does Harry blame me because I wasn't there when Jack fell?'

'No, of course not. It was my fault and I told him so. I'm not sure he will ever forgive me,' Priscilla said, a little sob in her voice. 'But I shall have to live with that – what I can't understand is where he is. Have you seen him?'

'Only at the funeral. I didn't speak to him and he didn't see me.' Jessie felt anxious. She couldn't believe that Harry would stay away from his home all these weeks. 'Where can he be? I know he has gone off before – but this is rather a long time, isn't it?'

'Yes, too long. I'm really worried about him, Jessie. I've never seen him as low as he was after the funeral, even when he was wounded at the end of the war. At first I thought he might have come to you, but there was no message and I knew I had to get in touch with you. Now that we've spoken I've got a horrible feeling that something is really wrong.'

'What do you mean?' Jessie shivered. 'You don't think he would . . . kill himself?' Alice's words after Jack's death rang in her head. What had Harry to live for now?

'I don't know,' Priscilla said. 'I really don't know. I'm worried about my parents. Alice has left them and Catherine is restless all the time. She screams and hits anyone who tries to comfort her. Nanny can't cope with her. My mother wasn't well when I left her, but I had to come home because of the

224

children and my husband. I know this is an awful cheek, but you wouldn't go back, would you?'

'To Kendlebury?' Jessie hesitated. 'I've started working for my aunt in her teashop. She needs me.'

'Catherine needs you more and so does Mother. Anyone can work in a teashop, Jessie.'

'But your mother . . . she might not want me around when she knows.' Jessie took a deep breath. 'I'm having a child, Priscilla.'

'Harry's? Yes, of course it is. Did Mary know? Is that why she got rid of you while she had the chance?'

'No, she didn't know,' Jessie said. 'I didn't know myself until after I left Kendlebury. But you see how difficult . . .'

'Stuff and nonsense!' Priscilla said. 'Mother may pull a face at first but inside she'll be pleased there's another baby coming, especially if . . . But we shan't get morbid. No doubt Harry will turn up when he's ready.'

'Supposing he doesn't want me to be there when he does?'

'He has a right to know about the child. Were you just going to forget all about him?'

'You know I couldn't do that. I love him and Catherine. It tore me apart to leave when I did.'

'Then go back, Jessie, please – just for a little while, until I can find out what has happened to my brother. I'm out of my mind with worry. At least I needn't worry about my mother if you're there.'

'Will you tell her about the baby? If she doesn't want me I shan't need to embarrass her.'

'Yes, of course, if that's what you want. Can I tell her you will come if she says yes?'

Jessie hesitated, then took a deep breath. 'I'll have to find someone to replace me at the teashop, but yes, I will come.'

'Bless you,' Priscilla said. 'You're wonderful, Jessie. I'll be in touch – can I telephone you?'

'You can ring this number and leave a message – just yes or no, that's all you need say.'

'I'll be in touch soon, but if you don't hear for some reason ring me again.'

'Yes, I shall,' Jessie said. 'You will find him, Priscilla.'

'My husband is already making enquires,' Priscilla said. 'Don't worry, Jessie. He can't have disappeared off the face of the earth, can he?'

Jessie laughed as she was meant to and then went back into the shop. Archie looked at her and smiled.

'Everything all right?'

'Yes, thank you, Archie. Mrs Barrington – Priscilla – may telephone with a message for me. Is that all right?'

'Yes, of course,' he said, and then came towards her. 'I've been wanting to ask, Jessie. Now that you're back . . . could we . . . I mean, would you come out with me sometimes?'

'I don't think that's a good idea, Archie.'

'You know I think the world of you.'

'You might not in a few months time,' she told him. 'I'm sorry, Archie. I'm in love with someone else and I'm having his child.'

Archie stared at her and she saw the hurt in his face. For a moment he seemed as if he didn't know what to say. 'Will he marry you?'

'I don't know,' Jessie answered honestly. 'But I can't marry anyone else. I'm sorry, Archie.'

'You've always been straight with me,' Archie said. 'I thank you for that, Jessie – and I want you to know that what you've told me changes nothing. I would marry you tomorrow if you wanted me to.'

'I know and I'm truly sorry it wasn't you,' Jessie said. 'You're a good friend, Archie.'

Jessie was thoughtful as she walked home. Had she been foolish to let Priscilla talk her into going back to Kendlebury? She would be letting her aunt down, and she wasn't proud of that, especially after Elizabeth had been so good to her.

Her aunt looked at her as if she were mad when she told her what Priscilla had asked of her. 'You won't go,' she said. 'Don't be a fool, Jess. I didn't call you a fool when you told me what had happened before, but I shall if you go back there.'

'I'm sorry, Auntie. I know I'm letting you down.'

'It's not me I'm thinking of. Girls for the teashop are ten a penny, though I would have liked it to be you and me. But you're laying up pain for yourself, Jess, after the way they treated you last time.'

'That was Mary. She isn't at Kendlebury now. She went off with her friends to France.'

'But she can come back whenever she likes,' Elizabeth reminded her. 'Supposing she does and tells them she wants you out? How are you going to feel then?'

'I suppose I shall be miserable and wish I'd taken notice of you,' Jessie admitted. 'But they need me at the moment. Catherine always needed me and Lady Kendle isn't well. All this upset is too much for her. I can't help it if I am a fool; I have to go. I'll wait until the end of the week. We can find a girl for you in a few days. I'll show her what to do and then I'll go – if I'm wanted.'

'You'll be wanted,' her aunt said wryly. 'There aren't many as will work for nothing – and that's what you'll get from that family.'

Jessie smiled and went to hug her. 'I love you, Auntie,' she said. 'I always have and I always shall – but I have to do this, for myself. I couldn't rest if I ignored them. I would feel I had betrayed them.'

'Then you'd better go,' her aunt said wryly. 'Maybe I'm as big a fool as you, because there will still be a home here for you if you need it.'

'Thank you,' Jessie said. 'Wish me luck, Auntie?'

'You'll need it, my girl!'

Jessie couldn't wait to get back to Kendlebury. The expected message had come that very evening and she rang Priscilla again to tell the family to expect her on Sunday.

When she got off the train Carter was standing on the platform looking for her eagerly. He came to take her cases, three of them this time.

'Good,' he said gruffly. 'You look as if you've come to stay.'

'I hope so,' Jessie said and smiled. 'Until I'm thrown out again, anyway.'

'I don't think that will happen again,' he said. 'You were daft to go quietly, lass. You don't know your own worth, that's your trouble.'

227

Jessie blinked in surprise but made no comment. She rode in the front seat with him, and as they approached the front drive her heart filled with emotion and she felt the tears prick her eyes.

'We're home,' she said softly. 'I've missed this place, Carter. I've missed all of you so much.'

'And we've missed you,' he said. 'God knows what would have happened if you hadn't come back.'

Jessie was out of the car as soon as he stopped and running towards the house. The kitchen door opened as she approached and Maggie came out with Catherine in her arms. She was grinning as she saw Jessie, and the little girl in her arms had started to wriggle and scream. Maggie set her down and Catherine walked unsteadily towards her. Jessie bent down to scoop her up, kissing her and hugging her for all she was worth.

'Jessie,' Catherine cried and tears were trickling down her cheeks. 'Bad Jessie. Not go away . . . Not go away.'

'No, darling,' Jessie said and kissed her again, wiping the tears with her fingertips. 'Jessie has come home. I won't go away again.'

'She's been asking for you ever since you left,' Maggie told her. 'We all thought she would forget after a while, but she didn't. Every day she asks for you and she screams when we try to look after her. She knows a lot more than some give her credit for, Jessie.'

'Of course she does,' Jessie said. She carried Catherine into the kitchen where Cook and Nanny were waiting for her.

'Welcome back,' Cook said. 'We've missed you sorely, lass. Haven't we, Nanny?'

'I think Jessie knows that,' Nanny said and smiled at her. 'As you see, I'm still here. I couldn't walk out on them when they needed me – and I knew you'd come back if Miss Priscilla asked you.'

'I never wanted to leave,' Jessie said and smiled as Mrs Pearson came in. 'The bad penny has turned up again.'

Mrs Pearson nodded. She smiled but the warmth didn't reach her eyes. 'We can certainly use some help since Alice left us,' she said. 'My niece may be joining us soon, but we shall have to see. Lady Kendle asked me to wait before I asked her.'

'I expect someone will be needed to replace Alice,' Jessie said. 'I'm just here to help the family until Captain Kendle comes back and things settle down again.'

Mrs Pearson nodded, but her manner wasn't as friendly as it had been and Jessie wondered if she had been told the truth of the situation. She decided that it would be best to make a clean breast of her news from the start, rather than let suspicion start once she began to show signs of her pregnancy.

'I have some news for you . . .' she said, but broke off as Mrs Pearson interrupted.

'Lady Kendle wanted to see you as soon as you arrived,' she said. 'Perhaps you'd better go up to her now.'

'Can't she have a cup of tea first?' Cook said. 'She's only just arrived.'

'I'm only telling you what her ladyship said.'

'I'll go up and see her,' Jessie said. 'I can come back for my tea later and we'll catch up on the news then.' She was going to give Catherine to Nanny but the child clung to her so she changed her mind. 'No, I'll take her with me. She should visit her grandmother more.'

If she was going to work here, she would do it on her terms this time, Jessie thought. No more hiding Catherine away when people came to the house. She was Harry's daughter and she was entitled to the love and care that had been denied her for most of her life.

Lady Kendle was sitting in her wheelchair by the window. She turned her head, looking eager when Jessie walked in.

'I saw you arrive,' she said. 'Oh, good, you've brought Catherine to see me. I haven't seen her for ages. I think they all thought it might be too much for me, but I enjoy seeing her. I expect she is happy to have you back. I was reluctant to ask you to come back, Jessie, but I knew Catherine must be suffering. Nanny is too old to look after her and Maggie is too rough to help me.' She smiled oddly. 'I'm afraid we're a selfish family. We had no right to ask this of you – we can't even pay you very much. Certainly not what Mary was giving you.'

229

'I don't care about that,' Jessie said. 'I never wanted to leave Kendlebury, ma'am.'

'No more of that,' Lady Kendlebury said. 'I think you should call me Anne in future. It is my name, you know, and you are to be part of the family now.'

'Am I?' Jessie asked. 'Priscilla did tell you?'

'That I should expect a grandchild? Yes, she told me. Harry is very irresponsible to leave you to face this alone – and I shall tell him so when he comes home. This is a most irregular situation, Jessie. Mary said she was going to divorce him after he tried to strangle her. I can't imagine what made him lose his temper that way. He is usually the mildest of men. I do hope Mary doesn't change her mind. She was never right for him.'

'Am I right for him?'

'Yes, I think so,' Anne Kendlebury said. 'I would never have admitted it in the ordinary way, of course. You come from a different class, a different world, Jessie. But you've proved yourself honest and true. To be quite frank, we need you. The house seemed to die after you went. I hadn't realized how much we had all come to rely on you. I wish you had consulted me before you left in the first place, but I understand your reasons for not doing so.'

'I shall try to be what you all need me to be,' Jessie said. 'When Harry comes back . . .'

'If he comes back,' his mother said and looked anxious. 'I must tell you that I am extremely worried, Jessie. He was in such a state when he left that night. I believed he was coming after you, though he didn't tell anyone what was on his mind. He had that terrible row with Mary and then he stormed out. At first we thought he must be with you. We expected a letter or a telephone call – but then we began to get worried. There are things that need to be done here, matters that cannot be resolved before Harry returns. I know he was angry, but he must be aware how difficult things are – and not just for us. He had promised work to the men he employed in that workshop. Until the barn is made ready they can't work.'

'Do we need to wait for Harry to return for that?' Jessie

asked. 'Surely the renovations could be set in hand now, if the money is available?'

'What money there is is waiting in the bank.'

'Then I think Sir Joshua should tell the men themselves to get on with it. I imagine they know what is needed as well as anyone. If they are ready to begin when Harry comes back it will be all the better.'

'I shall talk to my husband,' Anne Kendle said. 'He was half inclined to do as you suggest but I was worried that Harry might be angry if he interfered.'

'I should think he would be grateful to his father. After all, he cares about those men or he wouldn't have set up the workshop in the first place.'

'How sensible you are.' Anne Kendle smiled. 'Thank you for coming back to us. You can see how much we need you.'

'I never wanted to leave,' Jessie said and smiled. 'Now, have you taken all your medicine? We can't have you neglecting yourself, can we?'

'Yes, I think so,' Anne Kendle replied. 'Maggie sets my pills out on the tray for me. I think there's just one left and that's for tonight so that I can sleep.'

'Perhaps a nice cup of tea, then?'

'Yes, I think I might like that. Ask Mrs Pearson to bring it up for me. I am afraid she isn't pleased with me. She was expecting her niece to come and work for us when Alice left.'

'Perhaps something can be worked out once the men have started the furniture business up again,' Jessie said. 'It need only be a temporary delay.'

'What do you mean?'

'I think I ought to talk to Harry first,' Jessie said and smiled.

Lady Kendle gave her an odd look. 'You are determined he is coming back, aren't you?'

'I pray that he is,' Jessie said. 'If he shouldn't . . . then I'll tell you my idea anyway.'

She shook her head as Anne Kendle looked at her curiously and went away to see about her tea.

Sixteen

Jessie took Catherine for a walk in the direction of the barn one morning. The men were working on the renovation and she could hear the sound of hammering and sawing as she approached. Some of the men were working outside in the spring sunshine and she stopped to ask how they were getting on.

'We'll be ready to start working on commissions next week, miss,' one of the young men told her. 'But I don't know when there'll be any orders for us to start on.'

'I suppose Captain Kendle gets the orders for you,' Jessie said and he agreed. 'But wouldn't the customer whose goods were lost like to reorder at least some of those things?'

'Don't know, miss. Captain Kendle always looks after that side of the business. He came up with the drawings for us, and we made miniature pieces to show the customer what it would be like in the wood, but the captain was the one with the ideas.'

Jessie nodded and left him to his work. Harry was badly needed here. Surely he must know that. Why hadn't he come home when there was so much waiting to be done? When Jessie returned to the house she went to see Lady Kendle and told her what was on her mind.

'Did Harry lose all his paperwork in the fire, or is it possible that some of it is here?'

'Sir Joshua would know,' Anne Kendle said. 'He was asking me what I thought he should do about various things, but I've no idea. Perhaps you would like to talk to him yourself.'

'Would he think me impertinent?'

'My dear Jessie, we are grateful for any help we can get. I am sure you will find my husband in his study. He had some

232

letters to answer dealing with estate business I believe. Why don't you go and talk to him?'

Jessie felt awkward as she made her way to the study. Her previous interviews here had not been pleasant and she had spoken very rarely to Sir Joshua. She was afraid he might think her foolish or impudent. However, he greeted her kindly and asked her to sit down.

'Will you have a glass of sherry, my dear?'

'No, thank you, sir. It was about the workshop. I wondered if you had considered trying to get new orders for the men.'

'I was just looking through some of Harry's papers,' he told her. 'And yes, there are records of customers he has sold to in the past, and some interesting letters. I hadn't realized how much the work he was doing was appreciated. Apparently a lot of people want good-quality, individual pieces rather than this mass-produced stuff they turn out these days.'

'Yes, so Harry told me,' Jessie said. 'I was wondering if the customer whose goods were lost in the fire might like to reorder some of the items he had requested. You would need copies of the designs, of course, and they may have been lost.'

'As it happens, my son has kept copies of everything he has ever sold, with all the details of the materials used and the suppliers. I hadn't realized how efficient Harry was. He was actually a good businessman.'

'And he drew all the designs himself initially,' Jessie told him. 'I am certain he will make a success of this – if there is a business for him to return to.'

'Are you suggesting we contact the customer ourselves?'

'It can't do any harm, can it?'

Sir Joshua looked at her thoughtfully. 'I suppose not. I am not sure if it would be better to write or telephone. I've never done anything of the sort before. I'm not sure I know how to start.'

Jessie looked at the beautiful partners' desk in the middle of the room. There was a blotter, pens, ink and good quality notepaper laid out ready, which Sir Joshua had obviously been using earlier.

'I think perhaps a letter of enquiry on paper like that. Good-quality paper makes the right impression, doesn't it? It is so nice to touch and use. Would you like me to write a sample for you? It can't be very different to writing applications for a job, can it?'

'Please have a try if you feel you can, Jessie.'

Jessie got up and walked over to the desk. She thought for a moment and then picked up the pen Sir Joshua had been using earlier. Her letter was brief but clearly and concisely put, setting out their aims to have the business ready within days, and their terms for payment, which were on delivery. She took the finished letter to Sir Joshua.

'I thought something like this, sir.'

'This is excellent,' he said after he had read it. 'You have a beautiful hand, Jessie, and your phrasing is good. Where did you learn to write like this?'

'At school. My teacher was very strict. If our writing was sloppy she made us do our work again. She believed it was disrespectful to write badly or to misspell our words. I always enjoyed her lessons.'

'And she was perfectly right,' he said with a nod of approval. 'A sloppy letter is a sign of carelessness. But you haven't signed it, Jessie.'

'I thought you should do that – as a director of the company in Harry's absence.'

Sir Joshua stared at her for a moment and then gave a startled laugh. 'Well, I never! It seems my son knows a good thing when he sees it. You are a very intelligent woman, Jessie. I think we've all of us underestimated you.'

Jessie blushed and shook her head. 'I know it isn't my place to suggest these things, sir, but Harry needs help. I've no idea where he is or why he hasn't come home, but I know this is what he would want.'

'You care for him very much, don't you?'

'Yes, sir.'

'To be perfectly honest, I was doubtful about having you back when my wife told me of the situation. I believed Mary would make my son a good wife, but I appear to have been wrong about many things. We must hope she is willing to divorce him.'

Jessie smiled and thanked him. She was still a little in awe of Harry's father. He had been both kind and generous in his acceptance of her and her ideas, but she knew his instincts would be against a marriage between her and Harry. They came from different worlds and she could not expect things to change overnight. If Harry's parents learned to accept her from necessity, many of their friends and neighbours would not. It was a problem that would need to be faced when Harry came home. She could only pray that it would be soon.

Life at Kendlebury was much as it always had been, Jessie discovered in the days that followed. There was an empty space in their lives that no one could ever quite fill, but grief for Jack could not rule their heads, only their hearts.

Jessie noticed a new respect in Cook and Maggie. They knew about her child and were aware that her status had changed. She was a part of the family now, but because she was Jessie she also belonged to them. She had somehow managed to bridge the gap between upstairs and downstairs. She was breaking old taboos and bringing a new regime to the house.

Jessie was the new mistress in all but name. She did not give orders; she asked as she always had, taking over many of the tasks Mary had reluctantly performed. She discussed menus with Cook and oversaw what was bought from the tradesmen, going through the accounts with Mrs Pearson.

She asked Mr Goodjohn his opinion of the grocer and butcher they were using and when he suggested an alternative she asked Mrs Pearson if might be advisable to try a single order to see how they got on. The difference in price and quality made it difficult for the housekeeper to argue when other changes were suggested.

Maggie's mother was invited to come in more often. She helped her daughter clean before the household was up, making it easier for Maggie to complete her other duties during the day.

Sir Joshua had fallen into the habit of eating his evening meal in his wife's room, which meant there was less work as only simple food was required. Cook was a little put out that she had no chance to practise her skills, but Jessie told her to be patient.

'I believe you will be busy again soon,' she promised, 'if things work out as I hope . . . But we have to wait for Captain Kendle to come home.'

Cook gave her an odd look and Jessie knew that she, like almost everyone else in the house, was beginning to think that Harry would never return. Almost two months had passed since the night he'd quarrelled with his wife and stormed out. Where was he? Why didn't he come home? Surely he would have done by now if he could.

Jessie was tortured by her doubts and fears as she lay in her bed at night and longed for him beside her. She was still in the nursery wing despite being asked by both Lady Kendle and Sir Joshua to move into the main part of the house.

'I'll move when Harry asks me,' she said. 'Until then it's best that I stay where I am.'

But when would he come home? There were moments when Jessie felt close to despair, when she wondered if all they were trying to do would come to nothing. Yet even at her lowest ebb she refused to give in. Harry wasn't dead. Something inside her would not admit it was the most likely explanation for his disappearance. She was convinced that he was alive somewhere and she believed that when they finally found him he would need her.

'I wanted to tell you at once,' Sir Joshua said. He had come to the nursery to find her that morning, knowing she would be with Catherine at this time of day. 'I've had a very interesting letter from Mr Hamilton. He wants the complete order and he says he'll accept it piece by piece as it is finished, payment on delivery.'

Jessie took the letter from him and read it, deep in thought.

'I think he was relieved he didn't have to pay for the items lost,' she said. 'This is wonderful, more than we'd hoped for.' Jessie kissed Catherine and put her down. Curious about the man she knew but seldom saw, the child stood staring up at him, her eyes wide. 'Yes, that's your grandfather, darling. Say hello to him, Catherine.'

Catherine chuckled. 'Ganda,' she said. 'Ganda come walk?'

'Well, that's odd,' he said, looking at her awkwardly. 'It's the first time she's spoken to me. She's a lot brighter these days, Jessie.'

'I expect she's a little shy of you. She doesn't often see you.'

'My fault, I dare say.' He patted the child's head. 'We'll have a walk in the garden later perhaps. I can't manage those long treks you go on, Jessie.'

'A toddle round the garden will suit Catherine very well,' Jessie replied.

'Mr Hamilton was obviously impressed with your letter. I think we shall have to make you company secretary. That reminds me, there's something else I wanted to—' He broke off as he heard voices in the hall outside. 'Isn't that Priscilla?'

Even as he spoke the door opened and Priscilla came in.

'I am glad you're here, Daddy,' she said. 'I've got some bad news and I don't want to be the one to tell Mother.'

Jessie's heart gave a sickening lurch and then began to race. For a moment she felt faint and was glad that she was sitting down.

'You've heard something about Harry. He isn't . . .' She couldn't say the word, her chest so tight that she could hardly breathe.

'He's not dead,' Priscilla said hastily as she saw her white face. 'But he was in a car accident the night he left home. His car went off the road and hit a tree. Someone pulled him out seconds before it exploded otherwise he would have died. He was desperately ill for weeks but no one knew who he was. He wasn't carrying any papers and the car was burned out. Even when he started to recover he refused to tell them his name.'

'The damned idiot!' Sir Joshua cried and then looked oddly ashamed as he felt Jessie's eyes on him. 'Didn't he know how worried we would all be?'

'I doubt if he was in any state to think about us.' Priscilla took a deep breath. 'He's going to be in a wheelchair when he leaves hospital, Jessie. His legs were damaged in the crash. The doctors say his spine was badly bruised, though not crushed, and he should be able to walk again in time – but he's going to be an invalid for a long while. There were

237

various internal injuries that have taken their toll. He will need care and rest and he won't be able to do much in a physical sense for months – though his mind is as sharp as ever.'

'My God!' Sir Joshua's face went white and he sat down abruptly as his legs failed him. 'I can't believe it. Why? Why did it happen? Was he driving recklessly?'

'The man who witnessed the accident and pulled him out said that he swerved to avoid a dog that ran across the road in front of him. His car hit a patch of mud on the road and he couldn't control it. You know Harry and animals. That's so typical of him.'

'Where is he?' Jessie asked, her nerves steadying. 'I have to see him. Please, I must see him now.'

'He says he doesn't want to see you the way he is. I've told him that we need you here, but he's adamant. He says he won't come home until he can walk again.'

'That's so silly. I can help him. He must know that.'

'He's proud, Jessie. He knows you would look after him, but he doesn't want to beg for help. He couldn't give you anything before and now he's too proud to come to you as an invalid. He told me he didn't want anyone's pity.'

'It isn't pity I feel,' Jessie said. 'He can't think that.'

'I telephoned Mary,' Priscilla told them, her expression grim. 'She's back in London now, staying with her family. She was horrified. She wants a divorce. I can't repeat what she said, it was too awful, but it was more or less that she didn't want to be tied to a useless cripple. She said she'd had enough of lame ducks and she wants to be free of this family altogether.'

'Good,' Sir Joshua said, surprising his daughter. 'The sooner their divorce can be arranged the better.'

'I must see Harry,' Jessie said. 'He doesn't mean what he says. He can't think I would stay with him out of pity.'

Priscilla sighed. 'I've been telling him that for days. We've had endless rows about it and the doctors finally threw me out for upsetting him. He said he would never speak to me again if I told you where he is.'

'But you will tell me, won't you?'

'He's in London. George had him transferred to a private

clinic once we found him – at our expense. George says it's partly my fault all this happened and he insists on paying Harry's medical expenses.'

'Then I shall go to him,' Jessie said. 'I'll take Catherine and stay at the London house – if that's all right?'

'Of course it is,' Sir Joshua said. 'I'll come with you, Jessie. That son of mine needs some straight talking to sort him out. Feeling sorry for himself, by the sound of it.'

'Would you mind waiting here until I bring him home?' Jessie asked. 'You are needed here. Besides, I would rather do this my own way. Harry is in shock. He has been through terrible experiences, more than any of us can imagine. What he suffered in the war, Catherine's illness, and the loss of his son, the guilt he's always felt because of the way his brother died. He has been hurt more than anyone can bear and this is a natural reaction. I've seen it before, during the war. Men who had lost limbs or been badly burned were afraid of rejection so they put up a barrier. This is Harry's way of protecting himself.'

'I think Jessie is right,' Priscilla said. 'Why don't you go and tell Mother the news? She will need you to comfort her, Daddy. I'll help Jessie to pack and then Carter can take us to the station. I'll come with you, Jessie – just to help you with Catherine. Don't worry, I shan't interfere. I've tried talking to him but he doesn't listen.'

'He may not want to listen to me,' Jessie said. 'But he can't hide for the rest of his life. Sooner or later he has to face up to the truth, whatever that may be.'

Jessie found the long journey hard to bear, but she refused to let the doubts creep in. Harry was alive, that was all that mattered. He was alive and she believed he still loved her even though he would probably deny it because he did not want her to sacrifice her life for his sake.

She had no illusions about the future. Life wouldn't be easy for them. It would take hard work and patience to get Harry on his feet again even if it could be done. While working in the field hospitals in Belgium and France Jessie had witnessed the pain and despair men in similar situations had faced. Only the very brave managed to get through, some finding it easier simply to turn their faces to the wall and die. But she wouldn't give up on Harry. She would make him do whatever it took, no matter how long or hard it might be for them both.

The first hurdle was to get him to see her. He had the right to refuse if he wished, but even if she had to lie and cheat, she would manage it somehow.

'This is my sister, Jessie,' Priscilla told the nurse on night duty. They had asked to see Harry earlier that day and been refused. 'She has flown over from France specially to see him and she has to go home tomorrow.'

'It's very irregular,' the nurse said, looking doubtful. 'But in the circumstances, perhaps . . . I know he isn't asleep because I looked in a few moments ago.'

'Come on, Jessie,' Priscilla said. 'Harry will be so delighted to see you.' She hurried her along the corridor before the nurse could change her mind. Outside Harry's door she gave Jessie a little push. 'You'd better go in alone. I'll wait here unless he wants to see me, which I doubt. I'm not going to be his favourite person when he knows what I've done.'

Jessie smiled as she pulled a face and squeezed her hand. 'Wish me luck,' she whispered and then opened the door carefully and went in. The room was lit by a shaded lamp, which cast just enough light to see Harry lying on the bed with his eyes closed, a book abandoned on the coverlet next to his hand as though he had been reading earlier. His face looked thin and pale and she could see the new lines of suffering about his mouth. For a moment she was afraid to approach. Supposing she'd read it all wrong and he really didn't want her?

'So she told you in spite of my threat,' Harry said, his eyes still closed. 'You shouldn't have come, Jessie.'

'How did you know it was me?' she asked as she went closer, her heart racing. She was filled with love for him, wanting to take him to her and hold him forever. He opened his eyes and looked at her as she stood beside him, a faint smile on his lips.

'I can smell your perfume.'

'I'm not wearing any.'

'You smell of soap and fresh air and flowers,' he told her. 'It's your own special scent. I could never forget.'

'That's a beautiful thing to say, like poetry.'

'You're beautiful, Jessie, but you shouldn't be here. I don't want you here. I'm no use to you. They've told me I could be stuck in a wheelchair for the rest of my life.'

'You don't know that,' Jessie said. 'It means hard work and the will to get better, but it isn't necessarily the end of everything, Harry. Even if you can't walk – and you may be able to, the spinal cord wasn't cut – there is still plenty to enjoy in life.'

'That's the nurse talking.'

'No, it isn't, it's the woman who loves you and wants you back in her bed.'

Harry laughed bitterly. 'You always did know how to cut to the point, didn't you, Jessie? How do you think I can make love to you in my condition?'

'I can think of ways,' Jessie said, her smile teasing him. 'Your hands are not paralysed and neither is the rest of you – not the relevant bits anyway. I dare say we could manage to please each other if we tried. Besides, it would encourage you to do the exercises you will have to do to get fit again.'

'That still leaves you stuck with an invalid for a husband,' Harry told her with a frown. 'That isn't fair to you, Jessie. I may never be completely well again. I wanted to give you so many things and all I've done is take from you. No, it's no good, I won't let you sacrifice yourself.'

'So you would rather I went back to London and was miserable?' Jessie asked. 'That's a bit selfish, isn't it? I love being at Kendlebury. We're doing so much, Harry. Your father has had the barn renovated and the men are ready to start work on their orders. We have all the drawings we need, but the men could do with some encouragement from you – and we shall need new ideas.'

'What are you talking about – what orders?'

'Mr Hamilton has reordered everything and he will take delivery of each piece as it's finished this time, and pay on delivery.'

'And who arranged that little miracle?' Harry's eyes narrowed. 'You, I suppose? My father wouldn't have done it on his own.'

'I only did what I thought you would have done if you'd been there,' Jessie said. 'But we couldn't run that business without you for long. Even in a wheelchair you can make new designs, supervise the men, and tell us what we need to do next.'

'You've got it all worked out, haven't you? Supposing I don't feel able to face up to a future of pain, frustration and being tied to a chair? Supposing I don't feel I can do all the things you and my family want me to do? Supposing I would rather take the easy way out?'

'All I'm asking is that you live one day at a time,' Jessie said. 'Let me take you home, Harry. The doctors say you can leave here in a few days, provided you have someone to see you keep up the regime of exercise and medication they've set for you.'

'So you're going to be my nurse now?' Harry said bitterly. 'No thank you, Jessie. I'll stay here and rot before I'll let you give up your life for that.'

'I'll be whatever you want,' Jessie said and sat on the bed, taking his hand in hers. 'Nurse, lover, personal dresser. Your father says I should be company secretary and Catherine calls me Mumma sometimes. All I'm asking is that you give me tomorrow.'

'Give you tomorrow?' Harry smiled wryly. 'And tomorrow and tomorrow and tomorrow – is that it, Jessie?'

'Only one at a time,' she replied and bent her head to kiss him. Harry gave a little moan and then his arms went around her, holding her to him as the kiss deepened. 'I love you, Harry,' she said as he released her at last.

'You know I love you, Jess, but it isn't fair to you. I would be taking advantage.'

'No, you already did that,' she said teasing him. 'And if you're not prepared to make an honest woman of me, your son is going to have something to say.'

Pain flashed across Harry's face. 'My son is dead.'

'Our darling Jack is dead,' Jessie said. 'You loved him, we

all loved him, and he will never be forgotten. He lives on in our hearts, Harry – but I wasn't talking about Jack.' She took his hand and pressed it against her stomach. 'You can't feel him yet, Harry, but he's there, growing inside me – our son. Surely you can't refuse to give him a father.'

'My child?' Harry stared at her in silence, his eyes filling with tears. Suddenly, they were flooding out of him as he spoke of his grief for Jack, his sense of hopelessness and his despair when he learned Jessie had gone. 'I thought at first that you had left me. Then Nanny gave me your letter and I knew what Mary had done. I wanted to kill her. I think I would have if Priscilla hadn't come in at that moment and stopped me. God, I hate her!'

'Mary doesn't matter,' Jessie said, holding tightly to his hand as his grief poured out. 'Apparently she wants to divorce you and she's told Priscilla she's going to name me.'

'Over my dead body!'

'Let her,' Jessie said. 'It doesn't matter what people think. They will all know the truth soon enough anyway. If it pleases Mary to do it that way let's just be satisfied that she is giving you your freedom.'

'You really don't care, do you?' he asked and smiled when she shook her head. 'You're special, Jessie. It was the best day of my life when you came into it.'

'Then you'll let me take you home?'

'I can only promise you one day at a time,' Harry said. 'I'm not as brave as you are, Jess. I'm not sure I can do all you want – but I'll try. I'll try for you and for my children.'

That's all I'm asking for,' she said and her lips curved in a naughty smile. 'We'll just have to see if we can make each tomorrow better than the last.'

Harry looked rueful. 'You'd made up your mind before you came, hadn't you?' She nodded and he smiled. 'I never had a chance, did I? You and Priscilla were determined that I was coming home whatever I said.'

'That sounds about right,' Jessie said and bent to kiss him, a long, lingering kiss that brought a moan from him. His terrible injuries hadn't killed his desire for her and she saw a look in his eyes that told her he had realized there might be more to

243

life than he had imagined, even in a wheelchair. 'We're two determined women, Harry, and you're only a man. In this modern new world of ours, the world you told me is coming, what chance should you have?'

Harry reached up and touched her face. 'I don't deserve you,' he said. 'I know what this means, don't think I'm under any illusions. I visited my men in the hospital in France and again in England, and I saw what some of those poor devils went through. We let them down out there, people like me, the upper class, their superiors. They trusted us blindly to lead them and we sent them to their deaths like sheep. They'll never trust us again and they'll change the world – who can blame them? They suffered for it.' He smiled oddly as she held tight to his hand. 'I shall probably be a terrible patient, Jess.'

'Oh, I've no doubt of it,' she said. 'Strong men are always the worst, because they get so angry. But you are strong, Harry. Stronger than you think. You'll get through it, my love.'

'I won't marry you until I'm on my feet, Jess.'

'Then you'll have to work hard,' she said, 'because our son won't wait forever.'

Afterword

The bride was eight and a half months pregnant when she finally stood in front of the altar with Harry beside her. His divorce had been arranged quickly and discreetly, with Mary being given the London house as her settlement. Harry had resisted giving into her blackmail at first because he knew she was seeing her lover, but Sir Joshua told him it was a price worth paying for freedom. Harry's marriage to Jessie had been arranged the moment it was possible.

Carter had wheeled him in at the side door, and the chair was pushed out of the way when the wedding march began. Harry stood straight, if a little awkwardly, as his bride walked down the aisle to take her place by his side and make her vows. She had asked her friend Archie Thistle to give her away. In the congregation Aunt Elizabeth sat and watched, weeping as she whispered how beautiful Jessie looked to the girl who sat beside her

'Jessie *is* lovely,' Alice whispered back. 'I couldn't believe it when she asked me to come for the wedding.'

'Jessie doesn't forget her friends,' Elizabeth said. 'You've left the baby with your mother, I know. Jessie was so pleased you kept her after all and she'll want to see your daughter tomorrow.' They had to stop whispering then because the vicar had begun the address.

Jessie had never looked lovelier, but it was a bride's beauty, the beauty of happiness as she gave her hand to the man she loved and saw that love reflected in his face. The battle for Harry's health was still far from won, but they never asked or expected more than tomorrow.

Harry was wheeled out of church in the chair. He had stood up for his wedding as he'd promised he would, but he couldn't

245

manage to walk down the aisle with her just yet – though he had promised he would do it tomorrow.

The wedding reception was quite small, just a few of their closest friends. Neither of them wanted anything more and it would have tired Harry too much to have to greet and talk to a large gathering.

The effort of cutting the cake and talking to those they had invited was as much as he could manage, and he was looking pale by the time the family were at last alone in the drawing room enjoying a glass of sherry. Jessie was drinking lemonade, because Harry had told her he didn't want his son getting into bad ways before he was born.

'You look worn out,' Anne Kendle said to her son. 'Do you want to go and rest, Harry? I am sure what Jessie has to tell us could wait until another time.'

'No, I'm fine,' he said. 'Jessie has been waiting for this. She wants to get Father in a good mood – and I doubt there will ever be a better time.'

Jessie had risen to her feet. She was showing a large bulge in her cream silk wedding gown and laid a hand fondly on it as she surveyed her family and closest friends.

'I've waited until today to tell you my idea, because today I became a part of the family.'

'You've been that for a long time, m'dear,' Sir Joshua said. 'Don't know what we'd do without you.'

'You might not be so pleased with me in a moment,' Jessie said. 'I've told Harry, of course, and he thinks it's a good idea, but he thinks you might not, Father.'

'Well, fire away,' he said gruffly. 'Nothing surprises me these days, Jessie.'

'It's a way of improving the family fortunes,' Jessie said and looked nervously at Harry, who smiled at her encouragingly. 'I know that a lot of people are interested in good craftsmanship, and they also like somewhere to go when they are on holiday. I learned that when I was working in Torquay at that guesthouse. I thought we could open the gardens at Kendlebury during the summer, invite people to look in the workshop and buy small gifts from our shop.'

'What shop?' Sir Joshua asked, frowning.

'Well, we have the old stable block. We could open a part of that as a shop,' Jessie said. 'Those apprentice pieces the lads make for the workshop would attract customers, and we could sell other things. Perhaps Cook's jams and cakes for a start, and there are other things we might sell in future. I thought we might invite more craftsmen to come here, probably local men who can't afford their own premises. They could rent part of the stables at low cost and sell their goods in our shop, giving us a commission on sales, of course.' Jessie took a deep breath. 'I thought we might open a teashop in the annexe and we could have plants from the garden on sale in the Orangery. Jed Wylie could work there and tell people about the plants. He knows a lot . . .'

There was complete silence as she trailed off. Lady Kendle was stunned and Sir Joshua was frowning. Jessie felt a little sick. They hated her idea.

Sir Joshua was the first to speak. 'You are turning Kendlebury into a commercial venture, is that the idea?'

'Well, yes,' Jessie said. 'People love to take a trip out when they're on holiday and we're not far from Torquay. They can get here by car or train and there's a possibility of a bus being laid on as part of a tour if we want. We should be included in tour guides and various brochures.'

'You've given this a lot of thought, haven't you?'

'Yes, I have. The workshop is doing well, but this could help us to manage until it is really established again. And it would only be for a few weeks of the year.'

'More's the pity,' Sir Joshua said.

'So you don't like the idea. I was afraid you wouldn't.'

'On the contrary, my dear. It's rather exciting. I thought it was a pity we couldn't get them here more often.'

'Well, I do know someone who would print leaflets for us and distribute them too. He wouldn't charge much – he owes me a favour.'

'Are you agreeing to this?' Anne Kendle asked her husband, clearly astonished. 'Goodness me, we shan't know ourselves.'

'You don't mind, do you, my dear?'

'I am merely surprised,' she said. 'I would never have expected you to agree.'

'I dare say I wouldn't have a few months ago,' Sir Joshua said. 'But a lot of things have happened since then. We can't take privilege for granted any more, Anne. If we want to survive we have to change and grow and Jessie is showing us the way.' He lifted his glass in salute to her. 'I can only say thank you, my dear Jessie, and I wish you all success with your ventures – of which I am certain there will be many more in the future.'

'Well, perhaps,' Jessie said and laughed. She knew that she might not have been accepted so easily if the family hadn't needed her, but she was too happy to question, knowing that however it had begun she was a much-loved part of the family now. 'But we have to get these off the ground first.

'First of all, we have to see you safely delivered of our son,' Harry said and looked at her lovingly. 'Though I dare say you'll manage that as easily as you do all the rest.'

'I can't guarantee that,' she said giving him a look full of love. 'But I'll do my best.'

Jessie smiled as she looked at the faces of the people grouped around the room. Aunt Elizabeth, who had been so good to her, doing well with her teashop in London; it was her success that had given Jessie the idea she had cherished since her return to Kendlebury. Then Priscilla, her children and husband, looking relieved that things had apparently settled down after all the traumas. Anne Kendle, surprised but pleased, and Sir Joshua clearly relishing the idea of being closely involved in the new ventures – and Harry, her darling Harry, Catherine sitting happily on his knee, almost asleep after her busy day being petted by all the guests at the wedding.

It was a comfortable scene of family life, a good place to be. And there was always tomorrow.

F SOL
Sole, Linda.
Give me tomorrow